I've travelled the world twice over,
Met the famous: saints and sinners,
Poets and artists, kings and queens,
Old stars and hopeful beginners,
I've been where no-one's been before,
Learned secrets from writers and cooks
All with one library ticket
To the wonderful world of books.

© JANICE JAMES.

# THE LONDON LINNET

When Taisie Brown ran away from Number 1 Clerivale Street and the depraved Mr. Gribble, she was ten years old. Clutching a golden guinea and wandering aimlessly about the streets of Victorian London she drifted into Victoria Station and boarded the first train she had ever seen. So began the story of the little street urchin who was transformed into a beautiful star of the London stage, a spirited girl whose dramatic life, tender heart and wonderful voice brought her wide acclaim as Taisie Brown—The London Linnet.

TANIA LANGLEY

# THE LONDON LINNET

*Complete and Unabridged*

# ULVERSCROFT
*Leicester*

First published in Great Britain in 1985 by
Panther Books,
London

First Large Print Edition
published November 1986
by arrangement with
Grafton Books Ltd
London

British Library CIP Data

Langley, Tania
The London linnet.—Large print ed.
Ulverscroft large print series: romance
I. Title
823'.914[F]          PR6062.A53/

ISBN 0-7089-1543-4

Published by
F. A. Thorpe (Publishing) Ltd.
Anstey, Leicestershire
Set by Rowland Phototypesetting Ltd.
Bury St. Edmunds, Suffolk
Printed and bound in Great Britain by
T. J. Press (Padstow) Ltd., Padstow, Cornwall

# 1

AT ten o'clock on the night of Tuesday, the 21st June 1887, rockets soared into the air from six hundred hills around Britain and exploded in a shower of stars. It was Queen Victoria's Golden Jubilee.

Earlier in the day the Queen, wearing black satin, white lace and diamonds, had driven to Westminster Abbey for a Service of Thanksgiving for the fifty years of her reign. Surrounded by her large family, cheered by thousands of her subjects, she still felt, as she had ever since Prince Albert's death, "so alone".

On the following day there was to be a children's party in Hyde Park. Thirty thousand children were expected to attend and each one of them would be given milk and a currant bun and a Jubilee mug to take home. All the lucky children of London, but not perhaps the ones who needed it most; not the children who lived at Number 1 Clerivale Street, Pimlico.

The house stood at the point where two streets met at the apex of a triangle. Although its address was Number 1 Clerivale Street it might equally well have been called Number 1 Marvale Street, since the front door was exactly at the point where the two roads joined. Because of its situation the house had no immediate neighbours, turning its back on the other houses in both Clerivale Street and Marvale Street, and further separated from them by a back yard, not sufficiently cultivated to be called a garden, and a high brick wall.

It was a secret house, closed in on itself and shunned by the local people. The blinds were never drawn to let in the sunshine, the only people who went in and out during the daytime were Abe Gribble and his housekeeper, Betsey Pawne. Faces were seen at the windows occasionally; a disobedient young hand would lift the edge of a blind and for a few minutes a child would gaze at the indifferent world outside, then the blind would drop back into place and the house would seem lifeless once more.

The Cockney urchins playing on the pavements never chalked their hopscotch squares outside that house, nor lashed their spinning tops past its front door, nor rolled their marbles in its gutters. The younger children avoided passing it at all, even though they only half understood why "ole Gribble'll get yer!" was a threat which made even their bold elder brothers look uneasy.

Their parents dropped their voices and looked over their shoulders when they spoke of what went on at Number 1 Clerivale Street. It was better not to know. But they did know, and even hearts hardened by grinding poverty could not quite condone the traffic in young bodies, the inert, drugged bundles carried into the basement after dark and, it was whispered, sometimes smuggled out as well, cold and lifeless, for disposal in the wilder reaches of the river.

As the Jubilee fireworks lit up the sky a ten-year-old girl wriggled away from the heavy arm of the man who had fallen asleep sprawled across the bed in a first floor room at Number 1 Clerivale Street. She slid to the floor and stood for a moment, trembling with cold and nausea, holding on to the brass rail at the foot of the bed. She looked over her shoulder, but the man did not stir. He was heavily built, his naked body covered with mounds of smooth, white flesh. His face was buried in the pillow, but she knew that he was dark, with bushy eyebrows, a thick black moustache and whiskers, and hair worn long. The dim light of an oil lamp turned low revealed the reason for all this luxuriant hair: some accident had removed half of his left ear. The mutilation, and the puckered red and white scar, added the last touch of horror for the child. She shuddered and then, moving slowly because her body was sore and she was very frightened, she began to dress.

Her only garment, a dress of cheap pink taffeta, slid over her head; she pulled on long white stockings, kept up by garters, and then the black patent leather shoes with little heels in which she had been required to dance before the creature on the bed. His discarded clothes were tossed on a chair. She felt in the trousers pocket and found his money, but with instinctive cunning she took only one coin, a golden guinea, which could easily be dropped and lost if she were caught on the stairs.

There was a light in the passage when she crept out of the room; she could hear music coming from downstairs; in another bedroom a boy was sobbing. She stole down the stairs, hugging the wall, right down to the basement.

Betsey Pawne should have been in the kitchen, but Betsey had been tempted out by the Jubilee celebrations and had stopped for a pennyworth of gin. The door, which should have been bolted, was open. Betsey's old black wool shawl was hanging over the back of her chair. The child took it and wrapped it round her, tying the two ends in a knot at the back. Shrouded in its darkness she slipped out of the door, up the back steps, across the yard, through the gate and into Marvale Street.

There were many people about, sauntering home after going to see the street decorations and the illuminations in the London squares. The child, drifting along with the crowd, presently found herself near the railway station which had been named after the Queen. Until then she had had no clear idea of where she would go or what she would do if she succeeded in

5

getting away from Clerivale Street. Now the thought came to her that the guinea still clutched in her hand put it in her power to leave London altogether. No chance then of Abe Gribble catching up with her.

She had never been on a train, never seen the inside of the railway station before, but she was quickwitted and, after watching for a minute or two, she saw that what she had to do was to go to the Ticket Office and buy a ticket. She went and stood behind a tall man in a loose, fawn overcoat, carrying a valise, and heard him say: "Sutton, single, please". The clerk asked a question and the man said, "Yes, First", which she did not understand. Then he turned away and Taisie Brown stepped up quickly, put her golden guinea down on the ledge and repeated: "Sutton, single."

The clerk did not bother to ask her what class she wanted. He tossed her a third class child's ticket and a cascade of change and she scooped it up, looking round anxiously for the man in the light coat. She caught up with him at the barrier and followed him down the platform, but when she would have climbed into the same carriage he looked down and said, quite kindly: "Are you travelling First Class, little girl?"

Taisie looked at him uncomprehendingly. "I gotta ticket," she said.

"Ah, yes, but that's for a different part of the train. Come along, I'll show you."

He escorted her down the platform and opened the door of the compartment for her. "Are you all alone?"

"Yes."

"Do you know where to get out?"

"Sutton."

"That's my station, too. I'll look out for you when we arrive and make sure you don't get carried on. That would never do, would it?"

He smiled and then, with a courtesy which stunned Taisie, raised his hat before going back to his First Class carriage. A proper gent. Not one of them.

The change from her guinea was almost more than her small hands could hold. She put it into a corner of the black shawl and tied it up securely. The railway ticket fluttered unheeded to the floor.

The journey took about half an hour.

Taisie looked out of the window, but it was dark and there was nothing to see. She drummed with her heels on the seat until a sharp-voiced woman told her to stop. When the woman got out at Croydon Taisie put out her tongue to her.

She could read, though not with any fluency, and she recognised the word "Sutton" as they drew in to the station and got out of the train. She was ahead of Mr. Greville Lawton on the stairs and had already been stopped by the ticket collector when he arrived at the barrier.

"Is something wrong?" Mr. Lawton asked, handing over his own ticket.

"Good evening, sir. Just this child trying to get through without a ticket. Says she had one, but I've heard that story before."

"She certainly had a ticket," Mr. Lawton said. "I saw it in her hand on the platform at Victoria." He bent down to look at the bewildered child. "What did you do with your ticket, my dear?"

"I showed it to the ovver man," Taisie said in a hoarse whisper. "I didn't know I'd 'ave to show it to this one 'ere. I must 'a dropped it."

"It seems a very natural mistake for an inexperienced traveller to make," Mr. Lawton said. He straightened up and looked expectantly at the ticket collector. "Could you accept my assurance that she did have a ticket and overlook its disappearance?"

"I s'pose so," the ticket collector said. He looked at the small, grotesquely dressed figure disapprovingly. "I don't know what a child like that's doing, travelling all alone at this time o' night. Where d'you live?"

Taisie backed away, terrified by his uniform, by the way they were both looking at her.

"Don't be frightened," Mr. Lawton said. "We only want to help you. It's very late for a little girl like you to be out alone. Where are your parents?"

"Me Mum's dead and me Dad loped orf 'fore I was born."

For a moment he was disconcerted, but he persisted: "Who do you live with then?"

"Me Auntie Lil and Uncle Fred."

"And where are they?"

"They've gorne to Australia."

9

"But where is your home?"

Again Taisie backed away from them, huge menacing men who might at any moment pounce and send her back to Clerivale Street.

"Come on, give us your address," the ticket collector said impatiently.

"Don't frighten her," Mr. Lawton said, and because he sounded kind, Taisie blurted out the truth.

"Auntie Lil sold me to Mr. Gribble for five quid so's me cousin Algie could go wiv 'em to Australia."

"*Sold* you?"

Greville Lawton sounded as bewildered as he felt. The two men looked at one another.

"It sounds to me like a case for the Police," the ticket collector said slowly.

"No!" Taisie tugged desperately at Mr. Lawton's arm. "I ain't done nothin' wrong, mister. Don't put the rozzers on to me."

The memory of the stolen guinea rose up and terrified her.

"We're only trying to help," Mr. Lawton persisted. "What is your name?"

"Taisie Brown."

"Well, Daisie, there must be someone . . ."

"Not Daisie, it's Taisie. An-as-ta-sia."

Her careful enunciation of the syllables
made Mr. Lawton smile.

"What I'm trying to say, Anastasia, is
that if you will tell us who you know in
Sutton we will find them for you and put
you in their care."

"Don't know anyone in Sutton."

"Then why did you come here?"

"'cause I 'eard you ask for it. I run
away, see, and I didn't know where to go
and I was be'ind you when you said
'Sutton' so I said 'Sutton', too."

The simplicity of her explanation left
Greville Lawton even more at a loss than
he had been before. It seemed, in some
strange way, as if he were responsible for
the arrival of this frightened waif on
Sutton Station. What was to be done with
her? There must be some provision in the
neighbourhood for homeless orphans, but
he had never enquired into it. It was, as
the ticket collector had said, clearly a case
for the Police. What troubled him was that
they might hand Taisie back to the master

who had driven her to the extreme step of running away.

"Was he unkind to you, this Mr. Gribble?" he asked.

It was difficult for Taisie to comprehend that there were people who had never heard of Abe Gribble. She crossed her small arms, clutching her body and shivering.

"'e's the Devil," she said.

"Proper little play actress, isn't she?" the ticket collector said.

"I'm not so sure," Greville Lawton said.

He bent over the child again, putting his hand under her chin and lifting her face to the light. It was a triangular face, with wide cheekbones and a pointed chin; too thin, even after a week of adequate meals in Mr. Gribble's house. Her hair, he thought fancifully, was the colour of beech leaves in autumn. It was clean, because Mr. Gribble had had it washed in preparation for her initiation by her first client, and it was falling out of the corkscrew curls into which he had had it tortured, back into its natural waves. Her eyes were an unusual colour, between grey and green, and her skin was very white, with the unnatural translucence of malnutrition. Her body was under-developed for her age and she was not as tall as she should have been, but she had escaped the rickets which deformed slum children and her limbs were straight and shapely.

"What will happen to her if we hand her on to the Police?" Mr. Lawton wondered out loud.

"Prob'ly put her in a cell for the night," said the ticket collector carelessly.

"No!"

Taisie tried to jerk away from Greville Lawton's restraining hand, intent on flight, but he held her firmly.

"We can't have that," he said. "I'll take her home with me. One of the maids can find a bed for her, just for tonight. It's too late now to knock on the door of an orphanage. Come along, Taisie; no-one is going to harm you."

Taisie went with him because there seemed to be no other choice open to her. She had the sharp knowingness of a child of the London streets, and after her recent experiences she was all the more suspicious of strangers, on the watch for the slightest move that might mean danger, but she was

13

also very tired, emotionally and physically exhausted, and she had no idea what to do next except to go along with this man, who seemed kind and might mean well.

It was a treat to ride in a cab and confirmed Taisie's belief that Mr. Lawton was a real gent. She was impressed, too, by the size of his house, although it was no more than a suburban villa, standing in its own grounds in a tree-lined road.

Greville Lawton opened the front door with his own key, but as soon as they were inside he rang the bell. The maid who came to answer the call was a round-faced, sturdy girl in her twenties. When she caught sight of Taisie, sitting on the edge of a chair with her feet dangling, she looked as if she could hardly believe her eyes.

"We have a problem, Hetty," Mr. Lawton said. "This little girl is without a home. Can you make up a bed for her, just for tonight? Tomorrow I'll consult the proper authorities about what is to be done with her."

Hetty and Taisie looked at one another. "One of the guest rooms, sir?" Hetty asked.

"Oh, I think not," Greville Lawton said and the surprise in his voice told Hetty just where Taisie was to be placed in the social scale, even though he immediately went on: "She might be lonely. Somewhere near to you would be more suitable."

"Yes, sir," Hetty said. "Come with me, little girl."

"Her name is Taisie Brown," Greville said. "Has Mrs. Lawton gone to bed, Hetty?"

"The mistress went up an hour ago, sir."

And just as well for you she has, Hetty thought, looking at the disreputable scrap of a girl the master had brought home with him. What her ladyship was going to say about it in the morning was something Hetty looked forward to hearing. It might cause ructions, but it would certainly add a bit of drama to a dull life.

As it turned out, Hetty was disappointed. Laetitia Lawton, unpredictable, capricious to a fault, decided to find amusement in the arrival of a Cockney waif in her home. She spoke of it immediately, as soon as Greville went in to visit

15

her the next morning. Laetitia was sitting up in bed, her hair, ash blonde fading imperceptibly into grey, spread out over her shoulders, a lacy Shetland shawl arranged over her bare arms, enjoying her early morning tea and toast.

Greville had been away for three days, but Laetitia made no enquiries about his journey nor the way his business had prospered. As he bent over her and kissed her on the cheek she said: "My dear, what's this I hear? Alice tells me you've adopted an orphan."

Greville suppressed a twinge of annoyance. He ought to have remembered that Laetitia's maid would carry the news to her at the earliest possible moment.

"Not adopted," he said. "The poor child appeared on Sutton Station without friends or family: I have given her a bed for the night, but of course it can only be a temporary measure."

"I want to see her," Laetitia said. "I have asked Alice to bring her up to me."

Taisie was having her breakfast in the kitchen, watched with morbid fascination by Hetty and the cook. Hetty, better versed in the problems of the poor than

16

her master, had taken the precaution, in spite of the lateness of the hour, of giving Taisie a ruthless wash and examining her for vermin before allowing her into the narrow bed in the attic room that opened out of her own. To her surprise, the child had been clean, but Hetty had made a discovery which she discussed in a hushed whisper with the cook the next morning.

"Blood all down her legs . . ." she whispered.

The two women looked at Taisie, munching her way through thick slices of bread and honey. She picked up her tea and drank thirstily, her face almost hidden by the large cup.

"Poor little blighter," the cook said. "No wonder she ran away."

They wouldn't have been able to resist questioning the child, but at that moment Alice arrived to take Taisie up to Mrs. Lawton and they kept quiet. Alice was not liked. She gave herself airs, thinking herself above the others because she was a lady's maid, and she was too much in the mistress's confidence to be trusted. Without actually saying so to one another, the other women decided to keep the secret of Taisie's violation from her.

Alice spoke sharply to Taisie as they went up the stairs. "Be respectful when you speak to Mrs. Lawton," she instructed her. "Call her madam and don't speak unless you're spoken to."

Taisie made a face at her back. Now that she was no longer stunned by fatigue she was able to take an interest in her surroundings and she looked round her with curious eyes. The house seemed like a palace, soft red carpet even on the stairs, a polished mahogany banister which produced a satisfactory squeak when she ran her hand over it, patterned paper on the walls, and pictures. Taisie would have liked to have stopped and looked at the pictures, but Alice was waiting for her, an impatient expression on her face.

Laetitia Lawton's bedroom was even more of a revelation. Taisie had never seen anything like it. It was a pink and cream boudoir, all shimmering satin and lace appliqué, and in the middle of it Laetitia sat propped up against her embroidered pillows, her fading beauty flattered by the subdued light filtered through the net

18

curtains, an imperious queen demanding to be amused.

Taisie advanced to the middle of the room, her eyes fixed on this strange woman who didn't seem to be ill and was yet in bed at ten o'clock in the morning, and dropped the careful curtsey which had been drilled into her in the past week. She was still wearing her pink taffeta dress, since she had no other clothes, her hair had been combed out by Hetty and rippled down her back, there was a faint colour in her wide cheekbones.

"Oh, what a little doll!" Laetitia exclaimed in her high, drawling voice. "And what a perfectly horrible dress! You should *never* wear pink, darling. Not that sugary pink. Greens or browns for you."

She stretched out a hand. "Come here and tell me your name."

Taisie went to the side of the bed and put her hand in Laetitia's. It was very soft, not a hand that had ever done any work.

"Anastasia Brown, mam," she said. "But I'm called Taisie."

"Anastasia! How unusual! I'm told you are an orphan, poor little thing, and you've run away from a nasty man who tried to make you work for him."

Taisie considered this version of her story. "Yes," she agreed cautiously.

"You were quite right! Men are such monsters! Even my own dear husband, though you mustn't tell him I said so."

Taisie took her hand away. She was beginning to think that the reason this strange woman was kept in bed was because she was touched in the head. She took a step backwards, ready to run if it became necessary.

"What's going to happen to you now?" Laetitia asked lazily.

"Dunno."

Taisie was looking round her, trying to take in all the details of this unimaginable luxury.

"Mr. Lawton talks of an orphanage, but I don't know . . . Would you like to stay here, Taisie?"

That brought Taisie's wandering attention back to her with a jerk. "Yes," she said.

"So definite! I'm flattered! Perhaps it can be arranged . . . I must talk to my husband. But the most important thing is to get you some different clothes. I shall get up. Alice!"

Downstairs in Greville's study Hetty had nerved herself to reveal what she had discovered the night before—and was "just one blush all over, as I'm sure you'll understand, Mrs. Baker" as she later told the cook.

"If you please sir," she said, nervously pleating the edge of her white apron between her fingers, "it's not a thing as I like to speak of, but it's my opinion that the little girl had been . . ." she swallowed nervously ". . . interfered with," she finished in a rush.

"Good God!" Greville stared at her blankly. It had not occurred to him. He had thought that the child might have suffered cruelty and neglect, but not that she had been exploited in such a repulsive fashion. In his shock he spoke aloud the first thought that came into his head.

"Your mistress mustn't hear of this."

"No, sir," Hetty said, quite expressionless.

"It would upset her," Greville added unnecessarily.

"According to Alice, the mistress has

taken quite a fancy to the little girl," Hetty went on in the same carefully noncommittal way. "She's asked for the carriage to be brought round and means to go out and buy new clothes for her."

Involuntarily Greville glanced at the clock. For Laetitia to be out of bed before eleven o'clock was so unusual that the whole household must be buzzing with the news.

"Alice has got the idea that the little girl might be asked to stay," Hetty said.

That made him sit up and take notice, she saw with satisfaction. Now that she had got over the embarrassment of speaking about the other nasty business, Hetty was enjoying the interview. Right in the thick of things for once and that was one in the eye for stuck-up Alice.

"Who besides you knows about the child's . . . misfortune?" Greville asked abruptly.

"Only me and Cook, sir."

"Then I'll be obliged if you'll keep it to yourselves." Greville hesitated. He did not want to make an outright request for the information to be kept from Alice, but he need not have worried; Hetty understood him. Anything told to Alice would find its way to Mrs. Greville as a matter of course.

"I'm sure it's not a thing I'd talk about, sir," she said. "Less said the better, if you ask me."

"As for the child staying on . . . I'll have to consult my wife about that."

Hetty bobbed respectfully and left him, but outside the door her expression was derisive. "Consult" was good: go and listen to what his wife had decided, more likely. Properly under her thumb, he was, and who could blame him, poor gentleman, seeing how nasty the mistress could be if she was crossed.

No-one seeing Laetitia later that morning when she drifted into her husband's study, exquisitely attired in fawn-coloured silk, her expression livelier than Greville had seen it in an age, could have guessed at the implacable will behind her languid manner.

"My dear, the fatigue!" she sighed, sinking gracefully into a chair. "And so hot! All shops are horrid, but the ones in Sutton are the worst I have ever encountered. If only I could endure the journey to London more often, but my wretched health won't allow it. I do think, Greville, that you should have listened to me when I asked you to move to Belgravia. So much more convenient in every way."

It was an old complaint and Greville knew better than to enter into an argument.

"Can I give you a glass of wine to refresh you, my dear?" was all he said.

"Wine! So heating. Of course, if it were iced champagne . . . but I've resigned myself to doing without such luxuries."

Again he refrained from answering her. He poured out a glass of Madeira and set it down on a table by her elbow and after a few minutes Laetitia picked it up and sipped it slowly.

"I've been clothing that odd little thing you brought home with you last night," she said. "What is to become of her?"

"I intended taking her along to the Police Station this morning, but you forestalled me by taking her out with you."

"She couldn't be allowed to go anywhere in that horrid pink taffeta. Such a nasty dress. I've had it burnt."

"You've been very kind and I hope the child appreciates it."

Greville was being cautious, feeling his way until he knew what Laetitia had in mind.

"She seemed quite overcome. Of course, I used a certain amount of discretion. Not the clothes I would have chosen for a daughter of my own, just a few garments suitable for her station in life. The way she talks is atrocious, but she seems intelligent: I think we should keep her."

"But in what capacity . . ." Greville enquired.

"Cook is always saying she needs more help in the kitchen. I dare say Taisie could be of use. And I shall take an interest in her, try to improve the way she speaks, perhaps teach her to read to me. It will be an amusement for me during the long dreary hours when you have to occupy yourself with business, my darling."

The fact that Greville had recently become a partner in his brother's firm of wine merchants was another bone of contention between them. Laetitia, whose grandfather had been a bishop and one of whose cousins was married to a baronet, objected to having a husband in trade, even though the wine trade did have a certain cachet to it. If Greville had agreed to her suggestion that his office in London made it a necessity for them to have a house in town she might have been reconciled, but for once he had withstood her demands, saying, with more truth than Laetitia could be brought to admit, that they could not afford it. Faced with the choice of a smaller house with fewer servants in an unfashionable part of town or the continuance of her present comfortable life in the suburbs, Laetitia had made a graceful, but not uncomplaining, withdrawal. She had let it be understood, to the few friends who were interested, that poor dear Greville had insisted on the martyrdom of travelling up to London by train rather than deprive her of the benefit of country air. It was an explanation that reflected credit on both of them and Laetitia had almost come to believe it herself, only referring two or three times a week to the different existence she might have enjoyed if she could have had the house in Belgravia she had desired.

The idea of taking Taisie into his household did not commend itself to Greville, but it was a small concession to his wife's caprice, compared to the major victory he had won over the house in London, and he was prepared to let her have her way.

"Has Taisie told you anything about herself?" he asked cautiously.

"Only that she has no parents and her aunt and uncle have emigrated, leaving her in the care of a Mr. Gribble, who seems to have treated her badly. I asked Taisie if he beat her and she said 'Not so's it would show'! So quaint!"

It might be quaint to Laetitia; it made Greville shudder. He knew that he must not even hint at the more sinister side of Taisie's exploitation. Child prostitution was something no lady could be expected to know about and Laetitia, in particular, would be outraged. The revelation would certainly lead to a fit of hysterics and, all too likely, a revulsion against Taisie. Sex was repugnant to Laetitia, as he knew to his cost, since her delicate state of nerves had driven him into a separate bedroom and any approach from him made her prostrate with nervous debility for days.

He certainly knew that this Gribble character should be caught and punished and that it was his duty to take Taisie to the Police and help her to make a statement. But if he did that and the story leaked out, perhaps even got into the newspapers, Taisie would no longer be welcome under Laetitia's roof. He tried to weigh his public duty against the welfare of one small child and in the end he did what Greville usually did, he let it slide and Laetitia got her way.

Taisie, with two new print dresses to her name, promoted to a bedroom to herself, which was something she had never known before, well fed and kindly treated, was less grateful than she might have been, since she regarded all these benefits as stemming from her own initiative in running away from Clerivale Street. In a surprisingly short time she had settled into the household as if she had always been there and the memory of her past life began to fade from her mind. Only one image persistently came back to haunt her and she sometimes woke up in the night from the nightmare recollection, shaking and afraid: a man's face, white, plump and gloating, with a heavy black moustache and, on the left side, only half an ear. She never spoke of it, but there were still days when she looked all eyes and while the memory of the dream lasted she liked to stay close to Hetty.

She was ignorant, but she was sharp, and, as Mrs. Baker said to Hetty, she only had to be told once. Before long she had her own small tasks which kept her occupied and were useful to the other servants. She swept and dusted her room and Hetty's next door and also the stairs from the attic to the part of the house "the Family" used; she peeled potatoes and helped with the washing up; Alice, discovering her to be neat-fingered and sharp-eyed, condescended to teach her to sew and it was only Taisie who guessed that it was Alice's fear of her own fading sight that made Taisie's neat stitches acceptable to her. Laetitia, as she had promised, took an interest in her. In her languid way she had made up her mind that Taisie was going to be a credit to her and so, whenever she thought of it, she called Taisie away from her other duties and made her read aloud, correcting her mistakes and modifying her deplorable accent. It was not difficult because Taisie, as the other servants soon found out, was a born mimic.

The first time she sailed into the kitchen after a session with Laetitia, she sank down on to a chair, raised her hand to her head and sighed: "Oh, my dear, the fatigue!" Hetty snorted with laughter and then leaned over and smacked Taisie smartly on the arm.

"That's to teach you not to be disrespectful," she said. "The mistress has got more to bear than what you and I understand."

But for all her stern words her lips were quivering with amusement. Voice, attitude, the way Taisie had lifted the back of her hand to her forehead, all had been exact. It was Laetitia to the life and Hetty could not help laughing.

Greville saw little of her and he put the uncomfortable recollection of her despoilment to the back of his mind, except once when in an unthinking moment he smoothed his hand over Taisie's head and remarked that she had pretty hair. The panic-stricken way she jerked away from him shocked Greville and, after he had got over it, annoyed him, since he had truly meant no more by his careless gesture than the kind of compliment which might have been made by a mildly affectionate uncle. After that he took care to keep out of her way until he, too, was dragged into her education. Laetitia complained that the child could not write legibly and made him find an old, retired clerk who came twice a week and taught Taisie to write a beautiful copperplate hand.

It was Laetitia who discovered that the child could sing. Hetty and Mrs. Baker had grown used to hearing snatches of song from Taisie as she worked in the kitchen and joined in themselves sometimes: it was cheerful and it helped the work along. They thought nothing of it, and neither did Taisie herself.

When Laetitia sent for Taisie one afternoon she was at the sink carefully washing the lunchtime coffee cups.

"The missus wants you in the drawing room, Taisie," Hetty said. She sat down and put her elbows on the scrubbed white wood table. "Keep her busy till teatime, there's a dear; my feet are killing me."

Taisie removed the rough linen apron she wore for washing up, wiped her hands,

31

smoothed her hair and put on the white pinafore she adored. More than any other garment she owned this spotless pinafore signified to Taisie that she was one of the posh girls now.

When she reached the drawing room Laetitia was playing the piano. She smiled at Taisie, but did not stop playing. Taisie went and watched her fingers moving over the keys.

"I know that song," she said as Laetitia finished with a trill of notes in the upper register. "The Irish navvies who lodged with Ma Dailey use'ter sing it on the way home from the pub of a Saturday night."

"'Used to'," Laetitia said automatically. "Really, Taisie, the things you say! A little girl like you shouldn't know anything about public houses."

She played the opening bars again. "Sing it to me," she commanded.

Without the slightest selfconsciousness, effortlessly as a lark, Taisie opened her mouth and sang "The Londonderry Air".

When she finished Laetitia sat and looked at her. "A gift for music," she said. "I knew there was something that drew you to me the first time we met. I'm incredibly sensitive about these things—I *knew*. Taisie, you must have singing lessons; I shall insist."

"I don't know that I've got the time," Taisie objected. The idea of having lessons in singing was to her just one more example of Laetitia's strange goings on. Who needed to be taught to sing? Either you could or you couldn't. Taisie could sing already so why waste money on something so unnecessary?

Greville would have agreed with this view if he had known about it. Faced with a demand to find a suitable music master for the orphan child he had taken into his house, he objected that he could see no need to bestow such a luxury on a little servant girl.

"You don't understand," Laetitia said, leaning back and closing her eyes. "The child has a gift. How different my own life might have been if my musical ability had not been stifled. As it is, all that is left to me is to foster talent where I find it. Taisie must have singing lessons."

"I doubt whether you would have had the stamina to become a concert pianist, if that is what you're hinting; nor do I think you would have found it a suitable life for a lady," Greville said with an irritation he could not suppress.

"Alas, no," Laetitia agreed. "My wretched constitution, my exquisite sensibility. Even at this moment I feel one of my headaches coming on."

Greville got up from the dinner table and threw down his napkin. "I'll be in my study if you want me for anything," he said. "If you have a headache I suggest you go to bed. I will pay for music lessons for Taisie, but I really cannot spare the time to interview music masters; you must find a teacher yourself."

# 2

OF all the people living in the Lawtons' house the one to whom Taisie felt closest was Hetty. For one thing Hetty was the youngest and, although she was more than ten years older than Taisie, she had not forgotten her own childhood and would occasionally, when the Lawtons were out, chase Taisie round the lawn or join her in one of the singing games Taisie had picked up in the London streets. It was Hetty who realized that in many ways Taisie had a lonely life. Hetty saw no harm in making the child work; she had been in service herself since she was twelve; but she also realized the disadvantages of Taisie's position, half servant and half pet, exhibited like a performing dog in the drawing room and then dismissed at Laetitia's whim and forgotten.

"I'll say one thing for the mistress," she remarked to Mrs. Baker. "She hasn't lost interest in the child. I quite thought, knowing her, that young Taisie would be finished and done with before the summer was out. Yet here we are, getting on for Christmas, and no sign of parting with her."

"It's the music," Mrs. Baker said. "To give Mrs. Lawton her due she does know her stuff when it comes to music. She likes showing Taisie off to her friends. What is it she calls her?"

"My protégée," Hetty said. "Whatever that may mean. I've been thinking, Mrs. Baker, Taisie being only a child when all's said and done, that we might try and do something for her for Christmas."

"She'll have roast goose and plum pudding, same as the rest of us," the cook said. "What more does she want?"

"I just thought, some little present on Christmas morning."

"If she's to have presents I dare say Mr. and Mrs. Lawton will see to it. I can't see there's any call for you and me to lay out our cash on Christmas presents for Taisie Brown."

Hetty said no more, but that did not mean that she had given up her idea. The trouble was, it was difficult to think of anything suitable for Taisie. A doll might have been the answer for any other little girl, but there was something incongruous about the idea of Taisie cuddling a doll.

Hetty made an effort to find out what Taisie herself would like, but she was clumsy about it and Taisie guessed why Hetty took her along when she was sent out to deliver a note for Mrs. Lawton and why they stopped outside the toy shop and looked in the window when they ought to have been hurrying home.

"Looks pretty, doesn't it?" Hetty asked, elaborately casual. "I wonder what you'd choose if Father Christmas was to bring you a present? Bearing in mind, o'course, that things like that dolls' house are meant for rich little girls," she added hastily.

Taisie gave her one quick, shrewd look. Until that moment it had not occurred to her that Christmas might mean anything to her except a rich meal and extra washing up. She looked at the display of wax dolls and brightly painted wooden toys, but none of them appealed to her.

"I'd like a box," she said. "A pretty box to keep things in."

Hetty's face brightened perceptibly. It

was an odd choice, but practical, and it gave her plenty of scope to buy something she could afford.

As soon as they were back at the house Taisie darted upstairs and unscrewed the hollow brass ball on the rail at the end of her bed where she had hidden the change out of the guinea she had stolen six months earlier. If people were going to buy presents for her then Taisie was going to do the same for them. She counted the money anxiously and then reckoned up the people involved. There was Mr. Lawton and Mrs. Lawton, Cook and Hetty and, she supposed, Alice, who had a sharp tongue but had taught her to sew, Mr. Poplar, who had taught her to write and would like some tobacco, and Mr. Manders, who came every week to give her a piano and singing lesson. Looking at her little pile of silver and coppers Taisie regretted that she had been tempted into buying toffee at the sweetshop and now had so little left.

The following evening Mr. Lawton, on his way home a little earlier than usual, heard the sound of "Hark the Herald Angels Sing" sung with piercing sweetness by a child outside the station and felt automatically in his pocket for a penny. He had it in his hand before he realized that the child was Taisie, warmly dressed in her good wool coat and crimson tam o'shanter, and hopefully shaking a cardboard box under the noses of the passersby.

"Taisie, what on earth are you doing?" he demanded.

"Collectin'," Taisie replied. She was not in the least put out, until she realized his displeasure. "We always do it," she faltered. "I went round the houses with Algie and his pals last Christmas, singing carols, only Algie took it all off me when we was finished and I weren't any better off in the end than I was before."

"But that was different," Greville said helplessly. "You mustn't do those things now."

"It's not wrong, honest it isn't, Mr. Lawton. Some of the choirboys came round the other afternoon and Mrs. Lawton gave them ten bob!"

"It may not seem wrong to you, but I don't like you doing it," Greville said, abandoning any hope of making Taisie understand why he had been shocked to see her singing for money in the street.

"It's for Christmas presents," Taisie said in one last despairing attempt to make him see reason.

It took Greville by surprise, the idea that this child he had taken in for charity should want to be a giver as well as a taker. He looked down at the small, earnest face raised to his and saw that Taisie was entirely serious. She had improved in the months she had spent in his house. The hollows in her cheeks had filled out and the look of waiflike fragility had almost disappeared. Yet not entirely, for nothing would ever quite make up to Taisie for the neglect of her childhood, but her former attitude of shrinking defiance had become a sturdy independence and she argued fearlessly when she thought she was in the right.

"You do a lot of work for me," Greville said. "I know you are fed and housed— and clothed, too—and have other advantages over the other servants, but perhaps I ought to pay you wages. I'll give you sixpence a week. Since you've been with me for nearly six months, that means I owe you about twelve shillings and sixpence. Will that pay for your Christmas presents?"

"You're a real toff," Taisie said gratefully. "Will I go on getting the sixpence after Christmas?"

"Certainly," Greville said gravely, hiding his amusement at her wholehearted satisfaction. "Now come along home with me. How much did you collect for your carol singing?"

"One and fourpence. I hadn't been at it long," Taisie said regretfully. She still thought it was silly to neglect such an easy way of earning a penny or two, but with the promise of twelve and sixpence and more to come she was prepared to fall in with Mr. Lawton's wishes.

Greville found Laetitia in a gay mood when he arrived home and because she was in such a radiant humour he told her the story of Taisie's moneymaking effort. To his relief she received it with peals of laughter.

"Singing carols so that she could buy me a Christmas present!" she exclaimed. "Isn't she a little pet? Really I'm quite touched. But what a shock it must have been for you when you saw her! Poor Greville—so conventional!"

It would have surprised Laetitia to know that Taisie spent more on Hetty than on anyone else, but since Taisie was clever enough to consult Alice about what would be suitable as a present for Mrs. Lawton she was well satisfied with the pink satin lavender sachets she received and even said that Taisie had shown excellent taste.

The small incident jolted Greville into taking a closer interest in Taisie. He felt a thrill of pride when she came in after the dinner the Lawtons gave on New Year's Eve and sang to the guests, but he also felt uneasy.

"It's all very well to cultivate the child's voice," he said to Laetitia afterwards. "But she's had no real education. She's not fitted for anything but menial work. What will become of her in the future?"

"Really, darling, does it matter?" Laetitia drawled. "Alice tells me she sews very nicely. Perhaps we can turn her into a lady's maid, or even a dressmaker. She's only ten years old. I'm sure I shall be shown the way when the time comes to launch her into the world."

She sounded impatient and he thought that it was because she was tired after the New Year celebrations, so he kissed her on the cheek and left her, as he usually did now, to go to his own lonely bed in the room next door, but the truth was that Laetitia was growing a little bored with Taisie. She would not abandon her, that would have seemed unkind, and Laetitia valued her reputation for kindness, but gradually Taisie's visits to the drawing room became less frequent and the following summer when her music teacher fell ill and gave up teaching he was not replaced. Taisie was less of a pet and more of a servant, but she still received no wages except the sixpence a week Greville had absentmindedly ordered to be paid to her out of the housekeeping money.

Since Taisie had always been bewildered by Laetitia's capricious demands on her she was not sorry when they faded away, but she resented the loss of her music lessons. When she was sure that Laetitia was going to be out of the house for any length of time she sometimes abandoned her other duties to go into the drawing room and play on the piano. No-one was quite sure whether this was allowed or not, but Taisie carried it off with such a high hand that not even Alice cared to make trouble by mentioning it to Mrs. Lawton.

The atmosphere in the house was not happy. Greville looked grey and drawn and all the servants knew that there were arguments between the master and mistress about money. Nothing, it seemed, could stem the relentless tide of Laetitia's extravagance. She had the drawing room redecorated regardless of expense and Greville exploded in real anger when he received the bills. She took to her bed for two days as a result and for once it did not reduce him to remorseful apologies.

"Serves her right," was Hetty's verdict. "I don't know why he puts up with her ways. It's not as if they've got any real marriage—separate rooms, that's not the way to treat a man in my opinion."

"You'd do better to keep your opinion to yourself in front of the child," Mrs. Baker said. "Not but what I agree with you, but it's not fitting you should speak of such things, you being an unmarried woman an' all."

"I know what's what, same as any

44

woman does," Hetty flared up. Her unmarried state was a sore point with her, as Taisie knew.

"My Uncle Fred gave Auntie Lil a black eye when she said she wouldn't have him getting into bed with her when he was drunk," Taisie said reflectively.

It was the sort of remark she came out with occasionally which reduced the other women to shocked giggles, but it was rare now for her to speak of her past life. She hardly ever thought of them, Auntie Lil and Uncle Fred and cousin Algie in Australia, and had only the vaguest idea of where Australia was, except that it was a long way away and had kangaroos in it. And the memory of Abe Gribble's establishment had been buried deep in the recesses of her mind.

Taisie grew taller and larger and her clothes had to be replaced, but since Laetitia had stopped taking an interest in that side of Taisie's life it was Hetty who had to appeal to Mr. Lawton to give her the money that was needed, and she noticed that he parted with it reluctantly.

While Laetitia was still languishing on the sofa as a result of the quarrel over her new decorations she started calling Taisie in to read aloud to her, querulously correcting her Cockney accent which grated on Laetitia's sensitive ears. It gave Taisie some education, although since Laetitia's preference was for novels which dealt with High Society it was a onesided view of the world that she gained from her reading. Taisie secretly despised the sentimental passages and would sometimes repeat them as a comic turn in the kitchen.

"As good as a Music Hall," Cook said, wiping her eyes. "Do that bit about Sir Montagu and Lady Lilian, Taisie."

"'Her heart beat so hard that she feared she would swoon'," Taisie recited obediently, sinking back on one of the hard kitchen chairs and closing her eyes with a languishing air copied from Laetitia. "'Say you'll be mine', he whispered, bending so close that his soft golden whiskers brushed her bare shoulder. 'It cannot be!' she sighed. 'We must say farewell! Do not ask me why! I cannot tell you!'" Taisie clasped her hands over her heart and gazed up at the ceiling with a soulful look which convulsed Cook.

"Why can't she take him?" Mrs. Baker demanded.

"Because she thinks her brother killed his brother in a duel, only he didn't," Taisie said. "Silly ha'porth. What's it got to do with her if their two brothers had a scrap?"

"But it all comes out right in the end?" Hetty asked.

"Oh, yes—same as always. Up the aisle to the altar and happy ever after. Some hope!"

"Some people are happy when they're married," Hetty assured her.

"Can't say I've ever noticed it," Taisie said.

Taisie was fourteen when Alice at last admitted that she was shortsighted. The first time she wore her new spectacles Laetitia shrieked and forbade her ever to come near her again with them on.

"They make you look ugly and I can't bear ugly people," she said.

Stiff with resentment, Alice gave in her notice.

"You could have taken them off when you went to her ladyship and just worn them for sewing," Hetty said.

"I've had enough of madam's ways," Alice said. "No-one can stay young for ever, no matter what they put on their face out of a pot. Every time she finds a new wrinkle she blames me for it. My sister wrote only last week and said there was a vacancy in the village where she works. I was hesitating about it, but now I've made up my mind. I'm putting in for it and with my sister being known and recommending me I reckon I'll get it."

She went at the end of the month and the lives of the remaining servants were made hideous by Laetitia's efforts to find a replacement who suited her.

Since Laetitia insisted that she was unable to lift her arms above her head to do her own hair and Hetty was alleged to be clumsy, it fell to Taisie to help her with her elaborate daily toilet in the intervals between the departure of one maid and the arrival of the next. She learnt a lot, but she did not enjoy it. Laetitia was approaching her fiftieth birthday and Taisie, her fresh young face reflected in the looking glass beside her mistress's fading, fretful one, had little sympathy for dressing up mutton as lamb.

The birthday was the occasion of a celebration dinner. Greville's brother came with his wife and their son and daughter, and a few local friends. They sat down twelve to dinner, with Laetitia, her hair delicately tinted back to its original colour and a soft blush of rouge on her cheeks, looking remarkably well in the candlelight. She was wearing a pretty pearl and opal pendant which had been Greville's present to her and she had been well pleased with it until she caught sight of the diamond brooch her sister-in-law was wearing. After that her hand played restlessly with the pendant and Taisie, helping Hetty to wait at the table, saw the tightening of her lips and jealous glances which meant trouble for Greville later.

Perhaps it was his own realization that he had once again fallen short of his wife's expectations, perhaps it was that he had at last reached the end of his patience: Greville, rising to his feet at the end of the dinner, his glass in his hand, said: "May I ask everyone to join me in a toast? To my dear wife on her fiftieth birthday."

They drank the toast, but the sister-in-law said with lively amazement and the greatest possible enjoyment: "*Fiftieth* birthday? Why Laetitia, I thought you were no more than forty-five."

Greville's brother did his best to retrieve the situation. "I'm sure no-one would have been surprised if this had been Laetitia's *thirtieth* birthday, so well preserved as she is."

If he had not added the last few words he might have got away with his laboured gallantry. As it was, Laetitia thought he was mocking her. She shook visibly, the despised pendant trembling on her breast. With no thought in her mind but to avert a disastrous scene Taisie stepped forward with the water jug in her hand and, in filling her mistress's glass, contrived to spill the water on the polished table.

"Clumsy girl!" Laetitia hissed, turning on her. "Did I ask for water? No! Mop it up quickly or the table will be ruined. Was anyone ever so plagued as I am by stupid servants?"

Her sister-in-law, ashamed of her provocative remark, leaped into the breach with a story of the iniquities of her own servants and the dangerous moment passed, at least until after the guests had gone; then the storm broke over Greville.

For once he stood his ground. "You are fifty," he said. "And I see no point in hiding it. I'm tired of this cult of being young. You are beginning to make yourself ridiculous. You dye your hair, you paint your face—and it deceives no-one."

Laetitia became hysterical. She tore the birthday pendant from her neck, breaking the delicate chain, and flung it on the floor. Greville looked at her, her face contorted, her body writhing amongst the satin pillows on her bed, then he went out of the room and closed the door on her.

As he went down the stairs he staggered and put his hand to his chest, an expression of pain on his face. Hetty was passing through the hall and she said: "Is there anything wrong, sir?"

"No, I'll be all right in a minute," Greville said. He managed to smile. "Indigestion, Hetty. That was a very good dinner. Please give Cook my compliments."

He went into his study and poured himself a glass of brandy. He had not meant to think about money matters that

51

night, but unwillingly his hand went to the drawer where he kept his accounts. He had not been able to afford the pendant which Laetitia had despised, he had not really been able to afford the dinner. He felt deadly tired. The pain in his chest which had been plaguing him for weeks was growing worse. He raised his glass and sipped, but the spirit caught at the back of his throat and made him cough. The pain spread, stretching out tentacles across his chest, running down his arm. There was a band round his head, tightening until he thought that it would burst. Greville slumped forward over his desk, the glass fell from his hand and the brandy spread a slow stain over the carpet.

Hetty found him the next morning and by that time he had been dead for seven hours. It upset her badly, but she assured the other servants later that she had not been surprised.

"I knew there was something wrong," she said importantly. "Terrible he looked when I saw him coming down the stairs."

"To think that the last thing he said should have been a message to me," Mrs. Baker said, wiping her eyes. "He was a good master. We'll see some changes now he's gone, Hetty. How's *she* taking it?"

"Just like you'd expect," Hetty said. "Laid down on her bed, moaning away like it was the end of the world. He couldn't do anything right for her while he was alive, but he's her sainted Greville now he's dead and gone."

Greville's sainthood lasted until Laetitia discovered that there was far less money to come to her than she had been led to expect. Greville's solicitor explained patiently that they had been living on capital, but Laetitia could see no possible explanation for her comparative poverty but the grossest mismanagement.

When she was told that the house would have to be sold she had to be revived with smelling salts, but in the end she was brought to agree that no other course was open to her.

Cook was dismissed, the latest of Laetitia's personal maids had to go, the carriage and horses were sold, and Laetitia moved to a much smaller house with only Hetty and Taisie to look after her and a boy to see to the garden.

Taisie, with a coolness which earned

Hetty's shocked admiration, discussed her own position with the lawyer.

"If I'm to look after Mrs. Lawton and help Hetty in the house I think I ought to be paid proper wages," she said. "I'm fifteen years old and a good worker and I could get a place anywhere, but I won't desert Mrs. Lawton just now. Mr. Lawton was good to me when I needed a home and I don't forget that. For all that, I can't go on working for nothing for the rest of my life."

Laetitia moaned about ingratitude, but the solicitor was on Taisie's side and she knew in her heart that she would get no-one else who understood her so well at the wage Taisie had agreed to accept, and so it was settled.

Once they were established in the smaller house Taisie and Hetty found it very much to their liking. Hetty was a good plain cook and Taisie, too, had picked up the rudiments from watching Mrs. Baker; they shared the housework between them and Taisie waited at table and helped Laetitia to dress and kept her clothes in order. She and Hetty had some cosy times, sitting in front of the kitchen fire, making toast on the end of a fork and smothering it in dripping.

Laetitia, once she had recovered from the first shock, discovered that there were advantages in being a widow and, with the prudent management that had been forced on her, she was by no means as badly off as she had at first feared. Black was becoming to her and she wore it all the time, lightened after the first few months by a fine cameo brooch or a frill of white at the neck. She turned to religion and became assiduous in her attendance at the church near her new home.

"Like's having her hand held by the Vicar," Taisie diagnosed.

"He's ever so goodlooking," Hetty said. She spoke wistfully, which made Taisie smile derisively.

"Smarmy-parmy," she said. "I don't like dark men, especially with whiskers."

Life might have continued as harmoniously as it did for the first six months if the Vicar had not married. After that Laetitia grew fretful again.

"She makes my life a misery," Taisie complained. "Three times she changed her mind this morning about what she'd wear.

55

I sometimes wonder how much longer I can stand it."

"Don't leave me," Hetty said in alarm. "I couldn't put up with her without you."

"I don't know why you stay," Taisie said. "Why don't you go somewhere a bit livelier? A place where you'd meet more people?"

She meant men and Hetty knew it. It was true their lives were restricted and Hetty, seeing her thirtieth birthday looming up, was often downcast at the thought of remaining a spinster all her days.

"I felt sorry for her when the master died," she said. "And, of course, it's handy here for getting to Clapham to see Mum on my days off. All the same, you're right. I'll give it to the Spring and then I'll think seriously about looking round. Perhaps we could find another place together. That'd be nice, wouldn't it?"

Taisie agreed, but with no real enthusiasm for the idea. Mrs. Baker and Hetty had frequently told her that there was nothing like being in good service for a girl, but Taisie sometimes wondered whether there might not be something she could do to get away from the grind of looking after another woman's house. But what else was there? Shop girls worked long hours and were on their feet all day, and mostly for a pittance. There were no factories in the part of England where Taisie lived and, even if there had been, she would have hated working in one of them. She hadn't the education to teach, she didn't feel fond enough of children to become a nurse. She had a talent for singing, but what was the use of that? The best Taisie thought she could hope for was to become a lady's maid in a high-class household and then at least she might see something of life, but even that was something for the future, not a position she could aspire to before she had even had her sixteenth birthday.

Hetty had Wednesday afternoons off and usually went home to see her mother. On a cold day in February she came back shivering.

"Any tea goin', Taise?" she asked. "I'm perished. How's her ladyship been today?"

"She's nearly driven me mad," Taisie said, pouring out a generous cup of dark brown tea. "Said the egg custard I made was 'insipid', and I made it exactly the same as I did last time when she called it delicious. There's no pleasing her. Did you have a good time?"

"Oo, I did! It was ever so interesting. Have I ever spoken to you about Joe Barnsley? He's the eldest son of Mum's next door neighbours. I haven't seen Joe for years because he's always been working away, but his employer died and the estate's been broken up and so he was at home today and he came in for tea. He's a carpenter by trade, and he's got ever such a good new job, on some lord's estate in the Midlands, starting at the Quarter Day next month. In the meantime, he's doing odd jobs where he can and he's working for a theatrical group! Taisie, guess what, they're coming to Sutton next week, to the Public Hall, and Joe says he can get us complimentary tickets!"

Taisie's face lit up, but then she shook her head.

"She'll never let us both out on the same night," she said.

"That's the best part of it! Joe says the tickets'll be for Monday night and that's when madam's going to that dinner.

Carriages at eleven it said on the invitation and you know her, she'll stay to the bitter end. We can be home before she knows we're out."

The Public Hall had had to be "papered" with free seats given to landladies and local shopkeepers on the Monday night when Taisie and Hetty went to the performance given by Mr. and Mrs. Herbert Lamont and their troupe. However, they did not know that and were impressed by the size of the audience and by the fact that the seats Joe had given them were good ones. Having to steal out of the house secretly and knowing that there was a risk of being found out added to the excitement.

"You ever been to a real theatre?" Hetty asked Taisie as they settled in their seats and loosened their coats.

"I went to the pantomime once. Me an' Algie nipped in with the crowd and got up the stairs to the gallery without paying. I don't remember much about it."

"We used to go to the Music Hall reg'lar when I was still at home. I saw all the top acts—Vesta Victoria, Albert Chevalier, Dan Leno . . ."

"Sh! It's starting."

The curtains parted on the whole company assembled on the stage with a backcloth of a landscape of trees and classical columns and they broke into a rousing song about how glad they were to be there.

The whole evening was magic to Taisie. She was critical about the quality of some of the singing: Mrs. Lamont had once had a fine contralto voice, but Taisie thought that it sounded strained; Mr. Lamont did better with the dramatic monologue than with the two solo songs he attempted in a shaky baritone; only Leonard Luttrell, with a fine, high tenor and an appearance to make any girl's heart flutter, met with her unqualified approval.

"Isn't he handsome?" Hetty sighed. "When he sang all high I went quite wobbly."

Taisie did not answer. When Leonard Luttrell had turned away despairingly as he sang of his hopeless love for a lady far above him she had been struck through by a pang she had never known before. Somewhere inside her something stirred, like the first small flame of a fire which had been damped down but not extinguished. Taisie sat with her clenched fists pushed against the pit of her stomach, fighting a combination of nausea and an excitement she did not understand. With half her mind she was afraid of seeing Leonard Luttrell again because of the disturbance it caused her, with the other half she longed for him to come back so that she could feast her eyes on him once more. Even Tiny Totter, the comedian, in a coat ten sizes too large for him and boots in which he could scarcely shuffle, only made her smile, not laugh out loud as Hetty was doing.

"Isn't he a card?" Hetty asked, wiping her eyes as the curtain came down, but Taisie was incapable of answering, lost in a dream of singing a duet with the handsome tenor.

There was one omission from the published programme. "Owing to sudden indisposition, our dear daughter, Miss Lilian Lamont, is unable to appear," Mr. Herbert Lamont announced. "A much loved artiste has consented to appear in her place. Ladies and gentlemen, Miss Gertrude Pitt!"

61

She was atrocious and appeared to be unaware of it. A self-satisfied smile played round her lips; she simpered and was coy; she made play with an enormous feather fan; everything about her grated, from her off-key soprano voice to her assumption that the audience was overcome by her charm and talent.

"She'd have got the bird at the Alhambra," Hetty said.

"She reminded me of Mrs. Lawton," Taisie said.

Hetty giggled guiltily. "We'll have to nip off home smartly when it's over," she said. "Joe says he'll walk us back, which I thought was very nice of him."

"Sounds as if I might be in the way," Taisie suggested.

"Don't be saucy," Hetty said, but Taisie thought that she sounded pleased.

Joe explained about Lilian Lamont's "indisposition" as they hurried along the deserted streets after the show.

"She's not ill, she's run off," he said. "She's been billed as 'Little Miss Lamont' ever since she was twelve and now she's eighteen she's had enough of it. She walked out of her lodgings this morning and they didn't find her note saying she's gone off to marry a magician she met in Manchester until an hour before the performance. Gertie Pitt has been a dresser for the last three years, and lucky to get that. She offered to step in and Herbert Lamont agreed. His wife nearly took the roof off when she heard what he'd done."

"Will she be performing all the week?" Taisie asked.

"Not likely! They'll have to scout round for another replacement."

They were nearly home. Taisie was a few paces in front of the other two, who seemed to be moving more slowly as they neared the end of their walk. She stopped at the gate and then turned back and clutched Hetty's arm.

"The lights are all on!"

"Oh, my Gawd, she's come home early!"

They tried to get in quietly at the back door, but Laetitia heard them. She flung open the kitchen door, beside herself with fury. Nothing they could say pacified her.

"A theatrical performance! How dare you sneak out without permission to see a parcel of actors! I left my dinner party

63

early because I felt miserably unwell, and the house was empty when I arrived home, *empty*. Anyone could have broken in. I could have been robbed, murdered!"

She put her hand to her head. "My nerves are in shreds. This would never have happened when my dear husband was alive. You would never have dared to treat him like this. Now that I'm a poor widow I am at your mercy."

She tottered away, leaving Hetty and Taisie looking at one another.

"Give her five minutes and then I'll go up and help her get to bed," Taisie said.

"You take it very calmly," Hetty said. "I'm all of a quiver. Do you think she'll turn us out?"

"Not if she's got any sense. Who else would put up with her ways? Besides, we could always find somewhere else."

"Not without a reference, my girl. Unless she gave you a good character you'd have a right old time finding another place."

Taisie sighed. "I'd better go and pacify her then," she said.

She put herself out to soothe her distracted mistress, not so much for her own sake as for Hetty's, and then assured Hetty before they went to bed that the storm had passed and they were to be forgiven.

That night Taisie lay awake a long time after Hetty had fallen asleep and when at last she slept, for the first time for years, she had the old dream about the man who had ravished her as a child. She woke up drenched in perspiration and pushed the end of the sheet into her mouth to stop herself from screaming when a shadow in the corner of the room seemed to move.

No-one had ever spoken to her about her experience, apart from an offhand remark from Hetty that she'd had a nasty time and must try to put it behind her. Taisie had believed she had done that. She had not brooded over the memory, she had buried it deep. It was not as if the experience had come to her in total ignorance. At ten years old Taisie had known what went on between men and women. She had been under-sized for her age, but that had not stopped her cousin Algie from fondling her in a suggestive way, until Taisie had raked his face with her nails. She had known what to expect from the man who had watched her with greedy eyes when she was paraded for his inspection by Abe Gribble, but the act itself had been revolting and she had shut it out of her mind. Now she lay awake in a state of febrile excitement and wondered whether, with a man like Leonard Luttrell, it might not be different, not a brutal horror but more like the romantic stories Mrs. Lawton had made her read and which Taisie until then had despised.

In every way the evening had been a revelation to her. As soon as the curtain had parted she had been transported into a world which, even though she recognized that some of it was second rate, seemed to her to be touched with magic. More than that: something in her had responded to the music, the atmosphere, the applause. Deep inside herself she felt an absolute conviction—this was something she could do, too. She could, if she chose, stand on a stage and stir people to emotion by the sound of her voice. She could make them laugh or cry. It was not merely that she wanted to do it, but that she felt a calm certainty that it was within her power to do it. She thought about what Joe had told them and before she fell back into an uneasy sleep Taisie had made up her mind. The following morning she again left the house without permission and went to see Mr. Herbert Lamont.

She was fortunate in catching him at the Public Hall, conducting a despairing rehearsal of a couple of songs to fill in the gaps left by his daughter's defection and Miss Pitt's hurried dismissal. Taisie, finding the front of the theatre open, walked in and joined him.

"I'd like to speak to you, please," she said.

"Who are you?" Herbert demanded, sparing one irritated glance from the stage.

"I'm a singer. I was here last night and I know you need someone so I've come along to offer myself."

Mrs. Lamont left the piano to ask: "What's going on down there, Herbert? We haven't got time for you to sit chatting."

"It's a little girl who says she can sing," her husband said.

"Anyone we know?"

"What's your name?" Herbert asked.

"Taisie Brown. Let me sing for you now so that you can see what I can do."

"Send her up," Vera Lamont ordered.

She looked Taisie over when she got on to the stage. "Take your coat off," she said.

Taisie had started putting her hair up in a bun, but she still looked very young. She was wearing a brown velvet dress which had once been her best, but which had had to be let down and then lengthened again by the insertion of a contrasting band at the hem.

"Are you in the profession?" Vera Lamont enquired.

"No, but my voice has been trained," Taisie said, with an inward qualm about the length of time that had elapsed since her last singing lesson and the lack of practice she had done recently.

"Very nice for the drawing room, no doubt, but what you need in a theatre is projection. We haven't got room for amateurs."

"Let me show you what I can do," Taisie asked. She did not say it in a pleading way and something about the way

68

she stood with her chin up, looking Mrs. Lamont in the eye, impressed that lady.

"I suppose we've nothing to lose by giving you five minutes of our time," she said. "Brought your music?"

Taisie nodded. "I'll do this one first," she said.

"What makes you think we'll listen to you twice? All right, miss, go to the middle of the stage. Herbie! Go to the back and see if you can hear her."

As soon as the first notes of "O for the wings of a dove" rose in the air there was a stir of interest. High and sweet and clear, Taisie's voice filled the hall, just as she had known it would. She could dimly make out Herbert Lamont's figure at the back and she sang to him, sure that he would hear every word.

There was a short silence when she had finished. "You've got a pretty voice," Mrs. Lamont admitted grudgingly. "Can you do the comic stuff?"

She gave them "Pretty little Polly Perkins of Paddington Green", with a swing of her skirts and a lilt to her voice that brought a murmur of appreciation.

Vera left the stage and went to consult her husband.

"Come down here, little girl," she called.

When Taisie joined them Herbert asked: "How old are you?"

"Sixteen in a fortnight's time."

"Are your family agreeable to you singing on the stage?"

"I'm an orphan. I haven't got any family. I work as a maid."

"You know already that we're in a bit of a spot, otherwise we wouldn't even consider taking an untried child into our company. As it is, we'll let you try your wings with us. Can you start tonight?"

"Yes. Can I sing the two songs I gave you this morning? I can't stay to rehearse because I've got to get back to serve luncheon."

"Laying down the law already!" Vera Lamont murmured. "Of course, you do realize that being an amateur and us allowing you to get experience with us, we can't pay you a wage."

"Green I may be, but not that green. Fifteen shillings is what I'm asking," Taisie said.

70

"*Fifteen* . . . fifteen *shillings*! Out of the question."

Taisie offered to come down to twelve shillings and sixpence, on the grounds that she was only appearing for five nights instead of six, and finally accepted ten shillings, which was half a crown more than she had hoped for.

Hetty was aghast when she heard what Taisie had done. "How're you going to get round the missus?" she asked. "She'll never give you time off to appear on the stage, never!"

"It's all the same to me if she doesn't. I've made up my mind and I'm going to do it."

"And what about my time off tomorrow? I suppose you think I'll give it up if you ask me nicely?"

The truth was that Taisie had completely forgotten about Hetty's free afternoon. Once she was reminded about it she begged and pleaded and in the end Hetty goodnaturedly agreed to stay at home.

Laetitia would not have been so easily won over, but the illness which had caused her to leave her party early proved to be

71

more real than Laetitia's usual ailments. She took to her bed with a heavy cold that lasted for the rest of the week and remained unaware that Taisie was quietly letting herself in and out of the house for the next few evenings.

Taisie was far from pleased when she discovered that she was billed as "Little Taisie Brown from Your Very Own Town —Only fourteen years old" and required to wear flat-heeled slippers, a frilled white pinafore of the type she had discarded years earlier, and her hair loose round her shoulders.

"I'm sixteen—nearly!" she protested.

"The public like child performers," Vera Lamont informed her. "You'll be able to pass for fourteen for some time yet."

It was the first hint that Taisie might be kept on for longer than the week at Sutton Public Hall and she was silenced by the realization that this might not be merely an exciting episode but the beginning of a new life.

It was not quite the same thing, going out in front of an audience, as singing in the Lawtons' drawing room. For one terrible moment Taisie thought that her throat was too dry, that when she opened her mouth nothing would come out, then she threw back her head and began and it was all right. The audience liked her. She could feel the moment when she "got" them, when she was not merely giving out but receiving back a wave of appreciation. The warmth of the applause intoxicated her; she took two bows and skipped into the wings, hardly knowing where she was or what she was doing.

Leonard Luttrell was there, tall and blond, with a dashing golden moustache, and a smile that made Taisie's heart turn over. He nodded and said: "Well done, little one" and Taisie was in heaven.

It was Friday night before Herbert Lamont said abruptly: "We're off to Birmingham on Sunday. Are you coming with us?"

Taisie already knew the essential question to ask. "How much?"

"I'll put you up to fifteen shillings provided you join in the two finales at the end of the first and second halves."

"Do I have to go on being 'Little Taisie Brown'?"

"It's what'll go over best. Here, this is the billing I've drawn up for you, and very lucky you are to get a mention at your age—'Little Taisie Brown, the London Linnet—Only fourteen and the Toast of the Town.'"

"'The London Linnet', I like that," Taisie said thoughtfully. "I still think it's daft to pretend I'm only fourteen, but I'll have to put up with it, I suppose. Who pays for my fares and costumes and all that?"

"Third class travel will be provided and you won't want anything elaborate by way of dress, just what you've been wearing this week, which belonged to my daughter. You'll pay for your own board and lodging, though as you're new to it Mrs. Lamont and I will see that you get somewhere suitable in Birmingham."

"Where are we going after Birmingham?"

"Liverpool, then Manchester. I've got a booking in Margate over Easter and we'll be in Scarborough for the whole of August. The other dates still have to be filled in."

Taisie drew a deep breath. It seemed a

momentous decision to make all in a moment, but she knew in her heart that she had made up her mind the very first night she had come to hear the Lamont Musical Troupe.

"I'll do it," she said.

# 3

IT took Taisie no more than a week or two to discover that fifteen shillings was barely a subsistence wage. She could just manage to pay for her board and lodging, and she was too inexperienced at first to know that it was sometimes better to provide her own food. She had had six years of living in the midst of plenty and of sharing in the comfort of the Lawtons' middle-class home. It was not easy to go back to beds which had to be examined for bugs and waiting in the corridor to wash at the only cold tap. There were times when she felt that she had made a mistake in abandoning the safe life of a domestic servant, but every evening when she got to the theatre and the tingling atmosphere of excitement closed round her once more she knew that this was what she wanted.

The theatres in which they performed were sometimes no more than barnlike rooms fitted out with tables and chairs and filled with beer-swilling customers who could be rough in their judgement on the performers. The first time a raucous voice shouted to "Little Taisie Brown": "Does your muvver know you're out?" Herbert Lamont stood by ready to order the curtain down if she couldn't cope. But Taisie had been reared in the streets of London and she had a nimble Cockney tongue and the courage to use it. She doubled up her fists, plonked them down on her hips and, arms akimbo, yelled back: "Mine does. Yours is outside waiting for her beer money!" It got a laugh and a shout of approval and Vera rattled into the accompaniment to Taisie's first song before the interrupter could try again.

They had some poor weeks and some good ones. There were occasions when no engagement was forthcoming at all and they were all on short commons, but they got through the summer months. Taisie was learning all the time. She could handle her audience now and she would frequently argue with Vera and Herbert about the songs she should sing. She was growing more and more tired of being called a "child performer".

"I feel a fool," she complained to Leonard Luttrell. "Scuttling out after the show with my head down so that no-one can see that I'm older than I'm supposed to be."

"Bear up," he said, with the caressing smile that never failed to churn up her stomach.

She thought that he must know how she felt about him and yet at even the most casual touch she shied away from him in instant alarm.

"Once we get the pantomime season over I might be making a change," he confided in her. "This outfit is going downhill. Herbert's past it and Vera isn't much better. Lilian was the one who kept them going—and now you. You're a draw, Taisie."

"So are you," she said loyally. Her face was flushed with pride at his praise and he noticed it and smiled.

"We might do all right together," he suggested.

He had not until that moment meant it seriously, but her incoherent delight set him thinking about it. She was growing up, no longer the awkward child who had presented herself at the Sutton Public Hall. She was taller and she was developing fast. There was something very appealing about Taisie's pointed chin and wide cheekbones, the flash of her green eyes, the lovely fall of her copper hair. The cotton pinafore had had to be let out to allow for Taisie's expanding chest measurement, her waist was slender and she had long legs and pretty ankles. Off stage, unhampered by her childish disguise, she was beginning to make heads turn. Singing duets together they might be an act which could move to the Number One halls. Leonard had seen her childish infatuation for him and had been amused, now he began to watch her more closely and his interest quickened.

Christmas was marked by the return of Lilian Lamont and her husband. The Lamonts had kept the reappearance of their daughter a secret until rehearsals started for the pantomime they intended taking on tour. The company was expanded each year for this event, but no-one had expected that Lilian would come back as the Principal Boy, Aladdin, with her magician husband as Abenaza, the Wicked Uncle.

"I wanted to be Aladdin," Taisie grumbled to Leonard.

"I wouldn't like to see you showing your legs like Lilian does," he said and the seriousness with which he spoke made her heart flutter again. "The Princess of China will be a good role for you. Can you act, Taisie?"

"I don't know. You couldn't really call it acting, could you? Not in pantomime."

"You'll have to learn your words and say them nicely."

"Don't talk to me like that," Taisie said. "Like telling a child how to recite verses for Grandma."

Her irritation made him laugh, but it excited him too. Taisie was losing her shyness of him. She wanted him to take her seriously, she wanted him to look on her as a woman.

Lilian Lamont and Taisie took an instant dislike to one another, Lilian because she had not expected to find on her return to her parents' company that her place would have been filled so satis-factorily by an outsider, and Taisie because she resented the other girl's ruthless determination to hog all the limelight.

"I thought this was supposed to be a duet," she complained after the first meeting of Aladdin and the Princess in the Streets of Old China.

"If you produced your voice a little better, dear," Lilian said, "you wouldn't find that mine was swamping yours."

She was taller than Taisie and more heavily built, with hefty thighs that were loudly approved by the rougher parts of the audience when she appeared in her abbreviated costume. She had a trick of edging slightly in front of Taisie, looking towards her as if in loving appreciation and then turning to the audience and letting them have the full benefit of her powerful voice, while Taisie, with a fleshy shoulder and gesticulating arm in front of her face, struggled to be heard.

Taisie soon learnt how to deal with that trick. The next time Lilian turned her head Taisie had glided away with tiny steps, fluttering her fan and looking deliciously pretty in the loose embroidered gown and high headdress intended to represent Old China. The smile she gave

Lilian might have looked like pantomime love, but Lilian recognized the triumph behind it.

They toured until the end of February, but by then even Herbert had to admit that the Christmas season was coming to an end.

"The question is, can we afford to keep Taisie on as well as Lilian and Bert?" he said to Vera.

"Lil's our own daughter, and although I didn't like her going off and marrying Bert it's an asset, having a conjurer in the troupe. Taisie's been very useful, but we can't keep up the pretence of her being a child much longer. She's always saying she's fed up with it. I think we should let her go."

"Lilian and Bert together will come more expensive," Herbert pointed out.

"Worth it if we get better engagements."

"I'll start putting out some feelers. 'Lamont Music and Magic'—how does that strike you as a new name?"

"First rate. Keep it quiet until after we've done our week at Croydon. We can't do without Taisie until the pantomime's finished."

The engagement at Croydon woke Taisie's conscience into an attempt to see Hetty. She had sent her one or two post-cards and on the only occasion when she had remembered to give her address for the following week she had received a short letter from Hetty, but a year had passed since Taisie had left to go on the stage and she knew that she had been neglectful.

She went on the Tuesday afternoon, with a couple of free tickets in her handbag for the following day, hoping Hetty would be able to find a friend to go to the pantomime with her.

The house looked just the same, but smaller. Taisie went round to the back door and tapped with an unaccountable feeling of nervousness, but she need not have worried, it was the same old Hetty who opened it.

"Taisie! Wonders will never cease! Of all the people in the world I've been wanting to see it's you. Come along in. Jenny's just going to take Mrs. Lawton's tea up—this is Jenny, who came to us after you left—and I've made a big pot for myself, and scones fresh out of the oven, just as if I'd known you were coming."

"I ought to have let you know," Taisie said apologetically.

"Never mind about that. Let me look at you. You've grown! Quite the young lady. You must tell me everything you've been doing. Is it as exciting as you thought it'd be?"

"It's hard work," Taisie said, sitting down in her old chair by the side of the kitchen range. "We're at Croydon this week in 'Aladdin'. Is Wednesday still your day off? I've brought you a couple of tickets."

"Oo, that'll be a treat. Thanks ever so much, Taise. Now, before Jenny comes back I must tell you my news. Not that she doesn't know, but I feel awkward talking about it in front of her, seeing that I'm going off and leaving her in the lurch."

"You're leaving here at last?"

"I'm getting married. There, how's that for news?"

"Hetty, I'm delighted. Is it Joe?"

"That's right. Funny, when you come

to think about it, him coming here last year changed both our lives. We fixed it up at Christmas and the wedding's to be the Saturday after Easter. Any chance of you coming, Taise?"

"If I'm in London nothing would keep me away. Hetty, something else before that little girl comes back. Should I go and see Mrs. L?"

Hetty wrinkled her nose. "She took it badly, you going off and leaving her, and she doesn't get any easier as time goes by."

Her eyes lingered on Taisie's clothes, adequate but undeniably shabby. "If you was to come back all rich and successful she might be pleased to see you, but . . ."

"But I look as if I'm on my uppers," Taisie said. "Which I am, very nearly. You don't make a fortune out of the theatre, not unless you're very lucky. I get by, but it's a bit of a struggle sometimes, especially since I keep on growing."

"Do you ever regret it?" Hetty asked curiously.

"No, on the whole I know I did the right thing. It's early days yet. I think—I *know*—I've got it in me to do better than I am at present. I'm going to have to break away from the Lamonts and take a gamble on making a success on my own."

The little servant girl came back and the talk passed to less personal topics. At the end of an hour Taisie had to go and Hetty admitted that she ought to be thinking about preparations for dinner. They parted with affection and renewed promises from Taisie to attend Hetty's wedding if she could possibly manage it.

As she waited for the train on Sutton Station Taisie wondered where she would, in fact, be in April. Not with the Lamonts, she had made up her mind about that, but it was a fearsome step, to strike out on her own.

Taisie had finished her make-up and was adjusting the black wig she wore as a Chinese Princess when Leonard tapped on her door.

"Can I come in? Anyone likely to interrupt us for the next few minutes?"

"The other girls are all on stage. I'm not due for another ten minutes. You're cutting it a bit fine, aren't you?"

"I'll be ready when I'm called. I'll tell you this quickly and then we'll talk about it after the show. I went up to Town this morning, had a word with Charles Morton." He brought out the name carelessly, but she could see that he was bursting with excitement. "He's sending someone along to see us tomorrow night."

"Us? The whole company?"

"No, just you and me. I told him we were going to work up a double act. Sorry I couldn't go into it with you first, but the chance of a chat with Charlie Morton doesn't come up every day of the week. I had to get it in quickly, while he was interested. You're game, aren't you, Taisie?"

"I should think I am!"

He took her out to supper after the show and poured it all out.

"I was having a drink and a sandwich with Tom Costello. I've known him for years and he's always been a good sort, not the kind to forget old pals even though he's top of the tree now. Mr. Morton came in and stopped for a word with Tom. Tom introduced me, which was civil of him, but you could have knocked me down with a feather when he said: 'Mr. Morton, you were saying the other day you were keeping an eye—or rather an ear—open for a good new singer or two. Len here could be what you're looking for.'"

Leonard paused and smiled. "I don't think Charlie Morton was all that pleased, but he asked a few questions, more out of politeness than anything, I could tell that, and then he gave me the old line about keeping me in mind but tenors were two a penny and what he wanted for the Palace was something novel, and quick as a flash I got in with the notion of a double act and he looked more interested. He got up to go, but he said 'I'll send a man down to Croydon tomorrow night to look the pair of you over. If he gives me a good report, I'll ask you to come for an audition.'"

"I almost wish you hadn't told me," Taisie said. "I'll be so nervous tomorrow. If anything goes wrong I might muck up your future as well as my own."

"Nothing will go wrong. You can knock spots off anyone else in the cast. The thing that bothers me is that we haven't had a chance to practise together. We'll have to find a room with a piano and decide what we'll sing for our audition."

"If we get it."

"We'll get it all right. There's just one thing, Taisie. I don't think we ought to tell anyone else there's a man from the Palace coming to the show tomorrow night."

"I agree," Taisie said. "If Lilian knows he's in the audience she'll trip me up and sit on me rather than let me have a hearing."

They walked back to Taisie's lodgings arm in arm, with no reluctance now on Taisie's side to being touched. Every few steps Leonard gave Taisie's arm an extra squeeze and she responded ecstatically. It was all happening, everything was coming true, just like a fairy story. She was going to be successful, and rich—and happy.

When they reached her door she turned to face Leonard and said: "I don't know how to thank you for giving me this chance. I'm more grateful than I can say."

He kissed her quickly, his golden moustache brushing against her lips. Taisie would willingly have prolonged the embrace, but Leonard drew away.

"You're such a babe," he said, with a teasing note in his voice. "Sleep well, little one. See you tomorrow."

He looked in to see her again in the dressing room the following evening. Taisie looked at him with wide, frightened eyes, and he bent towards her and said in a low voice: "Don't look like that. You'll be wonderful, same as you always are. Good luck."

"You, too," she responded mechanically.

There were other people about, so he just put his hand on her shoulder and squeezed it hard before he went out.

Taisie started her performance in a dream. She wanted desperately to be better than usual, but her legs felt like lead and her voice sounded shrill. It was not until Lilian tried out a new little trick of up-staging Taisie so that she was forced to turn away from the audience to speak to her that Taisie suddenly felt herself blazing with anger. She was not going to spend the rest of her life at the mercy of a petty little bitch like Lilian, nor was Lilian going to spoil the best chance of success Taisie had so far had. Her nervousness dropped away, her stiff gestures became fluid, her voice soared. She flirted not just with Aladdin, but with the audience as well. She felt the warm tide of response coming back to her across the footlights. They were a good crowd; she loved them. And because she loved them, they loved her back.

The report that went back to Charles Morton was favourable, though more one-sided than either Leonard or Taisie realized.

"Leonard Luttrell," the note read, "good appearance, good voice, puts the songs over well. Not a *lion comique*. Better at the romantic stuff. Taisie Brown —not quite seventeen and definitely to be watched. Tons of personality and got the looks to go with it. Handles her audience like a veteran, but hardly knows her own power yet. Strongly advise taking the pair for a short season and dropping the man when the girl has got more experience."

By the end of the following week Taisie and Leonard had been offered an engagement at The Palace, Theatre of Varieties, Cambridge Circus.

The other members of the cast were generous in their congratulations. Even Lilian swallowed her chagrin and muttered a few words.

"Very satisfactory," Vera Lamont said graciously. "I hope you'll always remember the training you had with our little troupe, Taisie. We hadn't bargained on parting with Leonard, but Herbert and I have never been ones to stand in anybody's way and I'm sure we wish you both every success."

They had a little party and Taisie drank her first glass of champagne. She thought it decidedly nasty.

"Disappointing," she said to Leonard. "I thought it would taste lovely and sweet, but it's just like sour lemonade with bubbles."

"You'll get a taste for it when you're more grown up," he said.

"I'm grown up now," Taisie said, touched on her tenderest point. "I wish you'd stop treating me like a child." She pressed closer to him, unnoticed in the crowded supper room.

Leonard put his arm around her. "I know you're not a child," he said. "But . . . Taisie, there's something I've got to tell you, not tonight when I'm a bit tight, but tomorrow when I'm sober and feeling sorry for myself."

He broke it to her obliquely the next morning as they walked round a local park.

"Money, first of all," he said. "We're going to start by getting twelve pounds a week for the pair of us. Now, what I want to put to you is that I'm far and away the more experienced and we ought to split it seven pounds to me and five to you. Agreed?"

Five pounds a week sounded like riches to Taisie. "Yes, all right," she said. "But if we get a rise we'll talk it over again."

"Fair enough. The thing is, I need more money than you do, Taisie, because I've got . . . responsibilities. I don't know if you're aware that I'm a married man."

From a long, long way away Taisie heard her own voice saying: "No, I didn't know."

"Let's sit down on this seat for a minute or two. My wife and I live separate lives. We don't get on and so we parted. I still support her, but we rarely see one another. It's a sad situation."

"Yes," Taisie agreed in the same distant, reasonable voice.

"It means that I'm not free to form any other attachment."

"No."

Leonard turned to her and took both her hands in his. "You know what I'm trying to say. You're a lovely girl, we're going to be thrown together. I can't help being tempted. You'll have to be strong for both of us."

"Oh, Leonard," Taisie whispered. She could only look at him, her lips quivering, tears ready to brim over. He raised her hands to his lips and kissed them passionately. When they left the park they were walking as closely arm in arm as they ever had before and Taisie's hand was clasped in Leonard's.

The only satisfactory thing to come out of that devastating conversation was Taisie's ability to say: "Oh, yes, of course," when Lilian remarked spitefully: "I suppose you do know Leonard is married?"

Taisie smiled as she said it and went on smiling, even though she was sure her heart was breaking. She had worshipped him for the past year, but now she thought that she had loved him like a child. It was nothing compared to the feeling she had had for him since he confessed to his unhappy marriage.

The Palace had been built only three years earlier as the English Opera House, but it had had its name changed and become a Music Hall in 1892. When Charles Morton, a small, neat, abstemious man and a master showman, took it over he billed the theatre as "the handsomest Music Hall in Europe" and under his management it went from strength to strength.

Taisie and Leonard's act was no more than politely received at first, but then Taisie discovered a new song in which she could play the part of a girl, innocent but naughty, luring her man on until she landed him at the altar. When Taisie, wide-eyed and irresistible, sang the refrain: "I didn't want to do it, but I did" and Leonard, the reluctant bridegroom, was forced to repeat the same words, the audience chuckled and applauded and they had their first success.

"It suits us because it's just like real life," Leonard said, hanging over the back of Taisie's chair and watching as she removed her make-up. He leaned closer so that he could kiss her shoulder. "You tempt me like the devil, Taisie."

It never passed through Taisie's mind that for a man bent on avoiding temptation Leonard was remarkably free with his caresses. They always kissed each evening when they met at the theatre. That had started on their first night, when he had wished her good luck and she had clung to him in an agony of nerves. Now she had grown superstitious about it and could hardly bear to go on stage unless they had kissed first. When he knew she would be alone he would wander into her dressing room without knocking and there were times when Taisie had to whisk behind a screen to avoid being caught in the nude. He would play with her as she finished changing, lifting her hair to press his lips to the nape of her neck, running his hands down her bare arms, until Taisie closed her eyes and shivered with longing for him.

He drew her to her feet and put his arms round her.

"We ought not to do this," Taisie said automatically.

"I know," he agreed. "One kiss, just one. Put your arms round my neck. Let me hold you close. I love you like this, without any horrid stiff corsets."

She pressed against him, nervous but daring, not drawing away even when his hand moved inside her dressing gown, cupping her breast. Every time they embraced his caresses grew bolder and although she murmured a protest she never drew away from him.

They both knew that she was his, to take when he wanted, but still Leonard held back, savouring the pleasure of the chase, until the night came when Taisie said in a strange, high voice, as his hands moved slowly over her: "I can't bear it!" and Leonard replied: "Neither can I. Darling, you know how I'm situated. Will you come to me, even though I'm not free?"

She nodded, past speaking, and he drew away from her.

"Not here," he said. "Come back with me to my rooms, now, straight away. Stay the night. No-one will know, or care. Taisie, Taisie, tell me you love me."

"I love you," she said. "Oh, I do, I do!"

She was still frightened, even though she dismissed from her mind any moral qualms about giving herself to Leonard. It was not only the dark cloud of fear that lurked deep in the recesses of her mind, the terror connected with the sexual act that had been forced on her as a child: the thought had also come to her recently that she might have been damaged. No-one had ever examined her, they had all been too eager to ignore what had happened. Suppose, having gone to Leonard so willingly, it proved too painful for her to bear when he tried to take her.

She shook in his arms, determined to go on with it, but terrified of what might be going to happen to her, and Leonard, mistaking the reason for the tremors that shivered through her body, whispered: "I suppose you are a virgin, aren't you, my darling?"

"Not quite," Taisie said reluctantly.

"What does that mean? Either you are or you aren't darling."

"Something happened . . . when I was a child."

"You poor little thing! Never mind, I'll make you forget all about it."

He had been a promiscuous lover, but this was something new for him, this union with a trembling, ardent girl in need of something more than the practised caresses he would have given automatically to any woman. He enjoyed exercising his skill on her, it gave an added thrill to what might have been a fairly routine seduction.

And it was rewarding. Released from her fears, transported into a world of sensual delight, Taisie was profligate in her gratitude. She had no-one else to love nor had she any measure of how much she should love him. What Leonard wanted, Leonard could have. For Leonard she was wanton, provocative, unstintingly generous. She lived out her days in a daze of remembered joy and her nights in renewed bouts of passion.

"You wonderful girl," Leonard murmured, his head pillowed on her breast, his hand still almost absentmindedly smoothing over the swell of her hips. "There's not another woman like you in the whole world."

"I'm glad you admit I'm a woman now," Taisie teased him. "Only a few weeks ago you were telling me I was a child."

"I'd certainly call you a woman, and a naughty one at that."

"I like that! You're the naughty one. The things you do!"

Leonard laughed and whispered in her ear. "Have I ever done anything you didn't like?"

"No, never," Taisie admitted. "It's all wonderful."

Their love blazed out on the stage and the sensuous quality of it excited the audience. Their success increased. They were asked to play a second house at another Music Hall and this meant bundling into a cab and crossing London to repeat their act each night. It also meant twice as much money.

"You must get some new clothes," Leonard ordered. "You're a lovely woman. Dress the part!"

It lasted for five months, from their first engagement at the Palace to the end of their love affair and the breaking up of their partnership.

It was a hot night in August. Business was slacker than it had been in the earlier months and that particular evening Taisie had found the audiences at both the Palace and the Oxford sluggish in their responses. She had had to work hard for the chuckles which normally greeted her sallies and the effort had exhausted her. Her stage costume was soaked with sweat. She took off the blue silk dress with the flounces at the hem and, hanging it up, plunged her hands into a bowl of lukewarm water.

There was a tap on the door. Taisie wrinkled her nose. Visitors! The last thing she wanted. But she and Leonard were getting near the end of their contract and she couldn't afford to be capricious with anyone who came to see her in case it was a feeler from a prospective manager. She dried her hands, pulled a loose wrapper over her underclothes and called out: "Come in!"

It was a woman who opened the door and stood uncertainly on the threshold. Taisie thought that she looked about thirty, very shabbily dressed, and ill. Her colour was bad and there were dark circles under her eyes. Taisie had already heard more than one hard luck story and had responded generously, as far as her means allowed, because she remembered all too clearly what it felt like to be poor and desperate. She thought this looked like another touch and cast an anguished thought towards the few pounds in her purse.

"Come in," she repeated, but she didn't ask the woman to sit down, hoping thereby to get rid of her quickly.

"You look younger than you do on the stage," the woman said. "How old are you?"

"Seventeen," Taisie replied. It seemed a strange question and not at all the usual approach. She felt quite at sea and all the more so when the woman sank down on a chair without being asked, covered her face with her hands and muttered: "Oh, God!"

Taisie went and stood over her. "Can I do something for you?" she asked uncertainly. "Are you in trouble?"

The woman lifted her head and looked Taisie in the face. "I'm Beryl Luttrell, Leonard's wife," she said.

Without realizing what she was doing, Taisie moved away from her. The last thing she had ever expected was to meet the woman who had refused to live with Leonard. She made an effort to retrieve the situation by saying: "Did you think this was his dressing room? He's three doors away, down the corridor."

"It was you I wanted to see," Beryl Luttrell said. "I know it's no use appealing to Leonard. I thought you might help, being in love with him, and seeing the wrong you're doing me . . ."

"I'm not . . ." Taisie began, but Mrs. Luttrell interrupted her.

"Oh, come on, ducky!" she said with a touch of spitefulness in her voice. "Leonard doing a double act with a luscious young thing like you and not getting her into bed with him—don't make me laugh!"

Taisie was beginning to feel not only sick, but strangely frightened. She wished desperately that Leonard would come.

"You haven't told me what it is you want," she said.

"Money."

Taisie drew herself up with an attempt at dignity. "If this is an attempt to blackmail me . . ."

"It's not," Beryl Luttrell interrupted

again. "Don't you try those lah-di-dah airs with me, miss. All I'm asking for is what's due to me. The only person I want to put the screws on is Leonard. He hasn't sent me any money for the last five weeks and it can't be because he can't afford it, playing twice nightly at the Oxford and the Palace. I've been lenient with him in the past, letting him run up the arrears, because I've known he's found it hard to make both ends meet, but if he's short now it must be because he's spending it on someone else—and I presume it must be you."

"Leonard doesn't keep me," Taisie said quickly. "I pay my own way."

She thought uneasily of the suppers at the Trocadero, the little sapphire ring Leonard had given her. They had been going it a bit and money did run away. All the same, she couldn't help remembering that Leonard had told her early on that he had a responsibility towards his wife and it was for that reason that their earnings had not been equally divided.

"I'll speak to him about it," she promised.

"Speak to him now," the other woman

said. "I'm not leaving here without a pound or two in my pocket. I can't keep the landlord waiting any longer. He'll have me and the children out in the street if he's not paid tomorrow."

"The *children*?"

Mary Luttrell looked at Taisie with a faint smile. "He didn't tell you about them? We've got two boys, six and eight. The spittin' image of their Dad, both of them."

Taisie was leaning back against the dressing table, trying to stop herself from shaking.

"It doesn't make any difference," she said, but she spoke in an uncertain whisper. "I feel bad about it, of course, but I love Leonard and he loves me . . ."

"I dare say he does, at the moment. Have you asked yourself how long it's going to last? Oh, don't think I blame you! D'you think I don't know how he can get round a girl?" She gave a bitter, jarring laugh. "I ought to! I got caught myself the last time he was home. That's what this is all about really. I'm pregnant and Len thinks he can starve me into getting rid of it. Well, I won't. What would happen to the other two if some back street abortionist did for me?"

"Pregnant? But you can't be," Taisie protested. She looked at the other woman in horror. The sickly look, the desperation, the fullness of her breasts and stomach. "If you are, it can't be his."

"Oh, yes, it is! I've never been with any other man. Not even Len would say that. He was with me at Whitsun. We only had a couple of days, but it was long enough. I couldn't say no, could I, him being my lawful husband when all's said and done. Besides . . . I always think, every time, that this time he'll stick by me, come home and see the boys more often, be a proper husband."

"He told me you'd agreed to live apart," Taisie said.

"I've never agreed to any such thing. I've let him go on tour without me. Well, I didn't have much choice if we were to eat. But I've always wanted him back, I still want him back."

She was crying, angry, futile tears. She brushed them away with the back of her hand. "Give him up," she pleaded. "With you out of the way and the baby to come, he might turn to me again."

Taisie shook her head, not in refusal but in disbelief at the appalling betrayal that was threatening to undermine the glorious happiness of the love she and Leonard shared.

There was a perfunctory tap on the door and, without waiting to be invited, Leonard came in.

"Are you nearly ready, darling . . ." He stopped.

His wife stood up and faced him. He looked quickly from her tear-stained face to Taisie, white and still, backed up against the dressing table.

"What's she been telling you?" he demanded, kicking the door shut behind him.

"That you got yourself another child at Whitsun," Taisie said. "Is it true?"

When, instead of instantly denying it, Leonard said: "Taisie, I can explain . . ." she knew that it was true, but she repeated the question, standing very straight and looking him in the face, noticing the way his expression changed from alarm, to exasperation, to anger.

"It's a small house," he said sullenly. "There was nowhere else to sleep. She got at me . . ."

"Practically the only bit of the Bible I can remember," Taisie said. "'The woman tempted me!' And you didn't tell me you were visiting your wife at Whitsun. Going to see an old pal who'd fallen on hard times, that was what you told me. You make me sick. If you'd really felt about me the way you said you did you couldn't have touched another woman. It was all lies, wasn't it? Just a way of getting me to make love to you."

"No, Taisie! I did love you, I still do! I was weak, I admit that, but she's my *wife*!"

"I looked upon myself as your wife," Taisie said slowly. "You told me you never saw your real one. And you kept quiet about your two little boys, didn't you? Why didn't you tell me about them?"

She waited, but Leonard did not answer.

"Because you thought it might put me off," Taisie answered for him. "You were right. It's put me right off. Get out of here. Take your *wife* with you and give

108

her the money you owe her, you despicable little rat. I never want to see you again."

"But, Taisie, our act!"

She stared at him. "You don't imagine I'm ever going to appear on the stage with you again, do you?"

"You must. We've got a contract. I'll be out of work if we break it and so will you."

Taisie felt behind her. Her hands closed round a cut glass scent bottle, one of Leonard's presents. With a wild swing of her arm she flung it at him. It caught Leonard on the cheekbone and he reeled back.

"Get out!" Taisie blazed. "Go on, both of you! I'll see about whether I can break a contract or not. I'll talk to Mr. Morton now, this minute, and tell him I'll starve in the gutter rather than go on with you again."

She didn't give herself time to think but stormed off to the manager's office, still in her loose dressing gown and stage make-up.

Charles Morton was used to actresses' tantrums, but behind Taisie's incoherent story he recognized a sense of outrage which had shaken her to the depths, and sighed to himself. She was so young, too young to shrug her shoulders at a man's weakness. He remembered the way she had been on stage only that evening, incandescent with love, and he would willingly have seen Leonard Luttrell hanged, not so much for the pain he had inflicted on the girl as for the damage he might have done to the artist.

"Pull yourself together, Taisie," he said. He poured a drop of brandy into a glass and handed it over to her. "Here, drink this."

"I don't like it," Taisie said.

"Drink it and shut up. Now, listen to me. You've found out your lover's been unfaithful to you. Hard luck! You think it's terrible that he's got his wife pregnant. I sympathize, but that's the way things go. You're not the first girl who's been let down by her first love. You'll get over it —oh yes, you will! It's not the end of the world, no matter what it may look like now. But you're more fortunate than a lot of girls who go through experiences like this. You've got something to fall back on.

You're an artist, Taisie, and you're good. I don't often praise my girls to their face, but because you're down at the moment I'll tell you that in my opinion you've got it in you to go right to the top."

Taisie wiped away some of the tears which had been running down her face in an unending stream. She took a tentative sip at the brandy.

"That's better! Now, you say you'll never appear with Leonard again and I accept that—though there are plenty who'd call me soft. I'll pay him off and find you a replacement. Be here at eleven tomorrow morning to run through your songs with him."

"I can't!" Taisie said. "I can't sing the same songs as I sang with Leonard."

"Yes, you can. Come on, Taisie. This is the time to show whether you're a professional or just another gifted amateur. You've had a disaster in your private life. Rise above it. You can't let your public down—nor me neither, come to that."

She still looked appalled and he saw that he was going to have to coax her.

"Finish the month," he said. "Then take a holiday for a couple of weeks. Do you know anyone who lives in the country?"

"Hetty," Taisie said. "A friend of mine. I could go to her."

"There you are then. When you come back you can make a fresh start."

Taisie got up to go. "You've been kind," she said. "You don't understand how I feel, not in the least, but thanks for the good advice."

At the door she stopped and turned round. "What about Leonard?" she asked reluctantly. "If he's out of a job his wife and children will suffer."

"He'll be no worse off than he was before he pulled himself up by your shoe-strings."

Taisie came back into the room. "No," she said. "I hate his guts and I never want to set eyes on him again, but I can't take everything and leave him nothing." Her eyes filled with tears again and her voice shook. "I did love him."

"Don't start crying again, or I'll get rid of you too! Have some more brandy."

"No, thank you. Couldn't I do the Palace and Leonard the Oxford?"

"You could if the Oxford management

agree," Mr. Morton admitted reluctantly. "It'll halve your income."

Taisie dried her eyes. "No, it won't," she said. "If you're getting an unknown to partner me then we'll split the money the same as Leonard did with me: seven pounds for me and five for the new bloke."

# 4

TAISIE went to Hetty and Joe at the beginning of September and stayed for two weeks. She was surprised to discover how tired she was once she allowed herself to relax. When she looked back she realized that this was the first holiday she had ever had and the long months of hard work had been a strain, even without the crippling misery of her betrayed love.

She still loved him. That, to Taisie, was the worst part of the whole affair, the thing that humiliated her to the ground. If Leonard had walked in, put his arms round her and begged her to forgive him, she would have taken him back. She missed him with a hunger that gave her no rest. Only her obstinate pride stopped her from getting in touch with him. He was a rotter, he was no good, he had played with her and made her fall in love with him, he was despicable—and she wanted him with every nerve in her body.

Hetty noticed her restlessness and her exhaustion and at last, reluctantly, Taisie told her the bare outline of the affair. She had thought that Hetty would be sympathetic, but Hetty was shocked.

"Of course, we all know things like that go on between actors and actresses," she said. "But I thought you would have been a good girl, Taisie."

"I'm just the same as I've always been," Taisie said. "I'm not wicked just because I fell in love, Hetty."

"He was a married man!"

"I wish I hadn't told you," Taisie said. She turned away, her lips quivering. "I thought you'd be sorry for me."

"You did bring it on yourself, didn't you? Anyone could have seen that no good would come of giving in to a man like that."

She looked at Taisie's averted head and said uneasily: "Taisie, you're not . . . you haven't fallen for a baby?"

Taisie shook her head. "No, I've got that to be thankful for. But Hetty, Hetty, I'm so unhappy."

Her wild grief was incomprehensible to Hetty, but she did what she could to be kind. Her own opinion was that Taisie had had a lucky escape.

"Put it behind you," she advised. "You're not the first girl to have made a mistake. No need for anyone to know."

Taisie held her tongue. Everyone in the two theatres where she and Leonard had played had known that they were lovers. It was not entirely approved of, the blatancy of their affair, but their colleagues had been tolerant. She discovered that she was thinking longingly of the easygoing world of the theatre, where eyebrows might be raised at her indiscretion, but no-one would condemn her outright for having been carried away by the force of her emotions. Not like Hetty, who didn't understand.

Hetty and Joe lived in a small cottage in the grounds of the big house where Joe worked. It was a life that obviously suited Hetty. She was blissfully happy with her own tiny kitchen, the cherished front room with its red plush sofa, and the two bedrooms under the eaves.

"I'm not saying it wouldn't be nice to have an inside lavatory," she admitted.

"But, there, you have to put up with these things when you're living in the country."

"Aren't you lonely?" Taisie asked.

She looked out of the window at the uninterrupted view of fields and trees, turning to gold in the crisp autumn air. Hetty's cottage was one of an isolated row of three and she had no other neighbours.

"Not me! There's the Hendersons next door, and the Watkins on the other side of them. I wouldn't call myself isolated, not like some. Besides, I've got Joe."

She fidgeted with her tea cup and added: "As a matter of fact, there'll be three of us next time you come. I'm expecting."

"Hetty! I'm so happy for you!"

Taisie jumped up and kissed her friend, her own troubles forgotten. "You'll make a wonderful mother."

"I wish I was younger," Hetty admitted. "But, there, I was hard to please until Joe came along and no-one could be luckier than I am with him. That's what you really need, Taisie, a good steady husband."

Taisie did not reply, but she knew that Hetty was wrong. Hetty's life would drive her mad, the monotony, the placid unfolding of the seasons, even Joe's undemanding affection. She had enjoyed having a rest in the quiet of the country, but already Taisie was anxious to get back to the life she had left in London.

"If I get married it will be to someone rich," she said. "I'll be giving up a lot if I leave the theatre. He'll have to make it worth my while."

Taisie got work again as soon as she returned to London, but not in the West End. She appeared as "Taisie Brown—the London Linnet: Serio-comic Soprano" at The Bedford, Camden Town, The London, Shoreditch, The Paragon, Mile End Road: all good houses, but Taisie had to broaden her style to suit her audience and she thought that her voice was coarsening.

Every week she looked through the programme, always fearing that one day she would find herself on the same bill as Leonard. Then she heard that he was touring the provinces and felt easier.

When Christmas came she tried for an engagement as a Principal Boy in a pantomime but, to her disgust, was once again cast as the Princess in "Jack and the Beanstalk". In spite of her belief that she could have handled the larger part Taisie was surprised to find that she enjoyed appearing in something that had a coherent whole, a few lines to say, a bit of character to establish.

She said as much one evening to the middle-aged actor who was playing the King, her stage father. He didn't have a lot to do apart from first of all refusing her hand to Jack and then being persuaded to change his mind on being presented with a cascade of golden eggs from the Giant's stolen goose. Still, he had one good song and made the most of it with a fine bass voice.

"I like being in something that has a beginning, a middle and an end," Taisie tried to explain. "Even though the story is quite daft! It's a relief not to have to chase from one theatre to another and sing the same songs twice or three times in an evening."

The older actor looked at her with kind, tired eyes. "You ought to try to get into this new thing George Edwardes has started at the Gaiety," he said. "Musical comedy, he calls it."

"'The Shop Girl' you mean? They'd never take me. Not classy enough."

"You'd get in on your looks alone and your voice is all right."

"It's felt a bit strained lately," Taisie said, putting her hand anxiously round her throat.

"Your own fault. What practice do you do, apart from singing your head off in a smoky theatre every night?"

"Practice? None, apart from learning new songs."

He leaned forward and tapped her on the knee for emphasis. "Now, you listen to me, my girl. You could do better than this, but it's no use thinking you can walk into it without working. You can't dance, for one thing."

"I can! I dance with Jack in this pantomime."

"You strike a couple of attitudes and show a bit of leg. That's not dancing. Take some lessons while you're young and sprightly. And find yourself a teacher who knows how to nurse a voice like yours. I'll give you an introduction to Rosa Grazini, if you like."

"Who's she?"

"One of the best when it comes to voice training. Believe me, it's worth learning a bit of technique. You'll be glad of it in twenty years' time."

It had not previously occurred to Taisie that she had anything more to learn about singing, although taking dancing lessons made sense, but once Rosa Grazini, with regal condescension, had agreed to take her in hand, she found that the regime of exercises and breath control gave her voice a suppleness it had never had before.

Dancing lessons in the morning, singing practice in the afternoon and a nightly performance in the pantomime filled her days and sent her off into a dreamless sleep at night. There was no time for thinking about Leonard, her heart no longer turned over every time she saw a fair-haired man in the street and she began to forget, but not to the extent of finding anyone to take his place. It was no use, she couldn't fancy any other man, not after that searing experience. Romantic love was over for

Taisie and she was glad to have got it out of her system so young.

When the pantomime came to an end in February 1895 Taisie took her stage parent's advice and tried to get into musical comedy. Why not? Ada Reeve, who was the rave of the town in "The Shop Girl", had made the change from the Music Hall, and what had been done once could be done again.

It was something quite new, this musical comedy, and it was George Edwardes who had brought it to the London stage. He had seen the shift that was taking place in public taste, away from the broad comedy of burlesque towards a more refined and glamorous form of entertainment. He dressed his chorus girls in the height of style, with long skirts and fluttering petti-coats, and created a legend: the Gaiety Girl. She was haughty, she was beautiful, she was exquisitely dressed; she had her pick of escorts and was seen supping at Romanos or Rules with rich and titled young men-about-town. She had jewels and furs, she sipped champagne and nibbled at *foie gras* and plovers' eggs. The more exotic her life seemed the more the audience flocked to see her, and not only her but the fun and wit and *joie de vivre* of the whole Gaiety show.

With every singer and dancer in London trying for a place it was not easy to get a hearing, but Taisie had enough of a reputation to get her a chance to be seen, not by George Edwardes himself, but by his lieutenant, J. A. R. Malone, a much harder nut to crack. He was a tall and good-looking Irishman, but he didn't have "the Guv'nor's" easygoing ways. No-one got round Malone, and that was why he was invaluable to his more susceptible employer.

He thought well of Taisie, but was not encouraging about her chances.

"You're not tall enough for a show girl and we haven't got a vacancy amongst the dancers," he said. "What I can offer you is a chance to go on tour, and with a solo spot at that."

It was not what Taisie wanted, and she couldn't help letting her disappointment show.

"Take it," Malone urged. "I won't forget you. More than one girl has moved from a touring company to the front rank. The experience will be valuable to you."

The only alternative was an engagement at The Metropolitan in the Edgware Road. Taisie took two minutes to think it over and then agreed to go on tour.

It was less gruelling than it had been with the Lamont Troupe and she was better paid, but Taisie felt that she was marking time, waiting for the chance to show what she could really do.

Her opportunity came in the autumn when Mr. Malone kept his word and recommended her for a part in George Edwardes' new show, "The Hotel Girl". The lead was again created by Ada Reeve, enchantingly pretty and bursting with talent, but Taisie had the *soubrette* part and she was one of the hits of the show.

It was difficult to believe on the First Night that she had really arrived at last. She had a curtain call to herself, she was inundated with bouquets, she was over-whelmed with congratulations, and she was exhausted. In the middle of the first night party Taisie realized that she could hardly keep her eyes open. She slipped away, called a hansom cab and went home to bed.

She had recovered by the following evening and, arriving at the theatre early, paused to speak to Jupp, the stage door keeper.

"Evenin', Miss Brown," he said. "There's a florist's shop inside for you, not to mention the notes and messages. All sorts of young men hopin' to take you out to supper. O'course you know that the Guv'nor allows *no* visitors to dressing rooms, but if so be you favour one more'n the other just tip me the wink and I'll see the gentleman gets the message."

"Thanks, Mr. Jupp. I don't suppose I'll know one from the other so how am I to choose?"

"Well, now, let's see if I can remember any that's sent flowers. There's Lord Edward Pope, a very pleasant young gentleman, but *rackety*, if you know what I mean; Sir Lewis Lewson—now he's married, which I don't favour for a nice girl like you; Mr. Maurice Gaymour, not the brightest of the bright, but oodles of money and very free with it. Takin' it all in all, I'd recommend Mr. Gaymour."

"Very well, I'll settle for Mr. Gaymour. Thank you for your help, Mr. Jupp."

There were flowers everywhere when she reached her dressing room, just as Jupp had said. Amongst the dozens of red roses, the yellow lilies, the heavy-headed chrysanthemums, and the sprays of white orchids which had come from Mr. Maurice Gaymour, there was a bunch of pink carnations and attached to it a note which said: "I always knew you'd get to the top. Congratulations. Leonard."

Taisie caught sight of herself in the looking glass. She was still of only medium height, but so slender and holding herself so well that she looked taller. She had a heavy head of coppery hair balanced on a long, slim neck. Her face had matured, her jawline was firmer and the faint hollows in her cheeks accentuated the lovely high line of her cheekbones. Her grey-green eyes looked larger now that she had learned to darken her lashes. She was wearing a cloak of dark green satin trimmed with grey fur which slipped down to show shoulders which were flawlessly white. She had been given the Gaiety gloss. She had style, she had an aura of success. She knew she had reached a point she would never have achieved if she had stayed with Leonard Luttrell but, because of a lingering feeling of regret, it was Leonard's carnations which were given the place of honour in a cut glass vase on her dressing table.

When she left the stage door after the show she was wearing a spray of Maurice Gaymour's orchids pinned to her shoulder. He was waiting for her and Jupp was on hand to point him out. He was a tall young man in his early twenties, with mouse-brown hair brushed back sleekly from an egg-shaped face. Taisie found the smile with which he greeted her most engaging. It made him look boyishly excited, very different from the blasé young man she had been expecting.

"I say, Miss Brown, you're wearing my flowers!" he said.

"Of course. They were much the prettiest I had," Taisie said.

She looked up at him through her lashes and his expression of pleased gratification made her feel like giggling.

He took her to Romanos and bought champagne and Taisie sipped it and decided that she didn't dislike it as much as she had the first time she had tried it. That had been with Leonard. Leonard, who had sent her pink carnations he could probably not afford. Leonard, whom she had believed to be the love of her life and who had betrayed her. Listening with half an ear to Maurice Gaymour's compliments, looking round her at the gay, well-dressed diners, the soft lights reflected in mirrors, the gold-topped bottles standing in buckets of ice, Taisie admitted to herself that putting Leonard's flowers on her dressing table had been a sentimental gesture which had meant very little. Leonard belonged to the past, and this was going to be her future.

George Edwardes liked his girls to be seen in the best places, enjoying themselves and adding to the glittering reputation of the Gaiety Theatre. He had strict rules about behaviour in the theatre and no hopeful young men got past the watchful Jupp and into the dressing rooms, no matter how high the bribe they were prepared to offer, but the private lives of the girls were their own affair and he asked no awkward questions about the jewellery and furs some of them wore. It had been his predecessor, John Hollingshead, trying to put a limit on ostentation, who had put up a notice saying that "Ladies earning less than twenty-five shillings a week are respectfully requested not to arrive at the theatre in broughams".

The first time Taisie discovered a jeweller's box nestling amongst a bouquet of yellow roses she sat down and looked thoughtfully at the diamond bracelet it contained. Other girls accepted the presents that were sent to them and gave as little or as much as they felt like in return. She wanted to keep it, but she did not want to pay the price that was attached to it. To Taisie, it smacked too much of high-class prostitution, while to take and give nothing for it seemed mean-spirited. She went out to supper with her suitor, smiled at him very sweetly and handed the bracelet back.

She did the same thing when Maurice Gaymour tried to give her an emerald ring.

"It's a beautiful ring, but I can't accept it," she said. "The only ring I'll ever take is one I can wear on the third finger of my left hand."

"Then let me put it on that finger," Maurice said.

His face was flushed and he spoke on impulse, made reckless by her nearness and the champagne he had drunk. Taisie held his hand and laughed at him.

"You know you don't mean it," she said.

"I do! I'm madly in love with you, Taisie."

"Bless you, dearie! You'll be just as mad after someone else next week."

"I won't! This time I mean it. There's never been another girl like you, there never will be. Marry me, Taisie."

She shook her head and refused to let him talk about it any more, but the seed had been sown in both their minds. When Maurice took Taisie home that night she let him kiss her, drawing away when his ardour grew too boisterous, and he repeated in a thick voice: "Marry me, Taisie. Say you'll marry me!"

She liked him rather better than any of the other men who pursued her, but she thought him very young, forgetting that he was three years older than she was herself. His kisses were pleasant to her and it was something of an effort not to respond to his mounting desire. If she ever felt like giving up the stage it would not be difficult to marry Maurice, or someone like him. Taisie, considering the matter in a dispassionate way which would have made Maurice despair, knew that she could be as good a wife to him as any other girl he was likely to meet, even though she did not come from his world, and Taisie believed that she could find satisfaction in such a marriage. It was not as if she was ever likely to fall in love again, not in the way she had with Leonard.

Maurice's father was dead and Maurice had inherited a large fortune. An only child, and the darling of his mother's heart, he was surprisingly unspoilt and generous to a fault—but then, as his friends and hangers-on remarked, he could afford it—a little wild, but not vicious, inclined to be selfish, thinking more of his own pleasure than anything else, and not over-intelligent. He had been educated at Harrow and had been up at Oxford, but had come down without taking a degree, and since reaching the age of twenty-one had lived mainly for amusement. Owning a house in Grosvenor Square, a hunting box in Leicestershire, and an extensive estate in Derbyshire which included a coal mine conveniently tucked away in a valley out of sight of the Gaymour mansion, he was nevertheless not quite out of the top drawer. There was a subtle distinction between the level of society occupied by the Gaymour family and the true aristocracy which Taisie was not equipped to understand. Maurice's father had lived the life of a country gentleman, but Maurice's grandfather had made his money from trade and it was not forgotten, even though Maurice's mother was well connected.

Although Maurice might not be clever, once his mind had conceived an idea he held on to it with great tenaciousness. Having once proposed to Taisie he was convinced that she was the only girl he would ever want to make his wife. All through the months that followed he continued to ask her to marry him and because the idea was not unattractive to Taisie she kept him on a string, refusing him with an air of regret that made him believe that she might be made to change her mind if he persisted.

When the weather grew warmer Maurice persuaded Taisie to go down to Maidenhead with him for the day one Sunday.

"Let's get one thing quite straight before we go," she said. "I'm *not* staying the night down there with you."

"Taisie! I wouldn't ask you. Haven't I always treated you with respect?"

"Only because I've insisted on it, young fellow. You'd be just like all the rest if I'd let you. As it is, you know perfectly well that no girl your mother would approve of would spend the day alone with you on the river."

"That's what's so splendid about knowing you. You're just as . . . . as good, and all that, as any silly debutante, and yet it's so frightfully jolly, being able to talk to you and not having to watch my tongue all the time, and being able to share a joke an' all that. You're wonderful, Taisie. My mother would love you if she knew you."

"Would she?" Taisie said drily.

They got to Maidenhead in time for lunch at Skindle's where they ate poached salmon and strawberries and cream washed down with delicious pale yellow wine. Taisie smiled at Maurice over the edge of her glass and had a twinge of conscience at the adoration in his eyes.

The lawns sloped down to the river and the punts were bobbing on the water. At the next table a noisy party were calling for more iced champagne. Taisie looked at them with a frown.

"Let's get away," she said.

They went on the river, Taisie in white piqué trimmed with yellow, and a shady hat to keep her nose from getting burned. As an added protection she put up a yellow parasol and held it between her face and the sun. Maurice took off his jacket and rolled up his shirt sleeves.

"You don't mind, do you?" he asked.

"Make yourself comfortable," Taisie said, lazily settling back against the cushioned seat.

"I knew you'd say that. It's so pleasant and easy, being with you."

When he found a shady spot by the bank, under the overhanging branches of a weeping willow, and came to sit beside her Taisie did not repulse him. Under the cover of the yellow parasol they kissed, and kissed again, but when Maurice's wandering hand came to rest on Taisie's breast she removed it and sat up.

"Now then, none of that," she said.

Instead of accepting the rebuff Maurice put both his arms round her. With his face hidden against her shoulder he said in a muffled voice: "I do love you terribly, Taisie."

There was a desperation in the way he spoke which troubled her. Instead of chaffing him, as she had done in the past, she said: "I know you do, dear, and I'm beginning to wonder what I ought to do about it."

Maurice looked up. "Marry me!" he said.

Taisie looked down into his flushed young face and shook her head. "You're such a baby," she said.

"I'm years older than you!" Maurice said indignantly.

"I've been out in the world a lot longer than you have and I've had a harder life. I've come up from the bottom, Maurice. I'm the bastard daughter of an ignorant girl and a foreign sailor and I was dragged up in a slum."

"That doesn't affect what you are now."

"It does, you know. I wouldn't be the girl I am if I'd always had it easy. I've clawed my way up and even then I wouldn't have got where I am if I hadn't been lucky."

Taisie paused, but to spell out the horror of her ill-use was more than she could do. "I got taken up by some very kind people when I was a child . . ."

"And they brought you up to be a lady. You are a lady, Taisie."

"No, I'm not, ducky. I put up a very good show, but I'm not born to it and it doesn't go very deep. Your mother would be horrified if you married me. Could you face her and tell her what you meant to do?"

"She'd come round," Maurice said, but he sounded uneasy.

"Think about it," Taisie said. "Ask yourself whether you could face the scenes there'd be if you said you were marrying an actress from the Gaiety."

"We could get married first and tell everyone afterwards," Maurice suggested.

"Oh, no! If I get hitched it's all going to be above board and a proper wedding in church and everything. I'm surprised at you, Maurice. I thought you said you weren't ashamed of me."

"I'm not! It's just . . . what you said about all the fuss. I do hate women crying all over me."

"There you are, then. If you can't stand upsetting your family then you'll have to give me up. As it is, I think perhaps we shouldn't see one another for a few weeks."

"I can't go on living unless I see you every day. I'll come to the theatre every night."

"I can't stop you doing that," Taisie admitted. She looked at him with an expression of rueful exasperation on her face. "I don't know what to do, and that's the truth. I tell you what, give me a month and then I'll give you a definite answer one way or the other. Either I'll marry you or I'll send you away for ever. But during that month I'm not going to see anything of you at all."

"I suppose I'll see you all over the place

going around with other men," Maurice muttered jealously.

"That's right. It'll give me a chance to sort out how I feel, which I can't do while I don't see anyone but you."

Taisie tried, all during the month they spent apart, to weigh up the pros and cons of marriage to Maurice. She was never going to fall in love again, that at least was certain, so a marriage of affection to Maurice would be no hardship. On the other hand, she was successful in her career and could hope to do even better in the future. She was very struck one evening when someone spoke in her hearing of Nellie Farren.

"Nellie was the darling of London," he said. "More than that, she was a roaring success wherever she went, all over the world. What an artiste! The audience cooed over her every time she came on stage."

"What happened to her?" Taisie asked.

"Crippled with rheumatism. Poor Nellie, she danced like a leaf in the wind. Now she can scarcely hobble. And she's only forty-five."

The more Taisie thought about it, the

more she realized how much her standing in the world would be improved by marriage to Maurice Gaymour. Not only would she be financially secure, but as a respectable married woman she would be lifted on to a different plane altogether. When the gentleman who had tried to give Taisie a diamond bracelet became amorous in his private brougham one night and had to be given a clout over the ear which made his teeth rattle, Taisie thought longingly of the difference a wedding ring would make to the way she was treated.

"The Hotel Girl" was still pulling in the audiences, but it had been intended as a stop-gap and there were rumours in the air about a new show in the autumn. Taisie, putting out feelers, was disappointed to learn that she would, once again, have a secondary role.

"I could play the main part," she said wistfully to George Edwardes.

She lifted her big, grey-green eyes to his face, and he backed away hurriedly. It was very difficult for him to disappoint a pretty girl and it was well known that a girl who had been dismissed by his deputy only had to go and cry on George Edwardes' shoulder to be reinstated, until the implacable Malone got rid of her at a later date and made sure that she had no chance of appealing to the Guv'nor a second time.

"Not this time, Miss Brown," he said, with his impeccable courtesy. "It's promised to Ellaline Terriss." His face brightened. "Perhaps when 'The Country Girl' comes off . . ."

"But that might be two years!" Taisie complained, but she was talking to the air: George Edwardes had escaped.

Maurice saw the show three or four times a week and fresh flowers were delivered to Taisie every night. Exactly one month after their talk on the river she arrived in her dressing room to find his biggest offering to date: a gilded basket of red roses which stood waist high. The note attached to the handle said: "Tonight's the night. I know you are going to say yes. All my love, Maurice."

Taisie's dresser looked at the opulent basket, half envious, half disapproving.

"It beats me why you don't take anything but flowers," she said. "All that jewellery you send back, it's a criminal waste. You'll regret it one day, mark my words. Cash in while you're young and pretty, that's what I say."

She was offended when Taisie snapped at her, but the words had touched Taisie on the raw. "Cash in", that was the philosophy of half the girls she knew. Taisie thought it would be dishonest to take unless she meant to give. But where would that road lead her? She had no ambition to be any man's whore. As for falling in love, that part of her life was over. She had tried it with Leonard and look where that had landed her: broken hearted, even though she had been shown quite clearly that he was not worth it. She would never make that mistake again. She was fond of Maurice, it would not be difficult to be kind to him. There was no doubt at all that he would give her a wonderful life. As for his family, she would win them over.

Taisie caught herself up. Almost without realizing it she had begun to think of marriage to Maurice as a settled thing. She started putting on her make-up, striving to shut him out of her mind until the performance was over.

Maurice was waiting for her at the stage door. Taisie gave him her hand and he raised it to his lips. When they were in the cab she let him kiss her.

"I've been missing you so much," he said.

"You've been in the stalls nearly every night," she objected.

"It's not the same. Taisie, have you made up your mind?"

"I'm too hungry to think. Ask me again after supper."

Maurice had little appetite, but Taisie, as usual, was ravenously hungry and kept him waiting through several courses. As soon as she licked the last of the iced pudding from her spoon and put it down with a satisfied sigh he felt in his pocket and held out a small jeweller's case to her. Taisie opened it and blinked. Inside was the largest diamond solitaire ring she had ever seen.

"Do you like it? Is it all right?" Maurice asked anxiously.

"It's . . . it's unbelievable. Maurice, it must have cost a fortune."

"That doesn't matter. Not if you like it. Not if you'll let me put it on your finger and promise to marry me. Will you, Taisie? Please, darling, please."

Taisie held out her hand. "Yes," she said. "Put it on for me, Maurice. I'll marry you."

# 5

TAISIE was right in thinking that Maurice's family would be dismayed by the news of his engagement. Mrs. Gaymour, finding him adamant in spite of all her arguments and pleas, sent for her nephew, Blair Gregory.

He came in response to her agitated note, not without misgivings. His aunt had not said why she wanted to see him, but Blair had heard of his cousin's infatuation for an actress and he had a premonition that his summons might have something to do with that affair.

"He says he's going to marry her!" Mrs. Gaymour said, scarcely giving Blair time to sit down. "An actress! A Gaiety Girl! I'm distracted with worry. Something must be done."

"Maurice is of age," Blair pointed out. "There's not a great deal any of us can do if he's really made up his mind to get married."

"I refuse to admit defeat before we've

even tried," Mrs. Gaymour said crossly. "I thought I could rely on you to help me, Blair. With all your experience in the legal profession surely you can think of some way of getting him out of it."

Blair took her hand and patted it soothingly, but his reply was not encouraging.

"I'm a barrister, not a magician," he said. "Really, Aunt Gertrude, I always thought you were a woman of sense. What do you expect me to do? Forbid the banns?"

Gertrude Gaymour shook her head helplessly. She had never been a good-looking woman, but with approaching middle age she had achieved a certain distinction. Today her iron-grey hair was coming down in untidy loops and her hand fiddled nervously with the brooch on her bosom.

"If you could find out something that would discredit her in Maurice's eyes," she suggested.

"It's a possibility," Blair admitted. "Except that it might have quite the opposite effect, alienate Maurice from you and push him further into her arms."

Mrs. Gaymour closed her eyes and moaned.

145

"I had such plans for him," she said. "Lady Sarah Frolingham seemed really taken with him earlier in the Season."

"Sally Frolingham is a hardened little flirt," Blair said.

"A Duke's daughter!"

"And knows her own worth—such as it is. Has it occurred to you, Aunt Gertrude, that this girl—what's her name?"

"Taisie Brown—such a silly name."

"She might be just the thing for him."

Mrs. Gaymour sat up, stiff with indignation. "How can you say that? A girl from the gutter, flaunting herself on the stage, out for what she can get. Obviously she's marrying him for his money."

"You don't have a very high opinion of your son if you take that for granted. Perhaps she loves him."

"He's far too young to be thinking of marrying. I expect she's years older than he is."

"No, from what I've heard she's even younger, the merest babe. She's had an enormous success, you know. Everyone who's been to the Gaiety raves about her. Why don't you try making the best of it, Aunt Gertrude? Be nice to her, win her

146

over, teach her what she needs to know as Maurice's wife. She's said to be pretty, talented, got plenty of good red blood in her veins. If you're seen to take her up people will soon forget her origins."

"There are times when you talk like a Radical," Mrs. Gaymour said. She looked at her nephew with extreme disfavour. "Maurice's position is not as assured as yours. He's not the grandson of an earl. People have not yet forgotten how his grandfather made his money."

"His father took a step in the right direction when he married you," Blair said with a straight face which concealed his desire to laugh.

"That's true," Mrs. Gaymour said with a seriousness that nearly finished Blair's self control. "If Maurice marries into a really good family then *his* children will have an unassailable place in Society. But if he marries Miss Taisie Brown from the Gaiety then people will laugh behind my back and say blood tells and stupid things like that."

"Are we out to save Maurice or you?" Blair enquired.

"Maurice, of course. Naturally I shall

suffer if this absurd marriage goes ahead, but it's Maurice's welfare I'm thinking about. It must be stopped."

There was an unhappy silence which Blair did not break. He felt nothing but distaste for the whole affair. There was nothing new in Maurice making a fool of himself; Blair was mildly fond of his young cousin, but he had a low opinion of his mental capacity. He had dragged Maurice out of more than one scrape which his mother did not know about and this one was more serious than the others. Blair foresaw with misgiving that his aunt was not going to be satisfied unless he took an active part in her attempt to win Maurice away from the girl he had promised to marry.

"She might sue him for breach of promise if he broke it off," he pointed out.

"Could she? Yes, I suppose she could." Mrs. Gaymour looked thoughtful and more hopeful. "Money! That's the answer. You must try and buy her off, Blair."

"Why me?" Blair asked. "Isn't there anyone else you could employ?"

"No, we must keep it in the family. I might ask your father if he could ever be persuaded to come up to London, but he's become an absolute recluse. I'm sure my poor sister never expected to spend her entire life buried in the country when she married him."

"She likes it," Blair said mildly.

"And you know all about the law," Mrs. Gaymour went on, totally disregarding the interruption. "And you're so *reliable*, Blair."

He argued a little longer, but when he left his aunt he had made a promise to see Taisie Brown and to try to persuade her to give up his cousin.

"How much do you think she'll want?" Mrs. Gaymour asked.

"I believe ten thousand pounds is about the going rate," Blair said.

"Ten thousand pounds!" Mrs. Gaymour struggled with her sense of outrage and said resolutely: "Well, I'm sure it would be worth twice that amount to get Maurice out of the wretched girl's hands, though how I'm to raise it I'm sure I don't know."

"There's no point in promising the money unless you can pay it," Blair said. "Let us understand one another, Aunt Gertrude. I am to offer Miss Brown up to ten thousand pounds and you undertake to pay the money if she will break off her engagement to Maurice."

"Yes, yes. I'll raise the money somehow, even if it means selling my diamond necklace."

"There could be no greater sacrifice," Blair said, but he kissed her on the cheek before he went and Mrs. Gaymour was left with the comfortable conviction that Blair would settle everything.

Blair himself had little hope of succeeding in his mission. Ten thousand pounds represented only a fraction of Maurice's immense fortune. If money was what the girl wanted she had more to gain by holding him to the engagement; if she was genuinely attached to him then nothing would make her give him up. Blair considered briefly making an appeal to her better nature and dropped the idea more because he could not bring himself to frame the necessary phrases with any conviction than because he thought Taisie Brown would be deaf to such a plea.

He went to the Gaiety that evening. Unlike most of his contemporaries he had not seen "The Hotel Girl" and he thought

it might be as well to size up the opposition before preparing his case. He caught
a glimpse of Maurice in the foyer but
fortunately Maurice favoured the stalls and
Blair had secured a seat in the dress circle,
so he was able to avoid his cousin.

The story of "The Hotel Girl" was the
usual absurd nonsense. Blair smiled toler-
antly as it unfolded, although he had to
admit that the show was amusing, tuneful
and beautifully presented.

The leading lady was staying at the
Hotel—in the South of France—with her
wealthy aunt, who intended leaving the
girl all her money provided she married
suitably. The girl took one look at the
young man behind the Reception Desk
and fell head over heels in love with him.
He reciprocated her feelings, but for some
reason which never became entirely clear
to Blair was unable to tell her that he was,
in fact, the son of the man who owned an
immense chain of hotels and was only
acting as receptionist because he was being
made to work his way up from the bottom.
This was the basic story, but before it
could wind up with a happy ending there
were innumerable misunderstandings and

dozens of comical characters to be dragged in.

Taisie played the part of a pert chambermaid, continually flitting in and out at awkward moments, very much concerned in helping to unwind the difficult situations the other characters got themselves into. She wore a full skirted black dress, rather short to show her pretty ankles, a little white apron and a frivolous lace cap. The first time she came on to the stage Blair sat up straighter and stared harder: she was enchanting.

The chambermaid was in love with an Italian waiter and she, too, had her difficulties. Towards the end of the first act Taisie sang a wistful song which had everyone in the audience sympathizing with her:

Sitting and wishing, I've always been
    told,
Will never get anything done.
Yet I'm sitting here in the moonlight
    tonight
Wishing I wasn't alone.
Waiting for someone, waiting for love,
Hoping my lover will come;

Only the moon looking down on me
   sees that I'm
Wishing I wasn't alone.

The scene took place in the garden of the hotel. Taisie sat on a swing in subdued lighting, with the "moon" playing on her solitary figure. Then she danced, with her own feather duster, with her shadow, with a white rose plucked from a bush and, finally, ecstatically, with the Italian waiter she loved.

There was a moment of silence as the music died away and then a storm of applause. Blair joined in it, his face thoughtful. For a few minutes he had been taken out of himself, quite forgetting the reason he was there. The girl was something quite out of the ordinary.

But it was in the last act that Taisie sang the song that had made her name. Everything was going right, she had sorted out the rich young couple, she had pushed the wealthy father and aunt into one another's arms, her Italian waiter was going to be manager of the hotel. Taisie broke into triumphant song:

Let's be merry, let's be gay
Let's be cheery all the day
    Spread a little happiness as we go
    along!
Clash the cymbals, bang the drum,
Come along, boys, rumpty-tum,
    Spread a little happiness as we go
    along!
Do a dance and shout hurray!
Let's be merry, let's be gay,
    Spread a little happiness as we go
    along!
Let the bells ring out ding-dong,
Turn a cartwheel, sing a song,
    Spread a little happiness as we go
    along!

And at the words "turn a cartwheel" she did just that. There was a flurry of white petticoats, a glimpse of black silk stockings and Taisie went over in a magnificent wheel and was back on her feet, her hands outspread, laughing all over her face, in time to bring the song to an end.

They wouldn't let her go. Blair found himself clapping until his palms tingled and his face ached with smiling. The music swelled up once more and Taisie repeated the last part of the song: "Let the bells ring out . . . Turn a cartwheel"— over she went—"Sing a song, Spread a little happiness as we go along!"

When the show ended Blair wrote a few words on the back of one of his cards and left it with the stage door keeper to be given to Miss Brown, but it was not the usual plea to be allowed to take her out after the show and he did not wait for an answer.

Taisie, still lit up with excitement at the rousing reception she had been given once again that evening, read the message and then turned the card over.

"Blair Gregory—Barrister-at-law" and an address in Lincolns Inn. On the other side Blair had written:

"I am Maurice Gaymour's cousin. I would be obliged if you could find it convenient to call on me tomorrow afternoon between three and four o'clock."

Taisie's arrival in Blair Gregory's chambers at half past three the following afternoon caused a stir no other client had ever aroused. His Clerk knew that he was expecting "a Miss Brown" to call, but Blair had confided no more than that to him. When she gave him her name he murmured that he would let Mr. Gregory know she had arrived and requested her to take a seat.

Taisie looked round her with interest, taking in the ranks of law books and piles of papers. She thought it a fusty old place; the low, plastered ceiling and panelled walls meant nothing to her. One of the young clerks caught her eye and she gave him her wide, delightful smile. He turned pink and dropped his pen. As he bent to pick it up he hissed to his companion: "It's *Taisie Brown!*" Taisie smiled again at the other young man, tickled by the sensation she was causing. As she swept by them to go into Blair's room she turned her head and gave them a delicious wink. The second clerk dropped his pen.

Blair, getting to his feet as Taisie entered, was nearly as nonplussed as his two young clerks. He had wholeheartedly admired her performance on the stage, but he had expected to be disillusioned when he met her face to face. But Taisie, in tobacco brown silk, with enormous sleeves and a tiny waist, an impertinent little hat tipped forward on her forehead, was a sight to turn any man's head. Her complexion was dazzling and entirely without artifice, her burnished brown hair gleamed with coppery lights, her figure was perfection. When she smiled and held out her hand Blair felt as tongue-tied as a hobbledehoy.

Taisie sat down in the chair on the opposite side of Blair's wide polished desk and said: "Well, now, Mr. Gregory, what's all this about?"

Only her voice still betrayed a trace of Cockney twang. He was glad that there was something that was not quite perfect, at least it gave him a tiny advantage.

"I want to discuss your engagement to Maurice," he said.

"Oh, yes? I don't suppose you've called me here to offer your congratulations?"

"Not exactly," Blair admitted. He made an effort to pull himself together; it would never do to let this gorgeous chit have the initiative.

"One thing I must congratulate you on," he said smoothly, "and that is your performance in 'The Hotel Girl'. I saw it last night and I was full of admiration."

"Thank you," Taisie said.

She looked at him thoughtfully. Maurice had talked about his cousin Blair—"the brainy one of the family"—and she knew about his background. He was the child of Mrs. Gaymour's sister, who had married into the aristocracy. Taisie, comparing him with other young men of title who had besieged her, did not think highly of his appearance. He was tall, but his shoulders were too wide, which made him look shorter than he really was. He had dark hair, cut shorter than was fashionable in order to keep his head cool under the wig he was obliged to wear in court, and he was clean shaven. Although he was not yet thirty he had developed deep lines running from his nose to the corners of his mouth. When he was a boy his mother had called him "my little ape" with laughing affection, and there was something faintly simian about his appearance. The face of a highly intelligent and articulate monkey.

"However, in spite of my admiration for you as an actress," Blair went on, "I am not at all sure that your engagement to Maurice is a good thing."

"For him or for me?" Taisie asked.

"It could be a mistake for both of you. You must admit that your background is not what his family is entitled to expect in Maurice's wife."

"I'm marrying Maurice, not his family."

"It would distress him if he were cut off from his mother."

"That's up to her, isn't it. *I've* got no objection to Maurice seeing her."

"If Mrs. Gaymour refuses to receive you then Maurice, if he's half a man, will take your part."

"Why shouldn't she receive me?"

"Who were your parents?" Blair countered.

"My Mum was a Miss Annie Brown— yes, I did say 'Miss'—and my Dad was a sailor. She wasn't too sure of his name, but she always insisted he was Russian. That's why I was called Anastasia— someone told her it was a Russian name."

She saw with interest that her frankness had disconcerted Blair.

"It couldn't be much worse, could it?"

she asked sympathetically. "Enough to make a respectable lady have a fit."

"Quite," Blair said.

"On the other hand, I've come a long way since those days," Taisie pointed out. "And I'm not going to drag a lot of shady relations into Maurice's family. My Mum is dead and the only other family I've ever known went off to Australia, good riddance to them."

She paused and added carefully: "Seeing that there's only one of me and considering how I've improved myself, am I really too much for Mrs. Gaymour to swallow?"

"I'm afraid you are. An actress in the family is not something any mother would consider desirable. There's a certain prejudice, not entirely unjustified . . . the stage does not have a good reputation, from a moral point of view."

He thought he sounded like a pompous prig, but he battled on.

"I have made some enquiries and when I mention the name of Leonard Luttrell I'm sure you will know what I mean. You haven't led a chaste life, have you, Miss Brown?"

"Not entirely," Taisie said. "Have you?"

There was a little more colour in her cheeks, but she maintained her self possession and the calmly interested way she put her question tickled Blair's unfortunate sense of humour. The only way he could deal with it was by ignoring the question and asking: "Have you considered how unhappy it would make Maurice if he discovered your . . . unfortunate past?"

Taisie looked him straight in the eye, her face the picture of innocence, and lied.

"He was very sweet and sympathetic when I told him about it," she said gently.

Blair sat back in his chair. "That was clever of you," he said.

"You may not believe it, but I tried hard to persuade Maurice to give me up. It wasn't any use and in the end I came round to thinking he'd be just the husband for me."

"I'm authorized to offer you ten thousand pounds to terminate the engagement," Blair said abruptly.

"Who's been daft enough to ask you to do that? His mother? Silly woman, she'll lose Maurice if she's not careful, and it won't be my doing. I'm prepared to be friends. Give her a message from me. Tell her I'm going to try to make Maurice as good a wife as any Society girl she may have picked out for him."

"Am I to take it that you refuse the ten thousand pounds?"

"Yes, of course. It took me a long time to make up my mind to take Maurice and I'm not going to be talked out of it now."

"Are you in love with him?"

He did not miss the tiny, telltale hesitation before Taisie replied and in his heart he admired the honesty which prevented her from snapping back with an immediate "yes".

"I'm very, very fond of Maurice," Taisie said. "We'll do very nicely together."

"I believe you're making a great mistake and for a reason I doubt if you've considered. I'm fond of Maurice myself, but he's not got a lot in the way of brains."

"Otherwise he wouldn't have got himself entangled with me, is that what you're saying?" Taisie put in swiftly.

"No, it's not. I think you'll be tired of

him in a few months and what will happen then?"

He saw that he had made her think, but her reply revealed a depth of disillusionment which left him with nothing more to say.

"I don't expect to live happy ever after. Husbands and wives do get tired of one another. Loving don't last. Do you think I don't know that? Once the honeymoon's over you have to get down to living together and if you're poor that means worrying where the rent's coming from and how to keep the nippers in shoes and trousers. The man gets fed up and then there's rows because he starts drinking the money that should have gone on food for the family. The wife turns into a nagger and perhaps he knocks her about. Marriages may be made in heaven, Mr. Gregory, but, if so, the Lord makes mighty few happy ones. I'll take my chance with Maurice and at least I'll always be sure of a roof over my head and food in my . . . inside me. He's a gentleman and he'll be kind to me, even if the way he feels now does fade a bit."

"Suppose you fall in love with someone else?" Blair asked.

"I won't. That's something I've got out of my system."

"At nineteen? You could be wrong about that."

"It wouldn't make any difference even if I did take a fancy to someone else. I may have been dragged up in the gutter, but I know respectable married women don't carry on with other men. Of course, I know it's different in Society," Taisie said, in a kind voice which would have convulsed Blair if he had not been feeling so dismayed.

She stood up and shook out her wide skirts. "Well, that's that then. We understand one another."

Blair got to his feet. "You absolutely refuse Mrs. Gaymour's offer of ten thousand pounds to relinquish her son?" he said in one last attempt.

"Tell her to put it where the monkey puts his nuts," Taisie said.

She swept out of the room before Blair could get out from behind his desk. Smiling at the intoxicated clerks she said:

"I'm sure one of you gentlemen could find me a cab?"

They fell over themselves and the lucky one who got down the stairs first and handed her into the hansom cab walked about in a dream for the rest of the day.

Blair reported the failure of his mission to his aunt that evening, although he refrained from passing on Taisie's suggestion about what she should do with the money.

"I never thought it would work," he concluded. "I'm afraid there's nothing for it but to put a good face on it, Aunt Gertrude."

There were tears in Mrs. Gaymour's eyes and her voice shook as she said: "Perhaps if I appealed to Maurice . . ."

"He wouldn't listen," Blair said.

"What did you really think of her, Blair? Is she completely impossible?"

Blair hesitated, but in the end he said with more honesty than his aunt appreciated: "Any man who won Taisie Brown would be mad to give her up."

Mrs. Gaymour looked at him with hostility. "I didn't think you would be so

165

easily bowled over by a pretty face. Oh, Blair, what am I to do?"

"There's just one possibility. Invite her to the house. Seeing her against his own background may make Maurice realize that she doesn't quite measure up, especially if she makes some *faux pas* that shows how ignorant she is of how to behave. Mind you, I can't say it will answer, because she's a clever little minx and not easily put out of countenance."

No-one seeing Taisie as she entered the Grosvenor Square house the following week, attended by a besotted Maurice, would have guessed that she was as nervous as she had been on the first night of "The Hotel Girl". She shed her cloak in the bedroom to which she had been escorted and turned to look at herself in the cheval mirror, touching her hair with a shaking hand. Her gown was new and had cost a mint of money and there was no doubt that it was becoming, but seeing herself against that staid background of solid walnut furniture and soft chintz Taisie did wonder whether perhaps it was cut too low. She pulled surreptitiously at her bodice and then took her hand away: no point in worrying about that now and she had no need to be ashamed of the figure the gown revealed.

Blair saw her come down the stairs, in bright leaf green and looking like Springtime. She wore no jewellery except the great diamond ring Maurice had given her. By his side Blair heard Maurice give a little gasp.

"Isn't she the loveliest little girl you ever saw?" he muttered to his cousin.

"She's certainly beautiful," Blair agreed.

From the friendly way Maurice had greeted him Blair guessed that Taisie had not told him about their interview. He asked her about it as they mingled with the other guests in the drawing room after Taisie had been presented to Maurice's mother and had carried off the introduction with rather more aplomb than Mrs. Gaymour had shown.

"No, I didn't tell him," Taisie admitted. "Is it likely I would? Maurice thinks highly of me, but he's easily swayed. If he gets the idea that his family hold me cheap he might start thinking the same way."

"I wouldn't call ten thousand pounds cheap," Blair murmured.

Taisie turned her clear eyes on him. "You wouldn't have tried to buy me off if you'd had any respect for me."

"Would you believe me if I said that I regret having allowed myself to be talked into making the attempt? Even though I stand by my opinion that your marriage to Maurice is a mistake."

"I thought you looked a bit ashamed of yourself. Think no more about it. I'm prepared to forgive and forget. Tell me something. If you're the grandson of an earl why do you have to earn your own living?"

"I'm the younger son of a younger son," Blair said solemnly. "The merest riff-raff of the titled classes, my dear Miss Brown."

"Does that mean you'll never come into the title?"

"Not without a series of disasters. My cousin Augustus, who has the courtesy title of Viscount Akerne, is the heir and he's married, with two children already. Both daughters, I admit, but no doubt his wife will give him a boy next time. If he should be unfortunate enough not to provide an heir then the title would go to my father and then to my elder brother, who I am happy to say, enjoys excellent health and will also no doubt have a parcel of boys when he gets married."

"I see. Thank you, that's just the sort of thing I need to know and haven't come across before."

"I am happy to further your social education," Blair said gravely.

"Right, then you can tell me something else and because of what's already passed between us I'll trust you to speak the truth. Am I dressed right?"

"You shine down every other woman in the room."

"That's not what I asked."

Blair glanced round the room, full of gently murmuring people, the complement of guests nearly complete. They were burning with curiosity about the girl who had captured one of the most eligible men in London, but determined not to betray anything but a well-bred indifference. Most of the guests were of Mrs. Gaymour's generation, and a formidable, toffee-nosed lot they were, Blair thought irreverently. There were one or two younger married couples and three girls, but even they, he saw, were enjoying their third or fourth Season. No debutantes, presumably because Mrs. Gaymour was reluctant to expose them to the contamination of meeting an actress.

"You are—what, nineteen?" Blair said slowly in answer to Taisie's question. "Most young girls of your age wear white, or pink or blue. Muslins and things like that. You have more the air of a young married woman, very smart and sure of herself."

"I see. No use now pretending that I'm a sweet young innocent, because I'm not," Taisie said. "I'd feel a fool tricked out in white muslin. All the same, I can see I should have worn something a bit quieter. I'll know better next time."

Maurice came up to them, his face beaming. "I'm glad to see you two have made friends," he said. "Thanks, Blair, I knew I could count on you."

With the merest twitch of one eyebrow Taisie conveyed a sardonic amusement which made Blair choke. He murmured an excuse and moved away.

"You look wonderful, darling," Maurice

said ardently. "Mother is completely bowled over."

"I can see she is," Taisie said. "Knocked for six."

At a large formal dinner party the hostess sometimes provided some amusement for her guests in the drawing room after the meal was over, a famous pianist or singer engaged to perform to a room full of over-fed and indifferent listeners. Mrs. Gaymour had a different plan. With a cunning which most of her guests fully appreciated she turned to Taisie and said: "Could I persuade you to give us some music, Miss Brown? Please do, we've all heard so much about you."

The implication that the people present knew of her by repute, but that few of them had been to the Gaiety was not lost on Taisie and for a moment her eyes glittered with a green fire. Then Maurice broke in, his disingenuous face alight with pride.

"Yes, do give us a song, Taisie." He came up close to her and whispered: "I'm so proud of you. Show them what you can do."

There was a grand piano at one end of

the room. Very slowly Taisie went up to it, thinking hard. When she reached the piano she turned with the grace she had acquired in long, hard sessions in the dance studio and said, with beautifully calculated shyness: "I brought no music with me and must play from memory. If you are prepared to forgive my short-comings I'll be happy to sing to you."

The men were won over before she began, the women judged her more criti-cally. She was too well dressed, her appearance was theatrical. It seemed that she was not wearing paint, which most of them had expected, and she had got through the evening without making any serious mistakes of behaviour, but they were on the watch, ready to condemn her as soon as she put a foot wrong.

The first notes rippled out and Taisie began to sing, her voice pitched perfectly to the size of the room. Even more than in the theatre she was thankful for the lessons she had taken and the songs Rosa Grazini had made her learn.

Plaisir d'amour ne dure qu'un moment
Chagrin d'amour dure toute la vie . . .

The sweet, nostalgic tune hung on the air for a moment when she finished and then there was a spontaneous burst of applause. Maurice was clapping hard enough for the Albert Hall.

"I say, Taisie, that was first rate!" he exclaimed. "I didn't know you spoke French."

"I don't," Taisie said. "Just a few phrases and a couple of songs."

"Give us another. Just one," he coaxed.

Taisie glanced round at the faces which had been surprised out of their polite indifference and then she broke into the song she had sung for her very first appearance on the stage: "Pretty little Polly Perkins of Paddington Green".

In contrast to the French song it had a gay, swinging tune and the words were amusing and innocuous, at least in the version which Taisie chose to sing.

When it was over she got up from the piano stool and swept them a curtsey. She was smiling, knowing that she had triumphed over prejudice and distrust.

"A magnificent performance," Blair murmured as she was moving past him.

"But can you keep it up? And I don't mean at the piano."

"Yes, I can," Taisie said, pausing to look up into his face.

"Every day of your life? Always playing a part, always acting?"

"Until it becomes second nature," she said.

"But then you will no longer be Taisie Brown."

"That's right. I'm going to start being Anastasia Gaymour. Mrs. Maurice Gaymour."

Maurice and Taisie were married at the end of September. In accordance with Taisie's inexorable plan the ceremony was performed at St. George's, Hanover Square. The bride wore yards of ivory satin and was given away by Mr. George Edwardes, since she had no known male relatives. Guests on her side of the church were few, but one person who did attend was Laetitia Lawton.

Scraping round for a few respectable people to be her guests, Taisie had remembered what Hetty had said about Mrs. Lawton being pleased to see her if she ever became rich and famous. She took an afternoon off from the pleasant business of buying her trousseau to make a visit to Sutton. Laetitia, looking thin and sour, received her with condescension which wavered into unwilling admiration when Taisie displayed her engagement ring. She was envious of Taisie's success, but when Taisie was diplomatic enough to say that she owed it all to the Lawtons' kindness to her as a child Laetitia bridled and looked pleased.

She would never have been brought to admit it, but attending Taisie's wedding was the high spot of her year. She did not approve of the theatrical guests, but she was in ecstasies at being squired by the grandson of an Earl.

"She's a shocking old snob and I've got no patience with her airs and graces," Taisie had said to Blair. "But I owe a lot to her, and even more to her late husband, so I'll be obliged if you'll look after her for me."

"I'm not sure I intend coming to the wedding," he had said. "I still don't approve, you know."

"Don't be silly, there's no chance of

getting me to change my mind, so you might as well put a good face on it like Mrs. Gaymour's decided to do."

The honeymoon was spent in Paris and the South of France. The bride and groom spent a great deal of money, especially the bride; drank a lot of champagne, especially the groom; strolled along the Promenade des Anglais in Nice, gambled at Monte Carlo, laughed and played like a couple of children at the edge of the sea, went to the Opera and the Ballet in Paris, dined in all the best restaurants and returned to England at the end of October very pleased with themselves and with each other.

"Being married to Taisie is just splendid," Maurice confided to Blair. "She's so wonderful! You wouldn't believe how happy we are."

"I'm glad she's giving satisfaction," Blair said.

He would have liked to have heard Taisie's version, but one could hardly ask a woman how she had enjoyed her honeymoon. She looked happy enough, and so she should in Russian sables and a pearl necklace that had set Maurice back more than the ten thousand pounds his mother had been prepared to pay to buy off the girl who was wearing them.

They moved into the Grosvenor Square house and almost immediately gave a glittering party. It began late because most of the guests were Taisie's friends who came on after giving performances at the theatre. There was a lavish supper and the champagne flowed without regard to expense.

"Your hospitality is overwhelming, Mrs. Gaymour," Blair murmured to Taisie when she was able to spare a moment to greet him.

She responded with the disconcerting honesty that cut through his sarcasm.

"Have I overdone it? I didn't know what to order, so I just said lots of food and lots of champagne. Benson saw to all the arrangements. I thought he'd know what's what."

"He probably gets a commission from the caterers," Blair said. "However, there's nothing to be done about that. It's the established custom."

He looked round him at the noisy guests. "What you've provided does very well for the crowd you've got here tonight," he said abruptly. "But if you're entertaining Aunt Gertrude or any of her friends then take my advice and be a little less ostentatious, otherwise you run the risk of being thought vulgar."

His eyes dwelt for a moment on the revealing draperies of Taisie's gold satin gown, but he made no other comment. It was Taisie who said: "You think this dress is a bit much, too, don't you? I bought it in Paris, so I thought it was bound to be all right."

"It's infinitely becoming. It would do very well on the stage," Blair said deliberately.

"Meaning it makes me look like an actress."

"Meaning that it *reminds* everyone you were an actress."

"I'm not ashamed of that," Taisie flashed back at him.

"Why should you be? I'm only suggesting that if you want to be accepted in London Society you should learn restraint." He looked at her flushed, annoyed face and added: "It's Maurice who should be telling you these things, Taisie."

"Maurice never criticizes me. Maurice thinks I'm perfect. And who said you could call me Taisie? I'll have a little respect and be Mrs. Gaymour to you, thank you, Mr. Gregory."

She went over to Maurice and slipped her hand through his arm and as he turned towards her, his face alight with pride, she cast one scornful glance back at Blair over her lovely, bare shoulder.

Blair changed his champagne glass for a large brandy and went home without saying goodnight to his host and hostess.

# 6

TAISIE was blankly astonished to discover that Maurice took it for granted that they would spend the winter months in Leicestershire or Derbyshire.

"But I don't like the country," she said.

"Dash it all, old girl, you can't expect me to miss the hunting," Maurice replied.

"What will I do with myself?" Taisie demanded.

"Oh, you'll find plenty to do," Maurice assured her, with very little idea of how his mother had filled her days during the months when he was absorbed in sport.

She had, in fact, rarely spent more than a few days at a time in the house in Leicestershire. While her husband, and later her son, were taking tosses over fences and returning to the house muddy and bruised, but still undeterred from going out again the following day, Mrs. Gaymour had spent a comfortable time visiting her family and her circle of friends with country houses.

Taisie had no such resources. The only people she knew who did not live in London were Hetty and Laetitia Lawton, neither of whom would have welcomed her for an extended stay. She accompanied Maurice to Leicestershire and was so bored she thought she would go out of her mind. He had house guests, but they were all bachelors, and Taisie had a feeling that although they paid her compliments and were friendly in a hearty, slightly embarrassed fashion, they really found her in the way and would have preferred to have spent their evenings, comatose and a little drunk, without a hostess who had to be treated with civility.

Blair came for a week in December and Taisie made an effort to appear cheerful and busy, fearing his all-seeing eye and sarcastic tongue, but for once Blair was disposed to be sympathetic.

"This is no place for you with no woman to keep you company," he said abruptly. "Why didn't you stay in London and let Maurice have his hunting alone?"

Taisie looked at him in horror. "We've

only been married three months," she said. "I couldn't let him come away without me. It wouldn't have been right."

"You'll have to get used to it," Blair told her. "If you keep him on too tight a leash Maurice will start to fret."

"We're going to Starrid Hall for Christmas," Taisie said, changing the subject. "Maurice's mother is coming. I'm pleased about that."

She was grateful when Blair drove the men out of the dining room early that night, even more grateful when he asked for some music. She suited her songs to her company and coaxed them to join in. It turned into a convivial evening of music and laughter, but when Taisie at last got up from the piano, saying that she was growing hoarse and that the hour was late, she was met with a chorus of protest, Blair and Taisie's eyes met and the same thought flashed between them: Maurice should have done this.

But for all these little rubs, Taisie was not displeased with her marriage. Maurice was still dotingly in love and would do almost anything to please her; he just did not understand that she needed more support than he was giving her. She had known before she married him that his mental capacity was not great and there was no point in getting irritated because he did not comprehend the tedium that was so irksome to her.

She wanted more of his company, but when she got it at Starrid Hall, his home in Derbyshire, she found that she could be just as bored with Maurice as without him. She blamed it on the dreary countryside, because she knew that she had never felt like this in London before they were married. Looking back, however, she had to admit that most of the time she and Maurice had been surrounded by people and it was they who had supplied the wit and nonsense that had kept them amused. Maurice had always been ready to laugh— and to pay—but now Taisie asked herself how much he had contributed to her entertainment and she had to admit that it had been very little.

Christmas passed off with a reasonable degree of success because there was plenty for Taisie to do. Mrs. Gaymour was stiff with her but she had at least overcome her prejudice sufficiently to stay under the same roof as Maurice and his unsuitable wife. When she found Taisie genuinely anxious to learn from her she unbent and told her a little about the duties she had carried out herself in the past.

There was a party for the people who worked on the estate, all of whom knew that Mr. Maurice had married a London actress and were avid to see her. They thought her pretty, but too smart, a verdict with which the neighbours who called agreed. Taisie's Paris gowns were the height of fashion and would have earned admiration in London but in a country house setting they made her look as out of place as a peacock in a hen coop.

Mrs. Gaymour stayed until after the New Year and then went off to visit her sister, Blair's mother, to whom she complained bitterly about the daughter-in-law with whom she had been saddled.

"Flaunting about in velvet and satin," she said. "You can imagine how people stared. Maurice must have been out of his mind. Oh, well, I've vowed that I'll make the best of it and I must admit that the girl treats him well enough, even seems fond of him. Taisie! Did you ever hear such a name?"

"Blair has suggested that I should ask Maurice to bring her here," Mrs. Gregory said doubtfully. "I don't know . . . I suppose I must do it some time."

"Not while I'm with you, I beg," Mrs. Gaymour said. "But it would be good of you to have her. Since we've decided to countenance the marriage she may as well learn the proper way to go on and the only way she'll do that is by seeing how *we* comport ourselves. I gave her a hint or two while I was at Starrid. My dear, she hasn't the least *idea*!"

"How could she, poor child? Blair says she was an orphan and worked as a servant before she went on the stage."

Mrs. Gaymour closed her eyes and shuddered. "Don't dwell on it," she said. "When I think of the girls Maurice could have married . . ."

She dabbed at her eyes with a flimsy handkerchief. "I keep saying I'll make the best of it, and I will," she said resolutely. "Looking on the good side, she's beautiful, she's better behaved than I expected and she does seem to want to learn."

Taisie was eager to accept the invitation from Mrs. Gregory when it came, but Maurice made a grimace.

"I suppose we could take them in on our way back to London," he said. "Can't say I fancy two weeks in a country vicarage, but I dare say I can get some shooting while we're there if you really want to go."

"Vicarage!" Taisie exclaimed. "You don't mean to say that Blair's father is a clergyman?"

"Yes, why not? He was the third son, you see," Maurice explained. "One for the Army, one for the Navy, one for the Church—or the Law, like Blair. Of course, the Earl had a good living or two in his gift, so Uncle Edgar was well provided for."

"How strange," Taisie said. "A clergyman, I would never have thought it. I see now why you're doubtful about this visit. I suppose he'll disapprove of me."

"I don't think so," Maurice said doubtfully. "He's a rum old stick. Spends most of his time looking at birds."

Since Taisie assumed that Mrs. Gaymour's sister would adopt the same attitude towards her as her mother-in-law and she took it for granted, in spite of what Maurice had said, that a country clergyman would look down his nose at a girl who had been on the stage, all her pleasure in the invitation disappeared. It was not until they arrived at the Cotswold village of Kings Amberley, and she actually met the Reverend Edgar Gregory and his wife, that she began to recover her spirits.

To begin with the house was such a nice manageable size after the rambling enormity of Starrid Hall. The Gregorys kept a footman, two maids, a cook and a tweeney, a groom, a gardener and a gardener's boy, which would have seemed a sizeable household to Taisie before her marriage, but now that she had seen the armies of servants Maurice maintained in London, Leicestershire and Derbyshire, many of whom spent long months looking after unoccupied houses, the Gregorys' establishment seemed quite modest. She had her own maid with her, a forbidding female who had tried, just once, to patronize Taisie and had had to be shown her place, and Maurice had his valet, his coachman and his groom, all of whom were accommodated without question, although to Taisie it seemed a liberty to expect so many servants to be put up at the host's expense. She had tried to put this point of view to Maurice, but had been met by a stare of such blank incomprehension that she had hurriedly dropped the subject and never referred to it again.

Mrs. Gregory was a less formidable version of her sister, very much a countrywoman and apparently without the slightest consciousness that she was married to the son of an Earl. Taisie felt more at ease with her than she did with Maurice's mother and, very much to her surprise, the Reverend Edgar Gregory turned out to be a cultured gentleman in his mid-fifties who looked at her with kind, uncritical eyes and made her unobtrusively welcome.

The other thing that made her look round in bewilderment, was the way the house was decorated. Instead of the richly patterned walls and lavish upholstery which Taisie considered the height of opulent living, Mrs. Gregory's taste had dictated plain light colours and oak furniture with simple lines. In the drawing room the walls were not papered, but merely painted with a wash of a clear blue-green; there was a delicate carved screen in one corner, a strip of embroidered silk along the mantelpiece, balanced by a fine Oriental vase which echoed the colours of the curtains and cushions. Taisie had never seen anything like it before. She thought at first that the simplicity must mean the Gregorys were poor, but then she remembered that Maurice had said they were well off and, on closer examination, she realized that all the articles which looked so strange to her were of the finest quality.

Once she began to feel more at home with Mrs. Gregory she ventured to ask her about it.

"The art of decoration is something of a hobby of mine," Mrs. Gregory admitted. "You haven't come across these new ideas before? Morris started it, of course, and I do admire his work, but my own taste has ventured even further towards what one might almost call austerity, although I don't see any virtue in being uncomfortable. The drawing room furniture was specially designed for me and produced in Mr. Lethaby's Cotswold workshops, but in the dining room I kept the Chippendale; I really felt that one could hardly improve on it, don't you agree?"

"Er . . . yes," Taisie said. "I don't know much about taste," she added doubtfully. "I always thought that if you paid top price for anything then it was bound to be all right."

She looked round the bright, uncluttered room thoughtfully. "If this is the modern idea then I like it. I wonder whether Maurice would let me do up the London house like this?"

"My dear, do try to persuade him," Mrs. Gregory said earnestly. "If you can get rid of the hideous crimson flock paper you will be doing a service to mankind."

Taisie also managed to establish a rapport with Mr. Gregory when she conscientiously tried to make conversation about birds because Maurice had said he was interested in them.

"How many kinds of birds can you identify, Taisie?" he asked with a twinkle in his eye. "I may call you Taisie? And to you I must, of course, be Uncle Edgar."

"Thank you, yes," Taisie said. "I was wondering what to call you. Let me see, birds. Sparrows and pigeons . . ." She paused and looked doubtful. "Starlings . . . blackbirds, thrushes and robins," she added triumphantly.

"I can see I shall have to take your education in hand. Next time we go out I will take my field glasses with me and I think in the space of ten minutes or so we can double that list."

"How can you bear to shoot them?" she asked.

"I shoot for the table. I don't suppose you will refuse roast pheasant if I bring a brace or two home with me? Which reminds me, we've been promised a day's sport tomorrow and I must speak to young Maurice about the arrangements."

With her newfound confidence Taisie was persuaded the next day, while Maurice was out shooting, to accompany one of the parish ladies to visit a needy family.

"I suppose it's the sort of thing I ought to do," she said. "Mrs. Gaymour was talking about it at Christmas, visiting the poor and all that. I can't see myself making much of a fist of it, but practice makes perfect, or so they say."

"Oh, quite," Mrs. Gregory replied vaguely. "I didn't really enjoy it myself when I started, but one becomes accustomed and, of course, I had to do what I could to help Mr. Gregory. But if you will accompany Miss Bligh I shall be so grateful, Taisie. I'm afraid you'll find her dull. A dear soul, but so earnest."

Miss Bligh, a stout woman in her forties, with round eyes in a round face and a faint line of black hair along her upper lip, was far more suitably dressed, with her thick sensible boots, than Taisie was for an expedition up a muddy lane.

"Do loop up your skirt, Mrs. Gaymour," she said anxiously. "Oh, dear, you've caught it on a thorn. Stand still, I can free it for you. Such fine material! There, I think I can venture to say there's no harm done."

The cottage stood in isolation at the far end of the lane. To reach it they had to cross a wooden plank across a sluggish stream.

"Do be careful not to slip," Miss Bligh

said. "This wood . . . quite worn, you see. I believe this is where poor Tom fell and broke his arm."

Taisie looked critically at the cottage. It was of a pattern with which she was familiar in a town context; two rooms up and two rooms down and an outhouse which served as scullery and washhouse. At the far end of the garden there was a rickety shed with a broken-hinged door which she guessed housed the privy.

The family consisted of "poor Tom", a farmworker with a broken arm which prevented him from working, his wife and three children, with, as Taisie saw immediately, another on the way. The floor was covered with broken flag stones oozing with damp, the furniture was almost non-existent, and in one corner water seeped down, staining the corner green.

"The roof leaks something chronic," the wife said with a fatalistic resignation that made Taisie grind her teeth. "We're ever so grateful for the visit and for the vittals, Miss Bligh, and you too, ma'am. Aren't we, Tom?"

"Tha's right," Tom said.

"We've hardly known what way to turn, with Tom bein' off work. If only the pig hadn't died! But there, it's been a real bad luck year for us, hasn't it, Tom?"

"Tha's right."

"How do you manage to feed a pig when you've got so little for yourselves?" Taisie asked, genuinely out of her depth.

"That ole pig don't want anythin' but scraps, ma'am. Fattenin' up lovely, he were, and then he took sick and died and o'course we daresn't eat the carcase, though I won't say I wasn't tempted."

They stayed a few more minutes. Miss Bligh added a religious tract and a broad hint about better attendance at church to the basket of food she had brought. Taisie, raging inwardly that she had not thought to bring her purse with her, waited until her companion was outside the door and then turned round to look disparagingly at the tract.

"If I was you I'd put it in the privy," she said, and was gone before the family could do more than look at her with shocked, unbelieving eyes.

"Who owns that cottage?" Taisie

demanded as they negotiated the muddy lane once more.

"Mr. Perkins, who farms the land," Miss Bligh replied. "Oh, Mrs. Gaymour, don't you feel that such scenes of misery are sent to us to do us good?"

"They don't do me good. They make me furious," Taisie said.

"I mean, as a reminder of what we owe to God's goodness," Miss Bligh faltered. "Truly my lot has been cast in pleasant places and today I have been reminded that it is my privilege and duty to aid less fortunate creatures."

"That's all very well," Taisie said, "but what I'd like to know is why God can't dish out the luck more evenly?"

"Oh, Mrs. Gaymour, these questions are too deep for me! You will have to discuss them with Mr. Gregory."

"Yes," said Taisie. "I will. Where can I buy a pig?"

"A *pig*? I imagine Mr. Perkins might sell one. But Mrs. Gaymour, you can't buy a pig!"

"Oh, can't I? We'll see about that."

By the time they reached the Vicarage dusk was falling. A pony and trap stood at the door and Mr. Gregory had just got out and was standing talking to the driver, a large, red-faced man in thick tweeds and stout gaiters.

"Thank you, Mr. Perkins," Mr. Gregory was saying. "Good day to you."

"Perkins?" Taisie said, stepping forward.

The Vicar paused in surprise. "Yes, this is Mr. Perkins, one of our churchwardens, who has been kind enough to drive me home. My niece, Mrs. Gaymour, Mr. Perkins."

The farmer touched his hat with his whip, but Taisie ignored the civilities and said: "Do you own the cottage where the man with the broken arm lives? You do? Then why don't you repair the roof, which is leaking like a sieve, and build them a decent privy?"

The farmer turned helplessly to the Vicar, but Mr. Gregory looked down thoughtfully at the dead pheasants dangling from his hand and said nothing.

"Well, now, ma'am," Mr. Perkins said with uneasy joviality. "Money doesn't grow on trees, you know. Times are hard for farmers. I can't rightly afford to do anything to that old cottage."

Taisie's green gaze swept over him. "You've got a fine big belly on you," she said. "You don't want for much. Starve yourself for a couple of days and spend the money you save on a bit of roof straw and a few boards. Will you sell me a pig?"

"A pig?" Mr. Perkins said, echoing Miss Bligh's bewilderment.

"That family had a pig and it died. I'd like to replace it. I'll tell you what: I'll pay you double the market price if you'll spend the money on making that hovel habitable which at the moment, let me tell you, it is not."

A dull red flush was mounting to the farmer's face and his eyes had begun to glitter. Mr. Gregory intervened. "If I were you I'd close with that offer, Mr. Perkins," he said, with only the faintest tremor in his voice. "I'll see you don't suffer any loss over it, and I'll negotiate the purchase of the pig if Mrs. Gaymour will leave it in my hands."

Taisie nodded, but when they were safely inside the Vicarage she burst out: "I don't see how you can have a man like that as churchwarden when he does so badly by his tenants."

"There is always more than one side to a question," Mr. Gregory said mildly. "Come into my study, Taisie. I'd like to talk it over with you."

She followed him, but she was still seething. "What you don't understand is that I grew up in a place like that, only worse because we were surrounded by other families in the same case," she said. "I know what it's like to have water running down the walls and a slimy hole out the back."

"I understand your indignation and I was not sorry to hear you pointing out his duty so plainly to Mr. Perkins. I've spoken to him more than once about the plight of some of his tenants. However, it would be less than just if I didn't tell you that Tom broke his arm when he staggered home drunk, that he is at the best of times an exceedingly unreliable worker and Mr. Perkins has been most forbearing with him in the past. As for the pig, it was acquired in highly dubious circumstances, it was already sick when Tom brought it to the cottage, and it died of a fever which, if it had spread, would have put in jeopardy the whole of Mr. Perkins' herd."

Taisie's face was losing its mulish look. "If I'd known all that I wouldn't have been quite so rude to him," she admitted. She looked at Mr. Gregory doubtfully. "I suppose I've done nothing but harm, jumping in with both feet where I'm not wanted."

"On the contrary, I think we can turn it to good. And I certainly cherish the memory of your description of Mr. Perkins . . . person."

Taisie's face relaxed into a mischievous grin. "I thought Miss Bligh would have swooned," she said. "What a fool she is! Why do good people have to be so *silly*?"

"Poor Miss Bligh. The only daughter of elderly parents. Her mother is crippled with arthritis and her father has gone quite senile, poor fellow. Miss Bligh cares for them with a devotion which I am tempted to call saintly."

There was a short silence. Mr. Gregory was gazing at the ceiling. At last Taisie said: "I'm sorry."

"One should perhaps beware of making these snap judgements. As I said before, there are always two sides to every question. We are all more dependent on one another's charity than we realize."

Maurice noticed that Taisie was curiously subdued for the remainder of their stay with his aunt and uncle. He thought that it was because she was bored, but Taisie denied it when he tackled her.

"No, I've enjoyed it, and it's been useful to me," she said. "I've learnt a lot in this short stay. I wish we had a smaller house, Maurice. Somewhere where I could order the meals myself and supervise the servants and be more involved in the running of it."

"That wouldn't suit me," Maurice said decisively. "I didn't marry you to get a housekeeper, Taisie darling. What about all that entertaining we're going to do in London this Season?"

It was true that Taisie had looked forward with keen anticipation to a round of balls and receptions that Spring. It was the year of the Queen's Diamond Jubilee and promised to be a glittering Season. Once they were back in London the uneasy feeling that she was leading a selfish life began to fade, although it was revived when she encountered Blair and discovered that he knew about her meeting with Mr. Perkins.

She was very much on the defensive. "I only did what I thought was right," she said.

"Oh, quite! And there is plenty of scope for philanthropy if you have a bent in that direction. Did you, for instance, go and visit the miners' families while you were at Starrid? You didn't? Then I recommend that you do so next time you are in Derbyshire."

"I suppose that means they live in conditions just as horrid as that family in your father's parish," Taisie said resentfully. "You always manage to put me in the wrong. I do think it's unfair. I'm being a good wife to Maurice, aren't I?"

"I can see that Maurice thinks so," Blair replied.

"You should try getting married yourself," Taisie said with a touch of malice. "Your mother says she thinks it's high time."

Mrs. Gregory had, in fact, deplored the fact that neither of her sons had married.

"Frederick is thirty-two," she said. "Of course, he's been in India with the Army, but he'll be home this summer. I really must try to find some pretty girls for him. As for Blair, he's nearly thirty and I despair! A wife would be such a help to him, especially now that he's going in for politics. Did you know he was hoping to be adopted as candidate for a constituency where there's likely to be a bye-election soon? Oh, yes! And I do think a Member of Parliament ought to be married."

When Blair did not reply to the news that his mother wanted to marry him off, Taisie went on: "And you're going to be an MP, I hear. Why is that? Haven't you got enough work as a barrister?"

"I'm *hoping* to be an MP," Blair corrected her, getting up to go. "And I have plenty of Court work, thank you. It's quite usual to combine the two, you know."

"Shall I come and canvass for votes for you?" Taisie asked with a saucy look up at him.

"No, thank you! You're much too dazzling to do me any good with my earnest surburban constituents."

The exchange was similar to the way she usually sparred with Blair, Taisie thought regretfully. He had never quite forgiven her for marrying Maurice, which was petty minded of him, considering that she had not held it against him that he had tried to buy her off. And her marriage was a success, surely he could see that?

In spite of her misgivings about a young married couple splitting up so soon after their wedding, Taisie stayed in London after they left the Gregorys and sent Maurice off for some shooting in Norfolk, knowing that he would find the upheaval she planned in the London house quite unbearable.

"I've got a lot of planning to do for all the parties we're going to give," she said firmly. "And I do want to get the house to rights before I send out my invitations. I can redecorate it the way I want, can't I, Maurice? Do say yes!"

"You can have anything your little heart desires," Maurice assured her, but he was rather more doubtful when he saw the results of Taisie's orgy of decorating.

"I suppose it's all right," he said,

looking at the dining room walls hung with pale yellow paper like watered silk.

"It's the very latest thing," Taisie said. "And quite apart from that, I like it."

"If you're happy, that's all I ask," Maurice said.

He put his hand on her shoulder and squeezed it as he spoke, but when Taisie turned and put her arms round his neck, he said uneasily: "I say, watch it, Mrs. G. Not here," with a look at the half-open door.

It surprised her, the lack of spontaneity Maurice showed in their lovemaking. He was still ardent, but only behind the closed doors of their bedroom. Even the slightest show of affection in a place where they might be observed made him shy away. She had once made the mistake of kissing his cheek in public and had been given a blistering reproof once they were alone.

"I mean to say, not at all the thing," he said. "Vulgar!"

"Meaning I'm vulgar?" Taisie asked dangerously.

"No, of course not! Not at all! Not your fault you don't know people don't do these things. Not people like us, I mean."

Taisie let it drop and tried not to offend him in the same way again. She knew that he was more than satisfied with their relations, and so he should be considering the way she put herself out to please him, but he was not an imaginative lover. Taisie had not realized until after her marriage how sophisticated Leonard's lovemaking had been and she had to be very careful not to let Maurice realize how much more she had learnt than he would have thought proper. She thought him dull, and too easily satisfied, but as long as he came to her so often she could be sure that he was not wandering after anyone else, which was all that really mattered.

Since the Gaymours had disappeared into the country immediately after their honeymoon, Taisie was, in effect, making her debut in London society. She was on tenterhooks in case her invitations were not accepted or, even worse, in case she and Maurice were not invited back. She need not have worried. The word had gone round: Mrs. Gaymour had countenanced the marriage, the Gregorys had received her; Taisie would never move in the very highest circles, but standards were not as rigid as they had once been. She was beautiful, high-spirited, amusing, her marriage had made her respectable and, above all, although it was not something anyone said out loud, she and Maurice were extremely rich. It was only the very high sticklers who turned up their noses at an invitation to a dinner party where everything was of the very best, regardless of expense.

The newly decorated house, too, became something fashionable London had to see. Not to be able to say, in an offhand tone: "I do so admire Mrs. Gaymour's drawing room, don't you?" marked one as being not quite in the know. Some people saw the pale, clear colours and light silken draperies as no more than a theatrical background for Taisie's striking good looks: certainly Taisie's interpretation of the new movement owed little to the austere simplicity Mrs. Gregory had advocated.

To Taisie it often seemed as if she were living in a dream and her excitement at her own success led her into extravagance not only in spending money, but also in behaviour. Within a month of their first dinner party she and Maurice were setting the pace for a set of gay young married couples, spiced with theatrical people introduced by Taisie.

The fact that it was Jubilee Year affected Taisie in a way she confided to nobody, but which heightened her awareness of the contrast between her life at the time of the old Queen's Golden Jubilee and now, when her Diamond Jubilee was approaching. She tried not to let her mind dwell on it, but as the anniversary drew nearer she found herself remembering what had happened to her on the night of the previous Jubilee.

Ten years ago. Who would have thought then that the poor little ravished waif would be the wife of one of the richest men in the kingdom? Whenever she reached this point in her thoughts Taisie fingered her emerald necklace, her diamond ring, moved her limbs sensuously against the silk that covered them and thanked her stars for her good fortune.

In the middle of May Taisie and Maurice gave a supper party which ended by getting out of hand. It was attended by most of the cast of the current Gaiety hit and rather too many of Maurice's bachelor friends who were always, as they said, "ripe for a spree". Taisie knew that the atmosphere was becoming too hectic, but she had had an encounter that had shocked her so much that she thought she would faint, and her preoccupation with her sense of disbelief made her careless. Indeed, for a time she was almost totally unware of anything that was going on around her, moving amongst her guests with a fixed smile on her lips like an automaton.

Although the party was informal, Taisie and Maurice had stood at the top of the stairs to receive their guests. At first Taisie, in a dashing gown of shot bronze silk which gleamed with metallic lights when she moved, did not particularly notice the man who walked slowly up the stairs towards her behind a group who had come on from seeing "The Geisha" at Daly's.

The group moved on and he was in front of her, a tall man, heavily built, his bulging thighs straining the cloth of his evening suit. His black hair, streaked with grey, was long and carefully brushed forward. His face was bronzed, as if he had recently been in a hot climate, and although he must have been in his fifties it was singularly unlined, its smoothness accentuated by a luxuriant black moustache.

"My dear Maurice, this is the first opportunity I have had of greeting you and your charming bride," he said. "I come uninvited—isn't that a shocking confession?—but I was at the theatre with my good friends, Mr. and Mrs. Datchet, and they assured me that I must be welcome."

"Delighted to see you, of course," Maurice responded. "Didn't know you were back in London or we'd have sent you a card. Desmond Corley, my dear. My wife, Desmond."

"Ah, the pride with which he says it! And one sees why! Your very obedient servant, Mrs. Gaymour."

There was something about his manner which Taisie didn't like and she thought that the *galante* way he took her hand and bent over it, raising it to his lips, was overdone. Like a foreigner, she thought, suppressing an impulse to take her hand away and wipe it on her skirt.

As he bent over her his hair moved forward. The lower half of his left ear had been shot away.

Taisie's nervous start communicated itself to Desmond Corley. He straightened up and a shade of annoyance crossed his face when he saw the way she was staring at him, but he continued to smile as he bowed and moved away.

Taisie heard herself asking in a voice which seemed to come from an immense distance: "Who is he?"

"A cousin of my father's. He's a great traveller, spends part of every year out of England. In fact, he's got a villa in Sicily which is more his home than the lodgings he takes in London."

Through the wave of nausea that threatened to overwhelm her, Taisie forced herself to ask: "What happened to his ear?"

"Nasty, isn't it?" Maurice said. "It happened in Sicily years ago. Some fool of an Italian said Desmond had been molesting his daughter. Of course, they're very sensitive about that kind of thing, or so Desmond says, although he swears it was all imagination. Anyway, this Sicilian blasted off at Desmond with a shotgun, took away half his ear."

As she moved blindly amongst her guests, Taisie told herself over and over again that she must be mistaken. It could not possibly be the same man. Her mind had been dwelling on the past because of the coming Jubilee, she was letting her imagination run away with her. And yet, the mutilation was the same, the scar less vivid now than it had been ten years earlier, but just as distinctive. The colouring was right, the smooth heavy body was the same.

She had the feeling of being in a nightmare, surrounded by laughing, chattering people and yet totally alone, shut off from them in a cocoon of remembered terror. When she was offered a glass of wine she took it and drank it thirstily without realizing what she was doing and, putting down the empty glass, took another in the hope it would stop the shivering that had taken hold of her.

By the time she began to come out of her state of shock the party was reaching a climax and Maurice had had rather too much to drink.

An argument had broken out as to whether it was possible to toboggan down the stairs on a tray. There was only one way to settle the dispute: two men made the attempt and crashed in disorder. A girl from the Gaiety chorus insisted on trying and also crashed, her legs exposed to the thigh. One or two of the staider guests raised their eyebrows and made to depart.

"Taisie could do it," Maurice said, with drunken insistence. "Taisie can do anything."

There was a chorus of agreement, someone began laying bets. Taisie shook her head, but their insistence excited her and she did not realize how much of her bravado was due to her emotional state and the wine with which she had tried to mask it.

There was a particular reason why she knew she ought not to join in the dangerous game: she thought that she might be pregnant. She was not sure quite how she felt about the possibility. Pleased in a way, and curiously proud, but at the same time annoyed that it should have happened now, just when she was enjoying herself so much. Anyway, she was not yet two weeks overdue so it could turn out to be a false alarm. All the same, she was sure that she ought not to try riding a tray down the stairs.

"Come on, Taisie," Maurice was urging. "I've got a pony on you. Don't let me down."

Blair was standing close by. Seeing that she was wavering, he said in a low, urgent voice: "Taisie, no! You'll hurt yourself and this sort of behaviour can do you nothing but harm."

It was an intervention guaranteed to set Taisie's back up. With the green flash in her eyes that always appeared when she was angry, she seized the heavy mahogany tray and ran to the top of the stairs amidst cheers and encouraging shouts.

Crouched down with her feet tucked under her and her skirts anchored underneath, she was launched. She rode triumphantly, bumping from the edge of one step to the next, almost to the bottom and then, overconfident, let the edge of the tray tip forward and was somersaulted to the foot of the stairs, where she lay, unhurt but winded, and helpless with laughter.

It was Blair who picked her up, his face rigid with disapproval—or was it concern? —and over his shoulder Taisie saw the smooth brown face and dark head of Desmond Corley. She gave a little sigh and collapsed against Blair in a dead faint.

By the following morning Taisie knew there was no longer any hope of a pregnancy. Whether it was due to her bumpy ride or to the shock she had received from her encounter with Desmond Corley, or whether the lateness of her period had been no more than chance, she could not be sure. She confided in the doctor who came to see her and he shook his head at her foolishness and made her stay in bed until the following day. She did not tell Maurice, partly because he was frantic with worry any way and partly because she was ashamed to admit that she might have robbed him of the chance of a child.

All day she lay in her blue and white bedroom, with the outlines of lilies stencilled on the walls and a carpet like a field of bluebells, and debated what to do about Desmond Corley. She had never told

Maurice that part of her history and she did not intend to do so now. The one person she felt she could confide in was Blair. He was a legal man, he would be able to advise her, and with his experience in the Criminal Courts he was not likely to be shocked; but behind this rationalization of her motives there was a desire to justify herself in Blair's eyes. He had condemned her behaviour the night before; he might not be so self-righteous if he knew what lay behind it. Taisie penned a little note, more imperious than she realized, and sent it round to his chambers.

He came within the hour and she received him lying on the sofa in her boudoir. She looked unusually frail in the soft folds of her peignoir.

"You're looking far from well," Blair said in his abrupt fashion.

"That stupid toboggan ride came at an unfortunate time for me," Taisie said. "I've had a slight . . . disappointment as a result."

For a moment he did not understand her, but when he realized what she was hinting at a dull colour rose in his face and he looked at once appalled and diverted.

"Mrs. Gaymour, you really shouldn't . . . you can't tell *me* things like that! And how could you be so careless with your health!"

"Don't scold me," Taisie said. "And don't say anything to Maurice. He doesn't know. That's not what I wanted to see you about. Listen, it is possible to hire men to follow people about and report on what they do, isn't it?"

"Yes, but what on earth do you want with a private detective?" Blair sat down on a chair at the foot of the chaise longue. Taisie thought he looked tired and had a momentary qualm of conscience at dragging him away from his work.

"What are you up to?" Blair demanded. "You can't want Maurice followed, surely? I thought he was besotted with you."

"Of course it's not Maurice," Taisie said with an impatient wave of her hand. "It's someone else."

She looked at him doubtfully, not sure, now that she had got him there, how much she wanted to tell him.

"Are you in trouble?" Blair asked.

She took so long to answer that he began to fear that she was indeed in bad trouble,

216

especially when at last she said hesitantly: "There's a man . . ."

She stopped, and since she seemed unable to go on, Blair asked: "Is he blackmailing you? Is that it?"

"Blackmail?" Taisie repeated, quite at sea.

She looked at him with such astonishment that Blair said hurriedly, "I can see it's not. I'm sorry, Taisie, I thought perhaps something out of your past life had come up to worry you."

"It has," Taisie said, making up her mind. "I'll tell you, but you must promise not to speak about it to anyone else."

She leaned back against the pillow propped behind her head, closed her eyes and began to tell him in a slow, monotonous voice how she had been sold to Abe Gribble and what had happened on the night of Queen Victoria's Golden Jubilee. When she had finished she opened her eyes. Blair was sitting with his hands covering his face.

"I'd like to kill him," he said in a muffled voice.

"I wish you could," Taisie said longingly.

Blair sat up. His quick mind went straight to the weakness in her story.

"You can't really be sure it's the same man."

"I'm sure."

"After ten years . . ."

"I'm sure," Taisie repeated. "That ear of his. There can't be two like it in the world. I had nightmares about it for years. I've never forgotten it."

"But why do you want him followed?"

"To see what he's up to now. A vice like that, a man doesn't give it up overnight. I want to know if there's some other house he uses and, if there is, I'll put the police on to it."

"If you succeed it will cause a terrible scandal," Blair pointed out.

"Much I care about that! I thought, you being a lawyer and knowing about these things, you could put me on to a man who could be trusted to follow him and report back."

Blair got up and took a turn about the room. "You mustn't appear in this," he said. "I'll hire a detective and his report will come to me."

"And you'll tell me what it says."

"Yes, I suppose you have a right to know."

"And it'll be a secret between the two of us."

Again Blair moved restlessly about the room. "You ought to tell Maurice," he said, with his back to Taisie.

"Oh, no, I shouldn't! Maurice! He's got no more idea than a babe unborn. I don't suppose he even knows such things happen."

"Then he ought to be made to know."

"Not when it concerns his own wife. I think he would be . . . disgusted. It might turn him against me."

"That would be a pity," Blair said with the undercurrent of sarcasm in his voice that always made Taisie bristle.

"You don't like knowing about it yourself," she pointed out. "I can hear it in the way you speak."

"That's not true! I hate the thing itself. It makes me feel sick. But for you I feel nothing but compassion. I always knew you'd raised yourself up from degrading circumstances, but I never imagined anything like this."

He turned to face her again. "You are a

remarkable woman," he said quietly. "I am honoured by your confidence and I will respect it and try to serve you as best I can."

He took her hand in his, stood looking down at her with a strange intensity for a moment or two, and then he raised her hand to his lips and kissed it.

# 7

THE toboganning escapade brought a reproof from Mrs. Gaymour which stung Taisie all the more because she knew it was justified.

"Just when I'd persuaded people to accept you!" her mother-in-law said in despair. "Really, Taisie, these hoydenish ways won't do."

"I know it was very silly," Taisie said, hanging her head more to hide the fury in her eyes than out of shame.

Her apparent meekness mollified Mrs. Gaymour. "We'll say no more about it," she said and added, with resolute fair-mindedness, "I dare say Maurice was as much to blame as you. You've neither of you got any more sense than a pair of children. As for changes you've made to this house . . . However, you are mistress here now and I won't criticize. It must have cost a fortune."

"It did," Taisie admitted. "But it's been very much admired."

She gathered from her mother-in-law's expression that she could see nothing admirable in the new decorations but again, with admirable restraint, Mrs. Gaymour stopped herself from commenting.

"I was going to excuse myself from your Ball next week," she said. "But I suppose if I don't come now people will say it's because I disapprove of your conduct—which I do, but I won't have it whispered all over London. What I wanted to say to you was that I've heard from my sister that her elder son, Frederick, has arrived home from India. He's in the Army, you know. I dare say you'll want to send him an invitation."

She pursed her lips as Taisie made a note on a little gilt-edged note pad.

"How wise you are to write it down, so *affairée* as you are!"

As she got up to go she asked: "You've heard the news about Blair?"

"No, what's happened to him?"

"He's been accepted as Parliamentary candidate for Sandlands in place of old Sir Humphrey, who wants to retire. That means there will be a bye-election before the end of the year and we may see him a Member of Parliament by the time he's thirty. So gratifying!" She sighed. "I had hoped that once he was married and settled down Maurice might have been persuaded to do something similar, or at least to take life more seriously, but of course . . ."

She did not finish the sentence, but Taisie knew what she meant: if Maurice had married a more suitable girl he might have mended his ways, but with an actress for a wife he was condemned to a life of frivolity. Taisie doubted herself whether Maurice would ever change. He might give up betting on his wife's chances of sliding down the stairs on a tray, but because of his wealth he lacked any incentive to take up a profession, he was not greatly interested in the running of his estates, and he was highly unlikely to devote himself to public service.

Blair was out of town the following week, wooing his prospective constituents, and did not attend the Gaymours' Ball. Taisie was disappointed, even though she knew it was unlikely that he would have any news so soon about the watch on Desmond Corley. Corley himself she carefully refrained from inviting. Let him think it was an oversight or, as Taisie put it to herself, let him think what he damned well liked; she was not going to have him under her roof if she could help it.

Major Frederick Gregory, on the other hand, did attend the Ball and enjoyed himself hugely.

"Pity you had to miss it, old fellow," he said to Blair, who had offered to put him up in his roomy apartment until he was ready to return to the country. "Was it really necessary to go and see the voters this week?"

"I thought it would be a good idea," Blair said.

He was sorting through a pile of correspondence. As he picked up one letter and perused it he enquired in an offhand way: "What did you think of our new cousin?"

"Prettiest thing I've seen since I reached England," his brother said promptly. "How on earth did old Maurice persuade her to marry him?"

"Money," Blair said.

"Lucky devil. I must remember to send

her some flowers. I said I'd drop into her At Home tomorrow."

"I take it that means you've started a flirtation with her?"

"I wouldn't say no to the chance, but I don't think there's anything doing there, not seriously, you know. Full of fun and gaiety, but I don't think she'd step over the mark. Besides . . . not quite the thing, in the family, you know."

Blair was apparently absorbed in his letter, but Fred went on: "However, while we're on the subject of women, there's one thing I've promised myself while I'm on leave and that's a visit to the Empire. Are you game?"

Blair looked up. "I take it you're more interested in the women on offer in the Promenade than the show on the stage? I'll be in trouble if I get myself arrested."

"Don't be silly, old chap. They know how to arrange these things at the Empire."

"Don't be too sure of that," his brother warned him. "Things are changing. There's been a lot of fuss in the newspapers about soliciting in the Empire Promenade. They got it shut off from the

225

theatre at one time, but that didn't last long and things are back to where they were before."

"And how do you know that?" Fred demanded. "Been along and had a look, have you? I knew it! Enjoying all the delights of civilization while us poor devils are sweating it out on the Frontier. All right, just for looking so po-faced you can stand treat tonight."

"Try my patience too far and you'll find yourself out in the street," Blair retorted, but he was smiling and it seemed as if some strain in him relaxed in response to his brother's chaffing.

On 22nd June Queen Victoria drove to St. Paul's Cathedral for the Thanksgiving for her Sixty Glorious Years. Once again she rejected the idea of appearing in State robes and a crown. She wore black silk with panels of grey embroidered in silver, a chiffon cape and a bonnet trimmed with ostrich feathers and a diamond aigrette. She looked small, dumpy and curiously impressive, even though Keir Hardie, the Socialist, published a pamphlet attacking the Jubilee and calling her "an old lady of very commonplace aspect".

Taisie and Maurice had secured a room with windows overlooking the route of the procession and a party of friends to share it with them. It was very much a family party. Mr. and Mrs. Gregory had been persuaded up from the country for a few days and both their sons had come along, Fred looking very impressive in his uniform.

Taisie seemed more subdued than usual, but only Blair suspected that her withdrawal from the general mood of excitement might be due to something more than a desire to behave with decorum in front of Maurice's family. He seized a moment when the rest of the party was crowded round the window to have a quiet word with her.

In response to a tiny movement of his head she moved towards the back of the room and he followed her.

"Do you have news for me?" she asked in a low voice.

"Yes, but it's inconclusive." His eyes scanned her face. "You're looking tired. Are you all right?"

A glimmer of Taisie's mischievous smile lit up her face. "That's very uncomplimentary!"

Blair said nothing and after a moment she admitted: "I've been remembering . . . ten years ago. It haunts me. I can't sleep. I feel that if I can do something about that creature I'll be able to rest. What do you want to tell me?"

Blair glanced round and saw that his brother had already turned away from the window. "Not now," he said. "When can I call on you?"

"It would be difficult for me to see you alone while your parents are staying in the house. Is it all right for me to come to your Chambers?"

"Yes, there can be no impropriety in that. Tomorrow, around four o'clock?"

She nodded and would have moved away, but Blair said in a quiet but urgent voice: "Try not to dwell on what is past. To let it injure your health now would be foolish indeed."

Taisie smiled again and laid a hand lightly on his arm. "Considering how much you disapprove of me you are remarkably kind," she said.

"I don't . . ." Blair began quickly, but he stopped himself. "I have come to think that Maurice is a very lucky man," he said with a stiffness that made Taisie believe it was no more than a conventional formula.

On the other side of the room Major Gregory had observed the short tête-à-tête. There was nothing in it, of course. His brother had merely exchanged a few quiet words with his hostess. Except that there was something about the way they had stood together, talking confidentially; something about the way Taisie had smiled up at Blair and the way Blair had looked down at her; above all, the way Blair's eyes had followed her when she moved away and could no longer see his face. Frederick raised his eyebrows and pursed his lips and went back to looking out of the window.

One of the habits that Taisie had retained from her stage days was that she was always punctual. She had never been late for a rehearsal or a performance and she had carried this punctiliousness over into her new life. On the stroke of four o'clock on the day after Jubilee Day she presented herself at Blair's Lincolns Inn chambers

229

and remembered how she had done the same thing a year earlier. What a lot had happened since then, what a long way she had come. The two clerks were still there. They looked up, surreptitiously admiring her appearance, but she no longer aroused the same excitement in them as she had on her previous visit. Taisie noticed it with a certain rueful amusement, and a trace of regret. She was no longer Taisie Brown, she was Mrs. Maurice Gaymour, and that did not have the same glamour. She felt she had, to a certain extent, lost her own identity, sunk it in Maurice's, and the realization made her look pensive as she was shown into Blair's room.

"Still feeling under the weather?" he asked.

"I'm all right," Taisie said. "It's just that your two boys outside didn't fall flat on their faces when I walked in this time and it made me realize that I've become a nobody."

Blair looked at her, more restrained in appearance than she had been a year ago, but still with the same lovely hair and skin, the triangular cat's face and sparkling green eyes, the same exquisite body. He picked up the report from the private detective and plunged into the business that had brought Taisie to his office.

"As far as our man has been able to discover, Desmond Corley is not frequenting any . . . dubious houses," he said. "He has lodgings in Jermyn Street—very respectable—he belongs to a couple of clubs, which he visits regularly, he is invited to functions at some of the best houses in London and he occasionally visits a theatre."

"How disappointing," Taisie said.

"There's just one thing," Blair added slowly. "He is maintaining a house in St. John's Wood which is occupied by a middle-aged woman and her thirteen-year-old daughter. The girl calls him 'uncle', but the neighbours suspect that she is, in fact, his daughter."

"I don't believe that," Taisie said. "Oh, Blair, it's obvious! That poor, poor child."

"Just a moment, Taisie. The girl comes and goes quite freely, she is well fed, well dressed and seems cheerful. If she is a victim then she is a willing one."

"That doesn't make it any less horrible."

"I agree. It does mean that there is very little you can do about it."

"I don't understand you."

"I doubt very much whether you will get the Police to take an interest in the case. Think, Taisie: the identification of someone you saw ten years ago and an apparently respectable man who is keeping a woman and child in comfortable circumstances with no hint on the surface of any impropriety. I'm convinced they won't move, not unless either the girl or the woman accuses him, which seems unlikely in the circumstances."

Taisie was on her feet in one swirl of impetuous movement. "You're covering up for him because he's one of you," she said. "I won't let it rest there, I won't! I will see justice done!"

Blair did not move from his seat behind the desk. "Is it justice you want, or is it revenge?" he asked wearily.

"I don't see any difference," Taisie said. She looked at him doubtfully and sat down again.

"I am not trying to cover up anything Corley may have done," Blair said. "I'm merely pointing out the difficulty of getting a conviction."

"If the little girl was examined . . ."

"Without her mother's agreement—if she is her mother? The only thing I can suggest is that we probe deeper into the woman's background to make sure that she really has got a thirteen-year-old daughter. As I said when we spoke the other day, at the moment the evidence is totally inconclusive."

"It all looks obvious enough to me. I suppose I have to accept what you say. You're the expert. What did you mean about me wanting revenge?"

"You do, don't you? You want to see Desmond Corley behind bars because of what he did to you. If you wanted justice, then you might concern yourself a little more about the conditions that produce this kind of degradation."

"I don't understand you," Taisie muttered resentfully.

"You are unusual in that you were born into the direst poverty and are now a very rich young woman. You know what it is like to live at the bottom level of society. Now that you are at the top, what are you doing to improve the lives of those who have not been so fortunate? Nothing, as far as I am aware."

"Good works! I tried that in your father's parish and look what a mess I made of it!"

"On the contrary, you gave Mr. Perkins a salutary lesson. Father is delighted with the work he's done on his cottages since you—spoke to him. You could do a lot of good on your own doorstep, Taisie."

"I haven't been married a year yet! I've hardly had time to look round me."

"You've had time to turn your own house into one of fashionable London's talking points," Blair said drily.

"Criticism, criticism—that's all I ever get from you. And I'm not rich, not in my own right. Maurice will give me anything I want, that's true enough, provided he sees the point of it. What's he going to say if I start spending hundreds, perhaps thousands of pounds on . . . on Homes for Girls, or whatever it is you have in mind?"

"Try him and see. It's time he had an interest in life besides the cut of his suit and what won the 2.30 at Newmarket."

"You're very scathing about Maurice,"

Taisie said slowly. "You always have been. The first time I came here you as good as said he wasn't good enough for me. I don't think it's very nice of you to despise Maurice just because he isn't clever like you."

"I think it's a pity he doesn't make better use of his resources, that's all. If you could get him interested in philanthropy it would be something you could share . . ."

"We share *everything*!" Taisie said emphatically.

"Not everything," Blair said. "You haven't told him about Desmond Corley."

Since this was true Taisie was momentarily at a loss. Blair was not looking at her. Staring down at the scattered papers on his desk, a deep frown between his strongly-marked brows, he said in a low voice, "You do wrong when you give me confidences which you withhold from your husband."

It shook Taisie, and all the more so because it made Blair look so worried.

"I consulted you as . . . as a legal man," she said slowly.

"Did you?"

"And as a friend. I thought we were friends, even though you are so hard on me. I didn't know we were going to quarrel when I came to see you today."

The frown did not lessen, nor did Blair look up, but he said in a more conciliatory tone: "We haven't quarrelled. At least, I hope we haven't. I'm sorry, Taisie; I said more than I intended."

When Taisie did not answer he made himself look at her. As their eyes met she said: "I can't tell Maurice. You know that really."

A wry smile twisted Blair's lips. "It might be a tactical error," he agreed.

Taisie was pulling on her gloves and making rather a performance of it.

"You want me to go on with the investigation into the past of the woman Corley's keeping?" Blair asked.

"Yes. I don't want to give up yet. As for the other business . . . I know you're right when you say I ought to do something to help poor people. The trouble is, I don't like thinking about it. I don't want to go back and see people living like I used to live. It hurts too much."

"I never thought of that," Blair said. "I'm sorry. I didn't mean to distress you."

"I could give money to charity, but that's not what you had in mind, is it?" Taisie asked, still pursuing her own train of thought. "I don't know . . . what can one woman do?"

"Quite a lot. Octavia Hill, for instance . . . but I mustn't bore you with my hobbyhorse."

"No, tell me about her."

Blair went and looked in the bookcase on the far side of the room. "Here you are, you can read the book she wrote— 'Homes of the London Poor', although I doubt if it will tell you anything you don't know already from your own experience."

As Taisie took the book she was smiling. "You do know how to get your own way, don't you?" she asked. "You're determined to involve me in your charities and here I am promising to read a book that will probably keep me awake all night even though I've said I don't want to get involved. If I change my mind will you advise me how to go about it?"

"That's not what I intended," Blair said quickly. "I meant you and Maurice . . ."

"Now. Blair, do be sensible. Maurice is a dear and I'm devoted to him, but serious matters bore him and when Maurice is bored he is very difficult to handle. If I'm to be a new Octavia Hill I must do it on my own—or with your help. Do stop frowning. We are friends, again, aren't we?"

"Yes," Blair said. "Friends."

On her way home from Lincolns Inn, carrying the book Blair had saddled her with, half resentful and half in agreement with everything he had said to her, Taisie suddenly decided to confront her private nightmare. She asked her coachman to drive her to Pimlico, to Number 1 Clerivale Street.

"I don't want to get out, I just want to look at it," she said.

He was too well trained to express surprise, but he did wonder to himself what his mistress was up to now. A proper caution she was at times, but decent enough to work for and always remembered to say thank you, which was more than many a lady born would do.

He found the house and pulled up on the far side of the road. Taisie leaned forward and stared at it through the window of her brougham. The house was empty, that was obvious. One of the windows had been broken and boarded up. The blinds which had shut off the life inside from the world were still in place, but one of them hung lopsidedly as if it had been torn. The paint on the front door was cracked and peeling. It was not as she had expected; there was no trace of Abe Gribble and his repulsive trade. She felt a lightening of the load of guilt that had burdened her ever since Blair had reproached her for not doing anything for her fellow unfortunates. At least there was nothing here she could have remedied by speaking out.

She did attempt to involve Maurice in her new interest but, as she had expected, he was not impressed.

"Do you own any property in London?" she persisted.

"Not much. I get some rents from property in Stepney, I believe."

"What's it like? Have you ever been to see it?"

"No, I haven't! And what's more, Taisie, I won't have you going there. Now mind this, because I mean it. I absolutely forbid you to go poking about in the slums of London. There's no saying what you might catch from people like that."

"I was born in Wapping," Taisie said. "Not a very fashionable area."

"Yes, I know. I mean, I didn't know it was Wapping, but that's nothing to the point. You've left all that behind you and I don't see why you want to rake it up. Forget where you came from. You're my wife now."

Taisie saw that she had ruffled him and spoke swiftly to soothe him. "I'm a very lucky girl," she said. "I won't do anything you don't like, but would you object if I used the little bit of money I've still got from before we were married? I'd like to buy a house and let rooms to poor girls, perhaps girls like me who are on the stage and find it difficult to make both ends meet."

Maurice bent and kissed her. "That's just like you," he said. "You're the most generous girl. Keep your little bit of money, darling. I'll put up the ready for your house, just so long as you don't want to go trotting round there all the time

240

involving yourself in the running of it. Hire yourself a housekeeper and leave it to her."

He paused and chuckled, suddenly deciding to be amused by her latest whim. "I don't know when you're going to find time to go househunting," he said. "We seem to be up to our eyes in invitations for the next few weeks and I don't care what you say, I'm not spending August in London this year."

"I'm sure a suitable property won't be difficult to find," Taisie said.

"Get my solicitors to handle the purchase," he warned her. "No need to do anything except instruct them, say how you want it done and leave the letting to the agent."

There was more to it than that, but he was right in saying that Taisie had little time to occupy herself with the project in the remaining weeks they were spending in London. She conscientiously read the book Blair had lent her and was impressed by Miss Hill's experiments, which began when she bought three properties in Marylebone, repaired them and cleaned them up, and let them at fair rents. Taisie realized that Octavia Hill had become the friend of the people who were her tenants, not merely a faceless landlord, and that met with her warm approval. She would like to do the same herself and, in spite of Maurice's embargo, she was secretly determined to involve herself in the lives of the girls who might one day live in the house, or houses, she bought.

There was a Diamond Jubilee Ball at the Guildhall on the 5th of July. Taisie was surprised to receive an invitation, but Maurice had contacts in the City which made it expedient for him to attend and so they went and were received by the Lord Mayor in his gold chain of office.

"Just like Dick Whittington," Taisie said. "I'm glad to have seen him close to. Do you think he keeps a cat?"

"What a child you are," Maurice said indulgently. "Evening, Desmond, didn't know we were going to see you here tonight."

"Delighted to see you," Desmond Corley said. "Good evening, Mrs. Gaymour. How charming you look. I hope you are going to honour me with a dance?"

She didn't want to dance with him, his

touch was so repulsive to her that she could scarcely keep herself from shuddering, but it would look odd if she refused. Taisie smiled a stiff little smile and promised to keep him a dance.

It was while they were circling the room together, very decorously, with Taisie quite lacking the fluid grace that usually made dancing with her a delight, that something he said put an idea into her head which filled her with such excitement that she suddenly began to look more animated.

It was only a passing reference to a Charity Concert, but when Desmond said, with an unctuousness that made Taisie long to scratch his eyes out: "I think it's a cause worth supporting: I always like to help deserving young people" a whole plan of campaign sprang into her mind complete in every detail, a plan to confront Desmond Corley with his past and shock him into an admission of guilt.

# 8

THE news that Mrs. Maurice Gaymour required him to purchase for her a run-down property in Pimlico was received by Maurice's solicitor with polite puzzlement. He suggested that it would be easier to acquire other houses, possibly better suited to her purpose, but Taisie was adamant: Number 1 Clerivale Street or nowhere.

It proved more difficult than she had supposed and she fumed as the weeks slipped by. She and Maurice went to Scotland for the grouse shooting in August, which to Taisie was just so much time wasted, although she grudgingly admitted to the grandeur of the scenery and the warmth of the hospitality they received. They were back in London in September, in time to celebrate their first wedding anniversary. Taisie, having resigned herself to Maurice's obsession with sport, presented him with a fine pair of sporting guns from Purdeys, while Maurice's present to her was an unusual parure of topazes set in gold.

Bearing in mind her desperate boredom the previous year, Taisie decided not to accompany Maurice into Leicestershire at the end of the month. She was better supplied with friends than she had been when they were first married and there were any number of houses she could visit from Friday to Monday where it would not be thought unusual for a young married woman to be unaccompanied by her husband. Indeed, it was considered somewhat stodgy always to invite married couples together and if some temporarily unattached man and woman seized the opportunity to pursue a love affair the sophisticated hostess turned a blind eye and thought none the worse of either of them.

It was not an attitude that met with Taisie's approval. It had come as a surprise to her at first to discover that the respectability conferred by her wedding ring did not stop other men from pursuing her. She had known, she had had good reason to know, that married men in Society ran after actresses, but she had not thought it would continue once she became Maurice's wife. She had no desire to succumb to any of their advances. They all seemed to her to be very similar to Maurice, so that there was not even the interest of novelty about them. There was nothing *to* them, Taisie decided, ruthlessly dismissing her unwanted admirers. Really and truly she preferred men who did things, not these pleasant, well-mannered, idle nonentities. Not that she was in the slightest disappointed with the bargain she had made, she assured herself, especially when she was trying out in her looking glass the effect of her lovely new topaz set.

In November there was a family wedding which Maurice and Taisie attended together. Fred Gregory, with his return to India imminent, had pushed through a rapid engagement and marriage to the daughter of a neighbour in Gloucestershire.

The Reverend Edgar Gregory performed the ceremony and Blair was best man. The bride, dazed by the realization that by the New Year she would be on her way to a totally new life in an alien land and inclined to be tearful, was attended by her four younger sisters, none of them, as Fred admitted to his brother, pretty enough to be worth a second glance.

"Pity about that," he said to Blair during the time they had alone together while the bride was changing to go away. "Mother had in mind the old saying about one wedding bringing on another one, with you as the next victim."

"I haven't any plans in that direction at the moment," Blair said. "I've been too busy getting myself elected to Parliament."

"You did splendidly, old chap. Now you should start putting your private life in order."

"Are you implying it's disorderly?" Blair enquired with a smile that was not entirely convincing.

"I've seen plenty of what ails you in India. Young subalterns, married women. Always leads to trouble. Silly young beggars go out and get themselves killed sometimes."

"I'm not one of your junior officers," Blair said. "I don't know what you're talking about, but even if I did I wouldn't want your advice."

"Suit yourself," Fred said, completely unruffled. "But for what it's worth I'll tell you what you ought to do. Find yourself a nice girl who'll be useful to you in your constituency, marry her and raise a family."

Blair gave his brother a long, considering look. "What made you choose Mabel to be your wife?" he asked.

"She's a strong, healthy girl with a lot of good sense," Fred answered promptly. "That's not to say that I'm not dashed fond of her, but if I'd found myself falling for someone unsuitable I'd have run a mile. Mabel will survive in India and be a good wife to me. Dash it all, Blair, we're neither of us children, we both know that there's more to marriage than the first mad passion that sweeps a man off his feet. I got over that in my calf days and so did you—or so I thought."

"There's a lot in what you say," Blair admitted. "But it doesn't take into account . . . unusual circumstances."

"Unusual circumstances are what a man invents in order to excuse taking what he wants," Fred said with an acuteness that

248

raised a reluctant smile from Blair. "Don't do anything foolish, will you, old chap?"

"Of course not," Blair said. "As you say, I'm not a green boy."

With this conversation in mind he studied his new sister-in-law carefully as she made the rounds of her family and friends, saying goodbye. She was a fresh-faced girl in her mid-twenties, with brown hair and blue eyes and a sweet expression. She was sturdily built, with broad hips and a wide bosom. Her father was a local squire, only too happy to get his oldest daughter off his hands, with four more to follow and two young sons to be provided for. It was obvious from the way she looked up at him as he led her out to the carriage that however full of commonsense Fred's own feelings might be, Mabel adored her dashing major. Fred was probably a lucky man.

An imperious little hand tugged at his arm. "You're avoiding me," Taisie said. "And I know why. You haven't done a thing about following up that detective's report, have you? I know you've been very busy, getting into Parliament . . . congratulations, by the way, everyone says you did marvels, holding the seat for the Liberals when they are in such disarray . . . so why don't you let me deal with the man myself?"

"Certainly not. It would be highly improper. I *did* pass on your instructions and I assure you I will let you have whatever news there is as soon as I receive it."

Taisie slipped her hand through his arm and they strolled back into the house. She glanced up at his dark, simian profile, considering whether to tell him about the other ploy she had in hand, and decided against it. He would probably disapprove, so the least said the better.

The difficulty about buying the Pimlico House was that no-one could find the owner.

"The property was purchased some twelve years ago by a Mr. Abelard Gribble," the solicitor reported to Taisie. "He lived in it until about six years ago and then he . . . er, I'm afraid he was a very disreputable man, Mrs. Gaymour: he went to prison."

"Did he? Oh, good!" Taisie said.

"Er . . . yes," the solicitor said, sliding over the reason for Abe Gribble's term of imprisonment, which was not suitable for discussion with a lady. "He was released two years ago and from enquiries I have made it seems that he lived in the house for a few weeks, then he disappeared and the property has stood empty ever since. He is still the owner and it cannot be sold until he is traced."

"How very provoking," Taisie said. She thought deeply and then she said, "I might just possibly be able to find out the name and address of someone who might know Mr. Gribble's whereabouts. If I did that would you ask her where he is?"

"I would follow any instructions you gave me, naturally," the solicitor said. "But really, Mrs. Gaymour, I do think some other property . . ."

He stopped with a sigh as he saw the inflexible expression on her face.

Which was why, having waved goodbye to the bride and groom, Taisie said in her most beguiling way to Blair: "Is that poor young girl still living at . . . where was it, somewhere in St. John's Wood?"

"As far as I know, she is. And if you are trying to trap me into giving you the address I have to inform you that I was not born yesterday and I've dealt with wilier customers than you, Mrs. Gaymour."

He was laughing at her. Taisie frowned in disappointment and then, reluctantly, joined in.

"I should have known you would see through me. Give me the address, Blair. I won't go there, I promise you. I just want to know where it is. After all, I'm paying for the information."

"Are you? I haven't sent you a bill, have I? And what is more, I'm not going to."

"But I never meant you to stand the cost of the enquiry!"

"It's the only way I can be sure of keeping a tight hold on the results. I don't trust you an inch, for all your promises. If I give you the address you'll be round at the house intent on rescuing a girl who may turn out to be perfectly innocent, though possibly not legitimate."

"You don't really believe that."

"No, or I wouldn't be helping you at all. What about your idea of helping other girls? Have you forgotten about that?"

"It was your idea, not mine, but I haven't forgotten. I read the book you lent me—by the way, you must call round

252

sometime so that I can return it—and I found it very, very interesting. I intend doing something, really I do, and Maurice has promised to help me, with money if nothing else. I even have my eye on a house I might buy, so there!"

"Send the book back to me through the post," Blair said. "My parliamentary duties and my practice together hardly leave me time for social calls."

"It's a very strange thing that other Members of Parliament find time to come to my parties," Taisie retorted. "I shall lay siege to you in the New Year. You're spoken of as quite one of the coming men, you know. I intend to be right in the forefront of fashion next year; you must come along and let me lionize you."

"I didn't fight a singularly hard election in order to become an attraction at Mrs. Maurice Gaymour's dinners," Blair said.

Taisie looked up at him, her face alight with mischievous laughter.

"Oh, I see! You're taking a rise out of me! Baggage!"

Maurice came and joined them and Taisie transferred her hand from Blair's arm to his. "Blair is being atrociously rude," she complained. "Take me away, Maurice, before I forget I'm a lady now."

She held out her hand to Blair. "Goodbye, and next time I send you an invitation, accept it."

His smiling agreement committed him to nothing and, in fact, there was little contact between Blair and the Gaymours until after the New Year. Taisie and Maurice spent the months of December to February in Derbyshire and in February Taisie collected together a large house party to celebrate her twenty-first birthday.

Blair attended and also, to his surprise, Desmond Corley. Taisie, for some purpose of her own, seemed to be cultivating the man. Blair, who had news which threw a sinister light on Corley's establishment in St. John's Wood, deliberately suppressed it. If he were to pass it on to Taisie while the man was under her roof she was perfectly capable of having him thrown out. It would cause an uproar if it were not handled tactfully, and Blair placed very little reliance on Taisie's tact while she was blazing with indignation.

He was interested to see how well she

had fitted herself into the role of country house chatelaine. No London "larks" here. Taisie's marriage was nearly eighteen months old and she had, as she informed him when he congratulated her *sotto voce* on having captured the cream of the county for her ball, learnt what was what.

"But, oh, Blair, if you knew how I sometimes yearn to step into the middle of the dance floor and turn a cartwheel," she said.

They were standing together near the top of the staircase. Most of the guests had arrived and Taisie was debating whether to abandon her post and start enjoying herself, when the footman announced: "The Duke and Duchess of Garminster."

Taisie turned her head to look at Blair, her face solemn, but her eyes dancing, and gave him a slow wink. Then she moved forward, perfectly composed, to receive the new arrivals.

It was a triumphant occasion. Taisie was overwhelmed with congratulations, with compliments and with admiration which at times seemed fulsome. Only Blair knew that the evening had also given rise to some regrets.

On the stroke of midnight an enormous iced cake was wheeled in. With a flourish of music and a chorus of good wishes Taisie came forward, looking adorably confused, to cut it. There was a cry of "Speech, speech", but she shook her head with an appealing look at Maurice. Blair's eyes narrowed; the dear girl was doing it all too beautifully.

Then someone called: "Give us a song, Mrs. Gaymour" and she seemed to hesitate. An enquiring glance at Maurice, a quick word with the conductor of the orchestra and Taisie came back to the middle of the empty space which had been cleared for the cake cutting. She stood perfectly still, waiting for silence, and Blair admired her mastery of the restless, chattering crowd. A nod to the conductor and the first notes stole out: Taisie had chosen to sing "Home Sweet Home".

She had lost none of her skill, she held them spellbound, the Duchess was even seen to raise a hand to her eyes. "Be it never so humble, there's no place like home." Blair looked round at the marble pillars festooned with ferns and hothouse flowers, the crystal chandeliers, the painted ceiling, the gilded cornices, the guests in their satins and jewels, and choked.

To hide his unseemly mirth he retreated to a small salon and when Taisie, making a beautifully judged exit from the storm of applause that greeted the end of the song, came and collapsed into one of the armchairs, he was still there.

"A splendid piece of theatre," he said, with his voice still not quite steady. "How often did you rehearse it?"

Taisie grinned. "Three times," she admitted. "And, of course, I planted the man who called for a song. It went over well, didn't it? They loved me. Did you hear the way they clapped?"

A strange look came over her face, a look of puzzled regret. "I didn't realize how much I missed it," she said. "That feeling of the audience warming to you, the love coming back over the footlights. There's nothing quite like it."

"Are you sorry you gave it up?"

"No, of course not," Taisie said quickly. "There's another side to it, too. Backbreaking work, having to go on whether you feel like it or not, audiences who won't wake up, last night's sweaty costume to be put back on, the dreary routine of doing it again and again and again. I've no regrets. Have you seen this marvellous necklace—Maurice's birthday present?"

"Do you measure your happiness in diamonds? No, don't answer that. It's an impossible question and impertinent into the bargain. I have a present for you too, Taisie, though I'm afraid it's modest by the side of Maurice's magnificent offering."

"That doesn't matter. I love getting presents," Taisie said.

She opened the little box. It was only a small pendant of blue enamel and pearls on a gold chain, but Taisie exclaimed: "It's charming! Truly, Blair, it's one of the prettiest things I've had. Forget-me-nots! Is that a message? As if I would! Thank you, very, very much."

With the impulsiveness that was so much a part of her she bent over and kissed him on the cheek.

"Now, what I'd really like is a glass of iced lemonade," she said. "Will you take me to the buffet?"

She saw that Blair was touching his cheek and added, with a touch of asperity: "There's no need to wipe it away, I don't paint!"

Taisie slept until eleven o'clock on the morning after her triumphant ball. She rolled over and blinked at the watery sunshine filtering through her curtains and then rang for her maid. She was sitting up, sipping a cup of tea when Maurice came in.

"The most terrible news," he said. "Blair's had a telegram asking him to go home immediately."

"Not something wrong with Uncle Edgar or Aunt Judith?" Taisie asked.

"Not them, no. It's Fred."

"An accident? Illness? He can't have been in any fighting, there's not been time for him to rejoin his regiment, has there?"

"It was the plague. Taisie, he's *dead*!"

Taisie stared at him. "Oh no!" she whispered. "No, no, no!"

"It's true I tell you. Blair doesn't know any details, but he says Fred must have picked up the infection almost as soon as he landed in Bombay. I saw in *The Times* the other day that it was bad there this year and, of course, there was no way for Fred and Mabel to avoid passing through the town. I can't take it in. Poor old Fred."

"Blair will feel it terribly," Taisie said, throwing back the bedclothes. "I must go to him."

"You'll only hold him up," Maurice objected. "By the time you're dressed he'll be on his way. He sent his excuses and regrets an' all that. Poor old Fred. I can't believe it."

Taisie paused, half in and half out of bed. It was true that she could do nothing but hinder Blair's departure, and yet every instinct urged her to rush to him and try to offer what comfort she could. Reluctantly, she made herself stop and take the commonsense view.

"To think we were at his wedding such a short time ago," Maurice was saying. "Mabel will just turn round and come home again, I suppose. Poor little girl, it's been a short married life for her."

To Taisie it seemed that he was dwelling on the news with morbid relish, but she was even more alienated when Maurice went on: "A good job we didn't know about it yesterday. You'd have had to cancel your party."

Taisie looked at him with distaste. "That would have been a pity," she said, but her irony was wasted on Maurice.

The sad news cast a gloom over all the house party. Taisie was glad when most of her guests decided to leave early. She was even more thankful when the time came for her to return to London with Maurice. She told herself that it was only natural that her spirits should have been affected by the loss of someone who had come to be a close friend during the months he had spent in England, someone young enough to be looked upon as a contemporary, someone she had not expected to die. The circumstances were so sad; the recent marriage, the fact that it had happened far from home and so suddenly. It was enough to put anyone in the dumps.

In the circumstances, she felt she could not bother Blair about Desmond Corley, even though she at last had news which would make it possible to carry out the plan she had hatched the previous July. Abe Gribble was dead. He had died in a lodging house in Southend and had been identified by his police record. Exhaustive enquiries had failed to trace any of his family and since he had left no will his property passed to the Crown. If Mrs. Gaymour was still interested in purchasing the house he had owned she was at liberty to do so.

Taisie had gone to a lot of trouble to cultivate Desmond Corley and yet, now that the chance of confronting him with the evil he had done was at hand, she felt strangely unenthusiastic about it. It was because the first fire in which she had conceived the idea had cooled in the long months of waiting, she thought, but that did not account for the lacklustre way she was feeling about everything else. She had expected this second year of her marriage to be even more of a success than the first. She was launched now, she was a successful hostess, she had everything money could buy, but there was no doubt about it, there was something missing, some essential ingredient that would restore her enthusiasm for the life she had chosen.

Maurice himself, of course, was something of a drawback. Taisie was ashamed because she sometimes heard herself speaking to him more sharply than he deserved. Maurice had not changed. He was still the same amiable, lightweight pleasure-seeker he had always been. It was unfair to fret because he was no different. After all, she had married him with her eyes open and in spite of the warnings which Blair, for instance, had given her. She was glad, in a way, that they were not seeing much of Blair. It would have been galling to have his penetrating intelligence discover that he had been right and Taisie was secretly bored with her marriage.

The mood of disenchantment had dated back to her twenty-first birthday party. It had been a mistake to revive memories of her stage success. Taisie dwelt resolutely on the disadvantages of theatrical life which she had spelt out to Blair, but they did not quite shut out the pleasure of the response she had sensed in her audience that night. She had her diamond necklace brought to her, but in daylight it looked crudely ostentatious. "Do you measure your happiness in diamonds?" a scathing voice whispered in her ear. Taisie shut the jewel case with a snap and wore the simple little pendant Blair had given her. She also sent for Desmond Corley.

He came to her readily when she asked him to call. They had spoken several times about Taisie's plans for establishing a lodging house for young girls and he had promised any help he could give.

"I have the keys of a suitable property," Taisie said, fixing her grey-green eyes on his face. "I want to go and look at it and I wondered whether you would be kind enough to accompany me."

He agreed, but at the back of his mind he was surprised. Mrs. Gaymour was unconventional, but he had not expected to be invited to wander round an empty house with her unaccompanied by anyone else, not even a lawyer or agent. Still, she was a pretty thing and good for any number of dinners if he played his cards right. He smoothed his hair forward on the lefthand side of his head without even realizing that it was an automatic gesture and expressed himself willing to go anywhere with Mrs. Gaymour, to the ends of the earth if necessary.

It was the sort of gallant speech Taisie had come to expect from Desmond Corley.

It grated, but she managed to keep smiling in spite of her desire to smack his face for his impertinence.

He was surprised when she asked him to call a hansom cab, but Taisie had no intention of involving her own carriage in this adventure and was ready with a glib story about a lame horse if he queried it.

She glanced at him as they drew up outside Number 1 Clerivale Street. He was frowning, she thought he looked uneasy, and he tugged at the front of his collar as if it had become too tight. Yet all he said was: "The house looks half derelict and this is not a very desirable neighbourhood. Are you sure you want to go in?"

"Quite sure," Taisie said.

She produced the keys and opened the front door, not without difficulty. It creaked on its hinges as she pushed it open. Inside, the dust from the floor swirled up as the draught from outside disturbed it. Taisie gathered up her skirt in one hand and stepped inside.

The house smelt of dirt and damp and mouse droppings. Taisie pulled at one of the blinds to let in more light and it tore across and hung limply on its rail. A moth fluttered out and settled on the ceiling. The rooms which Taisie remembered, hung with red plush and lit by pink lamps, were empty.

"Hardly worth your while to go any further, is it?" Desmond Corley asked. "This can't be what you're looking for."

"You don't know what I'm looking for," Taisie said. "I'd like to go upstairs."

The stairs were rotten. Even Taisie was taken aback to discover how badly they had been affected by long neglect.

"The roof must be leaking," Desmond said. "Look, you can see where the rain has come in."

Taisie trod on one of the stairs and felt the sodden wood give beneath her feet. Woodlice scurried for cover as their lair was revealed.

"Tread on the outside edges," Taisie advised and went lightly up the remaining stairs while the heavy man behind her followed more slowly.

At the top of the stairs Taisie hesitated. The dark corridor was the same, but she was surprised to realize she was no longer sure which bedroom it had been. She put her hand on one of the door handles. It turned, but the swollen wood resisted her efforts to open the door.

"Put your shoulder to it," she ordered.

"Really, Mrs. Gaymour, I don't think . . ."

"Do it!"

The fierceness with which she spoke surprised him into obeying her. The door opened with a rush. Inside, the room was not entirely empty. It had been the one Abe Gribble had used for a few weeks after he had come out of prison and found his house robbed of every stick of furniture it had contained. In the corner there was a rough pallet bed, a small rickety table and a candle stub stuck on a saucer. A torn blanket had been tacked across the window. Taisie pulled it down and then she turned to Desmond Corley. In her hand she held a golden guinea.

"Take it," she said. "I owe it to you. Ten years ago I stole a guinea from you. Here, in this room."

"I don't understand you," he said mechanically. His normally high colour had, if anything, increased. There was a purplish flush along his heavy jowls. Again he ran a finger along the edge of his starched collar.

"It was the night of Queen Victoria's Golden Jubilee. I was ten years old," Taisie went on, ignoring his interruption. "You don't remember? I'm not surprised. I dare say I was one of many. Abe Gribble spoke of you as one of his regulars. A debaucher of little girls, Mr. Corley. You disgusting creature."

She flung the coin at him. It struck him on the chest and rolled unheeded to the floor. Still he tried to deny it.

"I don't know what you're talking about. You must be mad."

"Do you think I could forget you?" Taisie demanded. "That horrible ear of yours. Some poor Italian did that to you, didn't he? How old was his little girl, I wonder? At least he revenged her, which is more than my family did for me."

"I absolutely deny everything you say. Your imagination has run away with you. If some wrong was done to you as a child I am sorry, but you really cannot connect me with your misfortunes."

"Oh? And what about the woman and

child you're keeping in St. John's Wood now?"

He took a step towards her, his face livid. Taisie edged towards the door.

"You little fiend," he said. "Be careful what you're doing. If I go down so will you. A fine story it'll make. Mrs. Maurice Gaymour, the child whore. I can deny my part and hope to be believed, but you'll have to admit to yours if you want to do anything against me. Can you face that? Can Maurice?"

"Never mind Maurice. I can put up with anything just so long as I do you down. Publicity? I don't give a damn. But one thing I am going to do, Mr. Desmond Corley, and that's give you a taste of your own medicine."

She was in the doorway, ready for flight.

"I'm going to lock you in this horrible house and leave you to get out as best you can. You can see what it's like to be a prisoner, like the poor children who were shut up here."

She darted away from him, skimming down the dangerous stairs. She heard him shout and start after her. As she reached the front door there was a splintering crash and an even more agonized shout. Taisie whipped out of the door, slammed it behind her and locked it.

Walking swiftly, Taisie found her way to Victoria Street. Close to the Army and Navy Stores she picked up a hansom cab and drove home. She felt nothing but a fierce exaltation. She had confronted him, she had as good as got him to admit his guilt. Whatever the outcome she had shaken him to the depths of his filthy little soul. And with the back door boarded over and bars on the windows of the lower rooms he was going to find it extremely difficult to get out of the derelict house, unless he could attract the attention of a passerby. It would do his dignity no good to have to accept help from the sort of guttersnipe who might hear his cries. She saw him climbing out of a window assisted by a grinning boy and smiled to herself in satisfaction.

Taisie sent the keys back to her solicitor with a note saying that he had probably been right in thinking that the house was not suitable for her needs, a message which made the solicitor shake his head in despair at the whims of women.

As her first triumph subsided Taisie began to be conscious of reaction. She could not seem to get warm. A fine, uncontrollable shivering ran through her body. The slightest noise made her jump. Her head throbbed. It was alarming how much the scene with Desmond had upset her. She excused herself from a visit to the theatre and went to bed early, but she could not sleep.

It was not until the next day that she began to be seriously alarmed. Someone mentioned that Desmond, too, had been expected to attend the theatre the previous evening and had failed to turn up. She told herself that of course he had got out. The house was not impregnable. There were windows which could be broken. A strong man might even break open one of the doors. Probably he had been, as she was, too shaken to face an evening's pleasure. Served him right, Taisie thought, trying to recapture her earlier sense of achievement. All the same, she wished now that she had not been so hasty in sending back the keys. Try as she might she could not dismiss from her mind the sounds of a shout and a crash as she had slammed the door shut.

At last she gave in to her fears and went to the solicitor's office to ask for the keys to be returned to her. As it happened she saw only a clerk who gave the bunch of keys to her without comment and clearly without thinking anything of it. Mrs. Gaymour was known to be interested in that house and it was of no interest to him how often she went and looked at it.

For reasons she did not want to think about too closely Taisie travelled by omnibus from the solicitor's office. Again she hurried along the streets towards Number 1 Clerivale Street. Her hands were trembling as she unlocked the door a second time. It stuck as badly as it had the day before. She put her shoulder to it and pushed and it swung open with a suddenness that almost threw her off balance. Everything was dark and quiet. Desmond Corley must have got out, she told herself with a relief that annoyed her by its intensity.

As her eyes became accustomed to the dimness she saw that there was something wrong. Part of the rotten stairs had caved in. The pale, splintered wood showed up clearly against the older timber. Taisie crept up the stairs on her hands and knees, keeping to the side of each tread and clinging to the banister. The wood creaked under her as she leaned forward to peer into the hole. It was big enough for a large man to have crashed through into the hollow space beneath. He was there, she could see him. The light filtered down on to his upturned, contorted face. And she knew that he was dead.

# 9

IN the extremity of her terror, Taisie went back to the instinctive response of her childhood: if there's trouble, run. She crept down the stairs, shaking from head to foot, and then found herself outside the house without knowing how she had got there. There was no-one in the street outside. On the far side of the road a costermonger's cart trotted by, but the man never even glanced towards her.

She banged the front door shut and was going to lock it when the thought came into her head that she should make it look as if Desmond could have left the house, if he had not had that terrible accident on the stairs. There was no disguising the fact that she had been there with him the previous day, too many people knew about it. But there was no need to give away her visit that day or to be the one who found him.

For one moment she contemplated the possibility that he was still alive, then she put it from her. He must be dead. She had no real doubts about it. Nothing she could do now would help him. She must get away and think, cover her tracks, make it seem as if the accident had happened without her knowledge."

No-one knew where she had gone that morning. Early in her married life, Taisie had turned a deaf ear to hints that she should be accompanied by her maid when she went out alone on foot and by now her household were accustomed to her independent habits. She would go home, quickly and unobtrusively, and then think what to do next.

As soon as she got in Taisie enquired, in as casual a voice as she could manage, whether there was any message for her from Mr. Corley. When she was assured that there was not she forced herself to wait, with every nerve strung taut, for another hour before she sent a note round to his lodging to enquire why he had not waited on her that morning. The footman was instructed to wait for an answer, but when he came back he reported that Mr. Corley was not at home.

"How strange," Taisie said, twisting her

fine linen handkerchief between her fingers. "Has he gone out of town?"

"As to that, his man couldn't say," the footman answered, then the diplomacy that had been drilled into him disappeared and he added in a rush: "As a matter of fact, his man's worried, madam. He hasn't seen hide nor hair of Mr. Corley since yesterday lunchtime and not a word from him. He had a dinner engagement he didn't keep and he was goin' to the theatre and didn't do that either. His man's beginning to think he's met with some accident."

"But he was with me yesterday afternoon!" Taisie exclaimed. "How terrible if anything has happened to him. I must do something . . . is Mr. Gaymour in, James?"

"In the library, madam."

Taisie braced herself for the long and involved explanation she was going to have to din into Maurice's head. She pressed her handkerchief to her lips, nerving herself for the scene she was about to play, threw open the library door and hurried in. To her total dismay Maurice was not alone: Blair was with him.

Blair, of all people. The one person who knew all her story, who knew about her desire to be revenged on Desmond Corley, and who could be guaranteed to sense the falsity behind her apparent concern for him. It was too late to retreat. Without giving herself time to draw back Taisie plunged into the speech she had prepared.

"Maurice, I'm worried. Oh, Blair, good morning! What an age it is since we last saw you. Maurice, Mr. Corley seems to be missing and I'm concerned in case something has happened to him. He didn't keep his social engagements yesterday evening and he hasn't been home all night."

"No need for you to worry your little head about that," Maurice said in surprise. "A man like Desmond might easily take it into his head to spend a night . . . er, with some friends or something. He'll turn up all right and tight, don't you fret, and probably give his man a tonguewagging for letting it out that he'd not been home."

"You don't understand. Mr. Corley came with me yesterday afternoon to look at a house I might buy—you remember, I talked to you about it."

"That was ages ago. I thought you'd forgotten about it."

"The property I had my eye on has only just come on the market," Taisie said.

Blair shifted his position, moving round to a point where he could get a better view of her face.

"It turned out to be a horrible place," Taisie hurried on. "I left Mr. Corley there. He was supposed to come and see me this morning to talk about it."

"I don't see why you dragged Desmond into your scheme," Maurice said, puzzled. "Not his line."

Taisie's hands were clenched so tight that she suddenly became aware of the pain of her nails digging into the palms. Carefully she straightened them out and laid them smoothly one on top of the other.

"He was interested," she said. "That isn't important. The point is, I may have been the last . . . no-one else seems to have seen him since I left him there. It's not a nice neighbourhood. I'm afraid . . ."

Her voice trailed away. She caught Blair's eye and, unable to drag her own gaze away, she repeated, almost in a whisper: "I'm afraid."

Without looking away from Taisie, Blair said: "I think your concern is justified. Tell me the address and I'll go round there."

"Not you," Taisie said. "Not you, Blair."

"If not me then it'll have to be the Police. Let me go round on my own first."

In front of Maurice he could say no more, but he was convinced that Taisie knew more than she was saying. She was in a highly nervous state, far more than she would have been from pure concern about Corley. He would have liked to have known the full story before he visited this mysterious house where, for some reason, Taisie had taken the man she hated, but since it was impossible to demand to be alone with her he had to content himself with trying to convey reassurance silently.

"I'll give you the keys," Taisie said in a distracted way.

"If you left Desmond there, why didn't you leave the keys with him?" Maurice asked, showing acuteness at a time when she would have preferred him to be obtuse.

Taisie looked quickly at Blair and then away again. "I . . . didn't think," she said.

"We'll both go," Maurice said. "Got nothing else to do. Fit it in before lunch."

Blair was almost prepared for what they found at Number 1 Clerivale Street. That Desmond Corley had been hurt and that Taisie was aware of it seemed obvious to him, and something about the way her icy cold hand had clung to his as if she were trying to convey a message she could not utter out loud warned him that it was serious. He would have preferred not to have had Maurice with him, although in some ways it was better to have a witness.

"Bit unsavoury, isn't it?" Maurice exclaimed as they approached the house. "If I'd known Taisie was visiting places like this I'd have put my foot down! Not that she would have listened. She's so headstrong!"

Like Taisie they found Desmond Corley immediately, but Blair did more than she had been able to do; he swung himself down through the splintered hole and satisfied himself that the contorted body was lifeless.

"Cold," he reported as he clambered back again. "He must have died yesterday."

He sucked at a splinter in his hand, thinking furiously. Taisie had admitted to being in the house, there was no need to cover up any traces of her presence. The death was clearly an accident. It was going to be very unpleasant for her, but she was in no danger.

"I say, what a frightful thing," Maurice said. He passed a shaking hand over his face. "I mean to say . . . frightful!" He felt in his pocket and pulled out a flask. "Have a drop of brandy, old man. You deserve it, going down there, touching him . . ." He shuddered and, in spite of his offer, swallowed the first tot of brandy himself.

"I must fetch the Police," Blair said. "You go and break it to Taisie, Maurice. Do it carefully. It will be very upsetting for her."

"I suppose I know how to speak to my own wife," Maurice said. "If she hadn't been so obstinate this wouldn't have happened. She *would* have this house, nowhere else would do, and look at it! Run down, derelict, rotten stairs—and poor old Desmond dead. I hope she'll feel it as she ought and perhaps it'll be a lesson to her not to meddle in future. Charity! Why couldn't she let me give a thousand or two to something deserving, which I was willing to do? Oh, no, Taisie has to do it all herself, and look at the result."

"What you say may be very true," Blair said diplomatically. "But spare her your reproaches for the time being, I beg you."

He succeeded in calming Maurice down, but in the days that followed Taisie had a lot to bear. She knew, only too well, that she was responsible for Desmond Corley's death and did not need to have it dinned into her ears every hour of the day. In the end she flared up and she and Maurice had their first real quarrel.

Blair, timing his call carefully, managed to find her alone one morning. Her pallor and look of strain alarmed him, but she spoke steadily enough.

"Blair, I never meant you to be involved in my troubles," she said, her hand clinging to his. "On top of what you've already been through ... I've never spoken to you about Fred. I was so terribly sorry. Really heartbroken."

"Thank you. I had your letter and you will have heard from Mother, thanking you for the one you wrote to her. She was touched by what you said. Now, my dear, we mustn't waste time. Before we are interrupted, tell me what really happened."

"I wanted to handle it on my own," she said, by way of excuse before she began. "That house was the one where I was ... kept until the night I ran away. I took Desmond along there to confront him with what he had done and, Blair, it was all true. He as good as admitted it to me. I threatened him with exposure and then I ran away and locked him in."

"You locked the door?" Blair interrupted her. "It was open when Maurice and I went there."

"I went back the next day. I was frightened because he seemed to have disappeared. And ... I found him. He *was* dead then, wasn't he? He did die straight away?"

"Almost immediately. The doctor's

report says he broke a leg and two ribs in his fall, but what actually killed him was an apoplexy, probably brought on by the shock."

"I can't be sorry he's dead," Taisie said. "I can't! But the thing that makes me feel sick is that I heard him fall. As I shut the door I heard a crash and he cried out. And I ran away and left him. I ought to have gone back . . . I didn't realize! Oh, Blair, it's too awful. I really did kill him."

"Nonsense. The man died as a result of his own evil life. He might just as easily have been killed when he was shot in Sicily, and he would have deserved it just as much. I refuse to let you feel guilty for something that was clearly an accident. Pull yourself together, Taisie. This isn't like you."

"I don't feel quite myself," Taisie said, wiping her eyes. "And can you wonder at it? I suppose you're right in what you say. The man was a beast." She made a resolute effort to control herself. "What will happen now, Blair?"

"That's what I want to see you about. You will have to appear at the inquest, I'm afraid. There's no getting out of that. I want to coach you in what you should say. No word of Desmond's vices must come out, certainly not the slightest hint of any previous connection between you. Stick strictly to the story the world already knows. You were looking for a house for charitable purposes, Desmond was helping you; the only reason you visited Number 1 Clerivale Street was to see whether it was suitable; you were disappointed to find it so derelict and came away, leaving him to continue the inspection alone."

The inquest passed off without any untoward questions being asked. Taisie, already wearing deep mourning for Fred, for which she was profoundly thankful since it meant that she did not have to play the hypocrite in assuming it for Desmond, made an appealing witness. She was clearly deeply shocked by what had happened, her charitable intentions were honoured, she came out of the ordeal very well. The inevitable verdict was Accidental Death.

Only the family solicitor was not entirely satisfied. It had all gone off very nicely from his client's point of view, but he could not help remembering Mrs. Gaymour's extreme anxiety to secure that house and no other, nor the fact that she had returned the keys to him one day and asked for them back the next. There was something below the surface, something that had been kept from him. Blair Gregory knew about it, whatever it was. Clever young fellow. Looked as if he hadn't slept for a week.

Once the load of anxiety had been lifted, Blair felt justified in administering one small reproof to Taisie.

"You shouldn't have taken the law into your own hands," he said. "For one thing, it wasn't necessary. If it hadn't been for Fred's death I would have told you before this. We found out where the woman in St. John's Wood was living the last time Desmond spent a lengthy period in England. The arrangement was the same, but the 'daughter' was a completely different girl. With that evidence I think the Police might have moved."

Taisie hung her head. "I know I did wrong," she admitted. "Don't scold me. I've got enough to bear from Maurice at the moment."

The quarrel with her husband had not abated. To Taisie's horror it was discovered that Desmond had not left a will and, in default of any other family, Maurice was his sole heir.

"Not a big estate, but we should get about twenty thousand pounds and his villa in Sicily," Maurice told her, looking pleased.

"No!" Taisie exclaimed. "It's too horrible! We can't benefit from his death, we can't!"

"No need to get hysterical, my dear. It does seem a bit off when you first think about it, I admit, but it's all the luck of the draw. It was an accident, after all. No-one can object to our taking the money."

"I can't bear it. Please don't accept it, Maurice. Or, if you do, give it all to charity. Yes, that's a good idea! Donate it to some good cause and I promise you I'll never tease you to let me get involved in good works again."

"Twenty thousand pounds? Not likely! I'm as generous as the next man, I hope, but that's going too far. You'll change your mind when I bring you some pretty gew-gaw and tell you it's been paid for out of poor old Desmond's estate."

Taisie shuddered. "Don't do that. I'd never wear it. Please, Maurice. You can well afford it. You never expected this inheritance. Give it all away."

"Not on your life. Wealthy I may be, but it's an expensive business, having a wife. The amount you've spent in the past year would set any man back on his heels. This is my chance to recoup some of it and I'm certainly not going to let you talk me out of it just because of a morbid scruple."

The realization that it was impossible for her to explain to Maurice the real reason why she felt sick at the thought of benefiting from Desmond's death kept Taisie silent. There was a gulf opening between them. When Blair had told her once that she was wrong to keep secrets from her husband he had been right. But what was one to do, married to a man who would feel nothing but revulsion if he knew the truth?

Because of their double mourning Taisie's and Maurice's social activities were restricted. Maurice took it into his head that it was wearing unrelieved black that made Taisie look so pale.

"Fred was only a cousin, after all, and

poor old Desmond no more than a second cousin," he grumbled. "I can't see why you have to go around looking as if you'd been widowed."

"Mabel will be home at the end of April," Taisie said wearily. "It would be painful for her to see Fred's close family already wearing colours. After she's left London I'll think about it."

"I thought you were planning a lot of entertaining, too. The house has been as dull as ditchwater in the last few weeks."

"It's early in the Season, a lot of our friends are still out of town."

"There you are, I told you so. No use going back to London in March, I said; no-one there. But you would have it. If we'd stayed in the country like everyone else Desmond would still be alive."

Taisie bit back a sharp retort and said in a colourless tone: "Yes, I know. I'll collect a few people together for a theatre or something, shall I? And are you coming with me to hear Blair's maiden speech?"

"I suppose so."

But when the day came Maurice said vaguely that he had forgotten all about it and had made other plans and Taisie went alone to the gallery at the House of Commons to hear Blair speak on the Criminal Evidence Act.

He had told himself beforehand that he was too accustomed to getting to his feet in court to feel nervous, but that was not quite the same thing, he found, as speaking to the rows of lounging fellow Members and knowing that what he said might influence Government policy and, in a small way, affect the course of history. His first few words were almost inaudible. In the gallery Taisie recognized a case of first night nerves and gripped her hands together in her lap, willing him to overcome his weakness. Blair paused, cleared his throat, and then spoke out clearly.

It was not a long speech, but Blair had mastered his facts and marshalled his argument well. When he sat down there were the customary graceful tributes to a new Member and he felt that at least he had not made a fool of himself.

Taisie did not wait to hear the rest of the debate. She went home, dashed off a little note of congratulation to Blair and had it sent round to his rooms so that he would receive it when he got home that night.

That evening was not the only one when Maurice was vaguely otherwise engaged when Taisie wanted his escort. He had reverted to some of his bachelor ways, spending more time at his Club than he had during the first year of their marriage. Now he was going out in the evenings without Taisie, returning home late and, while by no means drunk, certainly a little elevated and amorous in a feverish way that made Taisie suspect he had worked himself up by joining in lascivious songs and watching the legs of the chorus girls in some lower class music hall.

It was no more than she had expected when she had first married him, but Taisie had come to have a higher notion of the married state than she had then. There were people, she saw now, who married for love and continued to live in affection year after year, couples who had shared interests, quite apart from their family. It must be pleasant, to have a husband to whom one could talk. Maurice was knowledgeable about horseracing, he would talk earnestly about whether or not trousers should have turn-ups, he could weigh up the relative merits of going to the Gaiety or Daly's, but it was doubtful whether he ever read a newspaper, unless it was an account of some Society scandal in which a friend was involved.

As for a family, in spite of Maurice's feverish attentions Taisie began to despair of ever conceiving a child, and whereas a year ago she was dismayed at the idea of being pregnant, now she would have welcomed it and thought that a baby would have been a steadying influence on Maurice as well as an absorbing interest for her.

She was still in bed one morning, sitting up and tossing over a pile of notes and invitations, when Maurice came in to see her.

"Doin' anything special this morning?" he asked. "If not, I'll take you for a drive. Got something I want to show you."

"The dressmaker is coming at ten and I'm lunching with Molly Conway. Apart from that I'm free. Do we want to stay with the Conways for Ascot Week? I think she's going to suggest it. What is it you want me to see?"

"It's a surprise. Might as well go to the Conways for Ascot. Jack's got a horse running and they always get a good crowd together."

Taisie wrinkled her nose. "Noisy," she said. "Still, I suppose you're right. We may as well go there as anywhere else."

They drove out together that morning in the open landau. It was one of the best days of early Spring, warm but with a touch of coolness in the air, a bright blue sky, billowing white clouds and fresh green leaves on the trees.

Not that there were many trees in the area into which the coachman turned his horses. Taisie looked around in puzzlement and then stiffened as she recognized the road which led to Clerivale Street.

"Where are we going?" she demanded.

"You'll see in a minute. There! You wouldn't recognize it, would you?"

They had drawn up at the place where Number 1 Clerivale Street had once stood. Nothing of it remained. It had been razed to the ground and the basement filled in. In its place there was an open garden, not large but with a semi-circle of grass, a stone path between flower beds, and a strong park bench. A small boy was bouncing a ball along the path and an old man sat on the seat smoking a pipe in the warmth of the sun.

Taisie stared and stared and then her eyes filled with tears. The house which had haunted her dreams had gone. These were no nightmares in this sunny open space.

"What a lovely thing to have done!" she exclaimed. "Maurice, thank you! I can't tell you how much better it makes me feel."

"I wanted to put up a plaque in memory of Desmond," Maurice said. "After all, it was his money that paid for it. But Blair thought it would be a mistake, might give people a dislike of it, he said, being reminded he'd died there."

"Blair knew about this?"

"It was his idea. Told me I must do it and then bring you to see it. He said you'd be pleased, which I can see you are. Makes it worthwhile. Not that it cost a lot. Not twenty thousand pounds, at any rate."

"It was like him," Taisie said. "Dear Blair. He's got so much . . . imagination."

"It's going to be properly kept up," Maurice said proudly. "There's a man who lives nearby who's going to come along and cut the grass and keep the flowerbeds in order and so on. Blair found him, too. Said he was a deserving case. So there you are, my love. You're pleased, aren't you?"

"Indeed I am. Thank you again, Maurice. Oh dear, have I made my eyes red? I meant to drive round the Park before going on to Molly's."

"You look as fresh as a daisy. I'll come round the Park with you. Drop me off at the top of St. James's. Goin' to have a game of billiards with old Bobby."

There was something heartwarming about that act of thoughtfulness which stayed with Taisie all through the first weeks of the London Season. She felt cherished, in a very special way. It made her gentler and softer, not only with Maurice but with everyone who came in contact with her. There was a radiance in her smile which, as Jack Conway remarked to his wife, made her look like a young girl in love.

"I suppose there's no-one . . . ?" he asked.

Mrs. Conway shook her head. "Not to my knowledge, and you know how acute

I am at spotting a new affair. If Mrs. Gaymour is in love it must be with her husband."

"Maurice? Nice chap. Can't see him inspiring a *grand amour* somehow."

The Conways were a dashing couple in their thirties. They had plenty of money and a large house not far from Windsor which was sometimes visited by the Prince of Wales. There were people who whispered that he found the Conways exceptionally understanding about his need for privacy for pursuing his amorous affairs and that was the reason for the social success of a couple who were somewhat *parvenu*. It amounted to no more than a whisper. The Conways were discreet: they valued their high connections too much to endanger them for the sake of a little gossip. They had three children in the nursery, seldom seen by either of them, and they had an amicable understanding that they would each pursue their own course unhampered by remorse or recriminations. Molly Conway suspected that Jack cherished a weakness for Taisie Gaymour, but thought poorly of his chances of succeeding with her. For herself, she was attracted to Maurice's cousin, Blair Gregory, and made sure that he was included amongst their guests for Ascot Week.

Taisie, overcoming a feeling of unreality at finding herself admitted to the Royal Enclosure at Ascot, entered into the excitement of the meeting with a zest that amused her host. She loved it all; the murmuring throng of fashionable people, dressed as if for a party, the noisier crowd outside, the parade of nervous, fine-boned horses, the jockeys in their colourful silks, the bookmakers, the thunder of hooves on the turf, the additional thrill of having a bet on the result.

Blair travelled down from London and drove straight to the racecourse. He had his pass for the Royal Enclosure and he knew that he would have no difficulty in locating his host and hostess amongst that select crowd. He saw them straight away, a little knot of elegant people, the ladies in sweeping gowns and large hats, the men tailored to the last inch in morning dress and grey toppers, exclaiming in unbridled amusement over the ladies' choice of horses on which they were to place their bets.

Taisie had bowed to Maurice's dislike of seeing her in black and had gone into half mourning. She was wearing a gown of cream tussore cut close to her figure in the princess line, with a huge bunch of violets at her waist and another under the brim of her hat. She turned away from the laughing crowd and found Blair behind her.

Until that moment she had not realized how much she had been counting on seeing him. She had known that she had been wanting to thank him for being the inspiration behind the garden in Pimlico; her mind had constantly formulated grateful phrases, her thoughts had turned towards him incessantly, but still without understanding what it would mean when she met him face to face. Her smile faded. She stood silently in front of him, her lips parted, but unable to speak.

Blair looked like a man driven to the last extremes of exhaustion, the skin drawn tight over the bones of his face, the lines from nose to mouth deepened into furrows.

Taisie put out her hand, not knowing what she was doing, and Blair took it. As soon as their hands touched they were lost. Without taking his eyes from her face he said, in a strange, hurried undertone: "You are unbearably lovely."

The noise of all the vast crowd, the laughter, the cries of the bookmakers, faded into the background. They were alone. Amongst the shifting, colourful throng they stood in complete isolation, unable to look away from one another, unconscious of their surroundings.

Someone was saying something. Taisie turned her head and looked blindly at Maurice.

"Wake up! Here, you said you wanted my binoculars. Hello, Blair. What do you fancy for the next race?"

Blair must have said something in reply, but Taisie had no idea what it was. All through the afternoon she moved amongst her friends, smiling and docile, like a charming mechanical doll, but nothing she said or did had any reality to her. The races were run and she heard with half her mind the exclamations and groans over the results, but for Taisie the spectacle had narrowed down to only one thing: a chance glimpse of a pair of broad shoulders, the back of a dark head, a sharp profile under a top hat worn at a careless angle.

She was still dazed by what had happened to her when she began to dress for dinner. She was so abstracted that her maid suspected she must have lost money at the races until she picked up Taisie's handbag and bit back an exclamation at the bank notes crammed inside.

"Oh, madam, don't you think it should be locked up?" she asked. "All that money!"

Taisie looked at the roll of notes as if she had never seen them before.

"Oh, yes, I remember now. I kept winning," she said. "How strange. You're right, it should be locked up."

She peeled off a five pound note and held it out. "Here, Jane, have a bit of my luck. Buy yourself something pretty."

She hardly spoke again, not even to say she was satisfied when Jane had finished doing her hair and helping her into her gown, although Jane thought it was one of the most successful she had ever had. Carefully chosen to complement the colours of the gown she had worn during the day, it was a deep violet ornamented with lace and cream silk roses and showed up the rich colour of Taisie's hair and her very white skin.

There was dancing after dinner, with other guests coming in from neighbouring houses. Taisie danced with her host and smiled at his fulsome compliments in a way that made Jack Conway suddenly hopeful of making headway with her at last, although the truth was that she had not heard a word of what he had been saying.

Two dances later Blair came up to her. One desperate look at one another and then Taisie put her hand on his arm and they left the dance floor, sauntering casually out of the room as if to go towards the supper room. Instead, Blair cast a swift look round and led Taisie into the conservatory, dimly lit and smelling of damp earth and green ferns. They had still not spoken.

Shielded by the graceful leaves of a palm tree they turned towards one another and clung together in an embrace so close that they seemed to be one body, one heartbeat that throbbed with a passion they had neither of them ever known before. Oblivious to the passing of time, they kissed, and kissed again. Blair murmured something which Taisie did not hear, so absorbed was she in pressing new caresses on him, but at last the first madness began to subside and a degree of sanity returned to her.

She drew away and, looking up into his face, she asked in blank bewilderment, "Why *now*?"

"Because my self control finally failed me," Blair said with his lips against her silken mass of hair. "I never meant you to know that I loved you, Taisie. My darling, my darling."

"It was bound to happen sometime," Taisie said. "How could I not have known that I loved you, that you loved me? Oh, Blair!"

She raised her face and their lips met once more, more slowly this time, lingering over the delight of their new love. At last Taisie drew away and as she did so she shivered.

"We must be careful. We shall be seen," she said.

"Come and sit down."

There was a wrought iron seat, painted white and scattered with cushions. They sat down, half turned towards one another, both of Taisie's hands held tightly in Blair's.

"How could it happen?" she asked. "How could I have fallen in love with you and not realized it? All this long time . . . and you, my dear, did you really know and not tell me?"

"I think I loved you right from the start. I always hated the idea of your marrying Maurice. I desired you, as any man might with eyes in his head, but I thought if I kept away from you it would pass. I didn't admire myself for coveting my cousin's wife. But it didn't answer. When I was away from you I was in hell, and when I was with you I was in torment. And, worst of all, I saw that you were beginning to turn to me. You looked to me for sympathy and help, you told me secrets that you kept from your husband, you cared enough to come and hear me speak in the House—and sent me a sweet note afterwards. My darling, don't laugh at me,

303

but I've kept it in my breast pocket ever since."

Taisie smiled and blinked. "It makes me want to cry," she said. "To be loved like that, what have I done to deserve it?"

"Nothing, except to be the sweetest, loveliest, most enchanting woman in the world. I love everything about you; your gaiety and wit, your courage, even your foolish side—perhaps your foolish side most of all."

"If you talk like that I'll never keep my head," Taisie said distractedly.

"Lose it," Blair said. "Do you really love me? Tell me!"

"Yes, I love you. More than I can find words to say. And looking back I think, like you, that there was something between us right from the start. A sort of challenge, something that made the sparks fly every time we met. This afternoon, seeing you unexpectedly, seeing the way you looked at me, it was such a revelation that I've been reeling from the shock ever since. The whole world has changed. I love you, I love you, I love you."

They were back in one another's arms,

kissing wildly, but at last Taisie drew away.

"What are we going to do?" she whispered.

"Leave Maurice and come to me."

Very slowly, Taisie moved away from him. "I can't do that," she said. "It would ruin you. What about your profession, your parliamentary career?"

"Damn my career. If I can't have you I don't care a fig for anything."

Taisie touched his cheek with a gentle hand. "Is this my sensible Blair? It won't do, my dear, you know it won't. If we behave foolishly I think one day you might blame me for what you'd lost."

"I wouldn't be the first Member of Parliament to keep a mistress."

"You might get away with keeping a mistress very discreetly hidden away, as long as she was what they call 'of a certain class'. You wouldn't survive once it became known that you were living with your cousin's wife. Look what they did to Parnell. It would be *criminal* for you to waste your life. I could never forgive myself."

"I can only say it again: I would give it all up gladly, for you."

He spoke resolutely, but Taisie caught a hint of reservation behind his words and knew that in his heart he agreed with her.

"It's too much of a sacrifice," she said. "It would destroy you and perhaps your love for me, too. Besides, Maurice has been a good husband to me, according to his lights. He doesn't deserve that I should betray him."

"Does that mean there's to be nothing for me?" Blair asked in a low voice.

"Nothing for either of us. We must be strong and stay away from one another. Blair, don't look like that! You know I'm right. My darling love, you *know* I'm right."

Blair stood up. "If that's your decision we'd better start straight away. We've been away from the ballroom too long already. People will start to notice. Can you do it, do you think? Smile, dance, pretend?"

"Not dance. Not with you. Never again, Blair. I couldn't stand it. Oh damn, I think I'm going to cry."

Blair had been moving out of the

conservatory, but at that despairing exclamation he stopped with a smothered laugh.

"Don't use those bad words, you little gypsy. I don't know whether to shake you or kiss you."

"Don't be angry with me for trying to do what I think is right. Please, Blair."

"I can't help being angry, not with you, but with the circumstances that have driven us into this corner. Come on, my treasure, put your chin up. Remember that I need your courage to help me."

He did not speak again until they were back in the crowded ballroom, both feeling dazed by the contrast between the carefree spectacle and the emotional turmoil inside them, and then he said, very softly: "We won't be able to keep to it."

# 10

IF they had been able to part that night and never see one another again the love between Taisie and Blair might have faded away into something that was no more than a regretful ache for what might have been, but that solution was not open to them. They tried, Taisie at first more conscientiously than Blair, but circumstances were against them. They had friends in common, they moved in the same social circle, it was not always possible to refuse the invitations that brought them together. As it was, Maurice complained that Blair was neglecting them and Taisie was forced to include his name when she sent out her invitations. She was reproachful when he accepted and hurt when he refused, so that Blair, trapped in a love that gave him no peace, accused her of deliberately tormenting him and they quarrelled in fierce, low-spoken whispers and were reconciled with hands that clung too long for a formal leave-taking and eyes that pleaded silently for forgiveness.

The ending of the Parliamentary session and the long vacation in the Law Courts gave Blair an excuse to get away. He went walking in the mountains in Switzerland, while Maurice went off to Scotland and Taisie, less because she was genuinely interested than because she felt it was something of which Blair would approve, went to Starrid Hall and devoted herself to the welfare of Maurice's tenants.

It was less rewarding than she had hoped. The estate was efficiently run, with snug farms and well-maintained cottages. Her personal interest was appreciated, but there was little she could do to improve the lives of people who were obstinately contented with their lot.

The miners were another matter. Maurice's steward agreed with her that their back-to-back houses were far from satisfactory.

"But my hands are tied, Mrs. Gaymour," he explained. "This property belongs to the Starrid Mining Company."

"In which my husband has a majority shareholding," Taisie said. "I know all about that. A very nice profit he had out of it last year."

She paused to think. "We can't pull down the houses, I quite see that," she said in a fairminded way. "But when I was talking to the women the one thing they all agreed about was the difficulty of heating up water so that their men could get rid of the coal dust when they came home. Some pits have baths on the spot, don't they?"

"They do, but Starrid is only a small mine. I doubt whether the directors would agree to putting in baths."

"We'll see about that!"

Maurice, tackled as soon as he returned home the following week, put up a feeble resistance to the scheme Taisie wanted him to sponsor.

"They've managed well enough without baths in the past," he grumbled. "It doesn't really bother people like that."

"Yes, it does. They go to an enormous amount of trouble to keep clean. You mustn't talk about 'people like that' as if they were a different species, Maurice. Not to me."

He gave in and the miners benefited,

but the trouble was that his assistance had to be paid for. They had been apart for several weeks and Maurice had not found any diversions amongst the almost exclusively male company of his shooting companions. He wanted to be thanked with more than a few smiles and a kiss on the cheek.

Taisie, with Blair's image always in her mind while she tried to do things of which he would approve, submitted to her husband's embraces and wept slow, difficult tears which had to be stifled in the pillow after he had fallen asleep. All too clearly now she saw that in marrying Maurice she had sold herself into a servitude to money which degraded her true value. Blair had said it, and he had been right. And it was going to last for the rest of her life.

She welcomed now the separations which had once seemed unnatural. When Maurice was invited to stay with friends in Norfolk she urged him to accept, while Taisie went to visit the Conways again. She was ashamed of the relief she felt as she parted with him, knowing that Maurice was no different from the man he

311

had always been, the man she had chosen to marry with her eyes wide open.

The Conways were expecting a houseful of guests. Molly Conway reeled off a list of names as she stirred herself to accompany Taisie to her room.

"We shall be positively crowded," she said. "I've put you in here, darling. You don't need a dressing room as Maurice isn't with you, do you, so I've given the room next door to Mr. Gregory. He's only here from Friday to Monday so I hope he will overlook its smallness."

"Blair Gregory?" Taisie asked carefully.

"Yes, of course. Who else? Such an interesting situation is developing in that family. Lady Akerne's just been confined, you know, and it's *another* girl. It really begins to look as if the delightful Blair will be an earl one day. Who would have thought that a year or two ago? So desperately eligible and really quite attractive, don't you think, in spite of that satirical way he has. Mrs. Curtiss is angling for him for Penelope, you know. I've asked them just for the pleasure of seeing him wriggle off the hook! Though really he *ought* to be married. Do come down as soon as you're

312

ready; there's tea on the terrace as the weather is so warm."

Taisie stood alone in the middle of the room. In a minute or two her maid would be coming to unpack and to help her out of her travelling clothes. She must pull herself together. Blair, not only in the same house, but in the next room. There was a communicating door. And the key was in the lock. Taisie shuddered and hid her face in her hands. It wasn't fair, she thought rebelliously; it simply wasn't fair, when she had been trying so hard to be good.

By the time Taisie drifted downstairs, smiling and *soignée* in a floating tea gown, Blair had arrived. He had not known, any more than Taisie had, that they were to be fellow guests, but fortunately Molly Conway had mentioned her name so that he was prepared for the moment when she came out on to the terrace, into the afternoon sunshine.

They had not met for six weeks and the question uppermost in both their minds was "Has he changed?" "Does she still feel the same?" Taisie, stealing glances at Blair, saw that he was leaner and fitter than he had been when he went away, and his face was burned brown by the sun of the Alpine meadows. On Taisie's face Blair saw the faint destroying imprint of sleepless nights and despairing days and his heart contracted. His hand was shaking as he put down his tea cup. He walked to the end of the terrace and stood looking out over the garden as if admiring the view. Taisie followed him.

Without turning his head Blair said in a conversational way: "If we walked as far as the rose garden could I kiss you without being seen?"

"I doubt it. Someone will look out of an upstairs window and see us."

"I'm in the mood to risk it."

They strolled across the lawn, mown to a texture like velvet. Inside the walled garden which sheltered the roses they turned to one another without another word and kissed. All their despair and the aching loneliness of the days they had spent apart was in that kiss.

"I was afraid you might have got over it," Taisie murmured.

"My silly girl. As if I could. Did you miss me?"

"Every day. Every *minute* of every day."

They kissed again and when they drew apart they were smiling.

"We could sit down for a few minutes, but we must be careful," Taisie said. "Molly has an eye like a hawk."

"She's in no position to be censorious," Blair said drily. "I think she'd be sympathetic if she knew."

"Don't be silly, darling, she wants you for herself. Besides, I wouldn't want to give her that hold over me."

With Blair's arm round her and her head on his shoulder, Taisie closed her eyes for a few blissful moments. And then she told him about their adjoining bedrooms.

"Dear God," Blair said blankly.

"I don't think God was watching when Molly made up her room plan," Taisie said. She sat up and pulled herself away from his encircling arms. "No-one should be asked to stand out against that much temptation. What are we going to do, Blair?"

"I don't think there is any man living, in my position, who wouldn't put his hand on that door tonight and hope to find it open," Blair said. "But the decision is still yours, my darling. If you leave it locked I'll try to respect your feelings, but it will be hard, damnably hard."

They wandered back to the terrace with Taisie still refusing to commit herself. As the evening wore on she saw the strain deepening in Blair's face. It was unbearable, that he should suffer; even worse than putting up with her own aching longing. When Molly accused her of being distrait, she admitted falsely to having a headache and made it an excuse to avoid playing cards and to go to bed early.

She rang for her maid and submitted to the slow ritual of preparing for bed. Her lovely gown was hung up, her underclothes put on one side for washing, her hair unpinned and brushed out. She sat at the dressing table in her fine silk nightdress and negligée and looked at her reflection. Her face was pale and her eyes looked huge and very green. When she moved her hands the huge solitaire on her left hand glinted in the light. Taisie took it off and laid it down with a click on the polished wood, but her wedding ring was tight and would not budge.

She got up and began pacing restlessly about the room. She heard voices in the corridor outside, the sounds of doors opening and closing. Taisie pressed her hands against her temples. She caught sight of herself in the long glass and recognized her histrionic pose for what it was: a pretence at being undecided when all the time she knew, had known ever since she had spoken to Blair in the rose garden, that she would unlock her door for him.

When Blair came to her she was sitting up in bed, her rich copper hair spread over her bare shoulders. He came quickly across the room and sat on the edge of the bed, stretching out his hand to run it through her hair.

"I've always wanted to touch it when it was loose. I've been in torment all the evening, not knowing what you meant to do."

"I thought I hadn't made up my mind, but of course I had," Taisie said. "If I'd really meant to hold you at bay, my dear love, I would never have told you that the key was in the lock. Blair, you don't think

Molly guesses do you? You don't think that's why she gave us rooms together?"

Blair held her close, soothing her moment of panic. "No-one knows," he said. "Not that I would care if they did, but I know you don't feel that way. We've been given this chance to be together and yet still keep our secret and it's up to us to make the most of it."

"You're right, we mustn't waste any of this wonderful time," Taisie said. "I hope I shan't shock you. I love you too much to be anything but shameless."

"I doubt if I'll be shocked," Blair said.

It seemed to Taisie that he had every quality she needed to make him her perfect lover. His body was hard from his long weeks on the hills. Taisie ran her hands over the smooth muscles of his back and gloried in his strength. She had always recognized a quality of ruthlessness in Blair and she sensed it in him now, a power used relentlessly to drive her into a state of mindless ecstasy. And yet he was imaginative, too, and sensitive to her needs. Not just a magnificent machine, but a man of wit and delicacy, who courted her gently and then swept her into a maelstrom of sensation such as she had never known before.

She heard herself cry out and Blair answered her with a sound deep in his throat, a rich, exultant laugh that sounded like a growl.

"Like a satisfied lion," Taisie said, smoothing back the damp hair from his forehead when at last they lay spent and weary.

"Satisfied? Taisie, Taisie, if I spent a lifetime loving you I could never have enough. My magnificent girl."

They kissed gently, reluctant to admit that for the moment they could do no more, and then with Blair's hands still softly fondling her, Taisie curled herself against him and went to sleep, and Blair tried to remain awake and failed. When he woke up the day was already dawning. Taisie was still sleeping deeply, but there was no help for it, he had to wake her up. She stirred and opened her eyes in response to his kisses. Blinking in the early morning light she yawned deliciously, showing her little white teeth, and then slipped her arms around his neck.

"I have to go," Blair said. "My darling,

319

we've slept too long. No, my treasure. I must leave you. And you have to lock the door. Now, before you slip back into sleep and forget."

She followed him to the door, naked and shivering, and he turned back to kiss her once more before he pulled the door closed behind him. Taisie turned the key in the lock, then she found her discarded nightdress and pulled it over her head. She climbed back into bed and lay in a dream of wonder that their love should have been so splendid.

There was a cricket match the next day, the last of the year and one of the reasons the Conways had gathered their house party together. Blair, with his powerful shoulders and accurate eye, was considered a useful bowler for the home side. Taisie thought he looked magnificent in his white flannels and she lay back in her chair, lazily admiring him, until Blair came and bent over her with a look of amusement on his face and said: "If you go on looking at me like that I'll be forced to take you behind the tea tent and behave disgracefully."

Looking up into his laughing face, still

bronzed from his days in the high mountains, Taisie felt as if all her bones were melting with longing for him. It was fortunate that the way he was bending towards her hid her face from everyone else. With the colour rising in her cheeks she said: "How can I help it when you look so beautiful? Blair, we'll draw attention to ourselves if we aren't more prudent. Go and talk to Molly."

She saw from the quick frown on his face that the reminder of their situation had displeased him, but he sauntered away and gratified his hostess with a little light flirtation, while Taisie looked up at the sky through the fringe of her parasol and tried not to feel resentful as she listened to Molly's delighted laughter.

It was not Molly Conway, but the watchful Mrs. Curtiss, jealous for her daughter, who said to Taisie with a snap: "I had no idea Mr. Gregory was such an intimate friend of yours, Mrs. Gaymour."

Taisie raised her eyebrows in calculated surprise. "He didn't at all approve when Maurice first married me," she said with a candour that silenced Mrs. Curtiss. "I've worked hard to win him over and I really think I can count him as a friend now. Of course, as everyone keeps saying, he should get married."

Her eyes dwelt for a moment on Penelope Curtiss, a nondescript lump of a girl in unbecoming pink. "Such a pity he can't seem to see anyone he fancies."

She felt that she had scored a small victory, but all the same she scolded Blair when they lay, blissfully happy, in one another's arms that night.

"I'd just as soon bring it out in the open," Blair said. "People do divorce these days, my darling. It isn't the complete social suicide it used to be."

"It is for people in public life," Taisie said obstinately. "I can't do that to you, Blair."

"Then after this weekend . . ."

She laid a finger across his lips. "We still have one more night. We've been wonderfully lucky to have any time together at all. Don't let's spoil it by thinking about the future."

But the memory of the shortness of the time they had left inevitably weighed on their minds. They were silent with one another the next day and they clung together in despairing passion on the last night they could be sure of sharing.

"We could meet," Blair said. "There are places we could go to. I could even take a house specially for us."

"In St. John's Wood, like Desmond Corley?" Taisie asked. "No, my very dear love, that's not for us. I won't indulge in a furtive little affair that has to be hidden in a corner. We've been strong before. We'll have to go back to the way things were before these wonderful few days."

"I told you then we wouldn't be able to keep to it, and we haven't," Blair pointed out. "And that was before we knew how wonderful we were together. Taisie, I love you so much. Not just here in bed, though goodness knows that's been a revelation, but all the time. I want to share my life with you. Please, Taisie, please, think again."

She could only shake her head and when he realized that the tears were streaming down her face Blair abandoned his importunity and comforted her. Once again a wave of passion swept over them. To Taisie it seemed as if she was being sucked down and down and down, in an endless spiral to the depths of a bottomless sea. There was an explosion of light behind her closed eyes and she floated up to the surface, peaceful and weary, her hands closed hard round the man who had striven with her in those turbulent waters. She kissed him once in gentle gratitude and then lay with her head against his naked shoulder.

When Blair stirred against her she said: "My darling, go now. Don't wait for morning. Leave me now, while I feel that I can bear it."

She had thought that he might protest, but Blair said: "Yes, perhaps it's best. Come and lock the door, my treasure, or else I might be tempted to come back to you again."

They kissed on the threshold as they had done on the two previous nights and Blair, holding her close against him, said in a low voice: "Do you really imagine I shall never make love to you again? It isn't possible."

He felt her deep sighing breath against his shoulder, but she did not answer him and after one more kiss he left her.

Blair departed early the next morning,

324

so early that he had gone before Taisie put in an appearance. She was glad to have been spared a public farewell, even more thankful that he had departed before Maurice arrived. There were two things which Taisie suspected that Blair, for all his clear-sightedness, had shut his mind to. The first was that he might have given her a child during their turbulent three nights together; the second was that she was still Maurice's wife and that Maurice, when he joined her, would expect to resume their married life.

He was as undemonstrative as ever when he arrived and found her taking tea with the other ladies in the drawing room, but when he came in to her room to see if she was ready to go down to dinner that evening he bent over and kissed her. Taisie knew her first moment of real panic. She felt herself go stiff and she drew away from Maurice so quickly that she expected him to comment on it, but he seemed to see nothing amiss.

All through the evening she kept thinking to herself: I can't do it. I can't. Not with Maurice. Not tonight, so soon after Blair . . . in the same room, the same bed.

In the end she resorted to the age-old excuse. When Maurice came to her, through the same door she had opened each night for Blair, Taisie put a hand to her forehead and said: "Maurice, I've got the most frightful headache."

"I thought you were quiet this evening," he said.

He put his hand under her chin and tilted her face up to the light, but he saw only the shadows under her eyes and not the desperation in her expression.

"I'll sleep in the dressing room tonight, shall I? Give you a chance to get a good night's sleep."

After Maurice had left her Taisie dragged herself into bed. He had been kind, far kinder than she deserved, but the moment when she would have to give herself to him had only been postponed. She was a faithless wife and she was going to have to pay a hard price for giving in to the temptation that had overwhelmed her. At that moment Taisie could almost have wished that she had held out against it. Almost, but not quite. Nothing could really make her regret the ecstasy she and Blair had shared.

The following night she did her duty, as she saw it, and it was not so bad as she had feared. What Maurice expected of her bore so little relation to the demands Blair had made that it was as if, for a brief spell, some quite different woman inhabited her body and Taisie, the real Taisie, was able to float away untouched by Maurice's inept heavings.

They departed once again on their round of autumn visits and this year Taisie went everywhere that Maurice went, too afraid of what might happen if she found herself alone in London within easy reach of Blair.

She tried to keep up an appearance of high spirits, but her old zest for living was missing. Every morning as she began to wake up she would be aware of a feeling of intense misery and then recollection would come rushing back and she had to face the familiar pain of yet another day with no sight or sound of Blair. She put on the clothes her maid laid out for her with none of her former interest in her appearance; the image that looked back at her from her glass meant nothing because Blair would not see it. When she was off her guard her face settled into lines of sadness and she was constantly telling lies about suffering from headaches to explain her dejection.

She had one brief moment of triumph when she was invited to sing at a charity concert in Manchester. Taisie hesitated at first because the request came from Viscountess Akerne, the wife of Blair's cousin, but then she told herself that she was getting morbid, unable to have any contact with any member of his family in case it led to seeing Blair, and the cause for which the concert was to be held was to provide hostels for young working girls, a need so near to Taisie's heart that she could not bring herself to refuse.

She was scarcely acquainted with Lord Akerne and his wife, since they preferred to spend most of their time in the country where Gus occupied himself in helping his grandfather to administer the family estates. A sickly-looking specimen, Taisie thought Gus, tall, thin and languid; nothing there to remind her of Blair.

His wife was quiet, but Taisie suspected that she was the stronger willed of the two, and certainly it was her doing that Taisie had been asked to appear on the stage once more. Maurice's mother thought it was a pity for people to be reminded that it had once been her profession.

"I'm not criticizing you, of course, Taisie, and no doubt it is a very good cause," she said. "All the same, I do feel that it's a pity to draw attention to . . ."

"My unfortunate past?" Taisie asked as her mother-in-law hesitated. "I think you're worrying unnecessarily. Actors have become quite respectable, they're received everywhere."

"Standards are so much laxer than they were when I was a girl," Mrs. Gregory admitted, with no sign that she thought it an improvement. "Of course, if Minnie thinks it's all right . . ."

Her voice died away and Taisie concealed a grin at the implication that a future countess could do no wrong.

"Such a pity, all those daughters," Mrs. Gaymour went on, pursuing her own train of thought. "Fortunately Minnie is still quite young. Next time, perhaps."

"She was only confined in September," Taisie was startled into exclaiming. "Poor girl, after having three children in five years I think she deserves a rest."

"That may be your opinion, but I'm sure Minnie understands where her duty lies," Mrs. Gaymour said. She looked pointedly at Taisie's svelte figure.

"I had hoped that Maurice and I would have been setting up our nursery before this," Taisie said smoothly, taking the wind out of her mother-in-law's sails, as she saw with naughty satisfaction, though the truth was that she scarcely knew what she would do if she became pregnant at this time.

Taisie was suffering a reaction from all her highmindedness in connection with Blair and she took a perverse delight in turning the tables on Maurice's mother and in shocking her. She sang two songs at the charity concert: "The Boy I Love is Up in the Gallery" and her own success from "The Hotel Girl"—"Spread a little happiness as we go along"—and drove Mrs. Gaymour to distraction by wondering out loud whether she dared attempt the cartwheel with which she had ended it at the Gaiety. Right up to the evening of the performance Mrs. Gregory was on tenterhooks in case her unpredictable daughter-in-law took it into her head to turn upside down and display her legs in front of an audience of her friends and neighbours. She gave a gasp of relief when Taisie indicated the cartwheel with a little circular movement of her hand and a naughty twinkle that made some of the men who had seen her at the Gaiety chuckle out loud.

There was one man in the audience she had not expected to be there. After it was over Taisie received a little posy of roses and forget-me-nots and a card. There was nothing on the card except Blair's name, but she treasured it just the same. What need of words, when the crimson roses said it all?

She reproached him when they met after the concert for not warning her that he was to be a guest at the house where she, too, was staying, but Blair refused to be repentant.

"Don't waste time telling me I shouldn't have come, but try to think of some way we can at least have a few minutes alone together," he said.

"It's a strange coincidence, but I've

been here before," Taisie said. "An old friend of mine is married to the estate carpenter. I mean to walk across the park tomorrow morning to see her. Will you come with me?"

"It's better than nothing, I suppose."

Taisie was still buoyed up by the excitement of her stage appearance, but when she saw the sombre expression in Blair's eyes as they rested on her she laid her hand lightly on his arm and said unsteadily: "Oh, my dear, don't look like that."

"I don't find it gets any better," Blair said in a level voice. "Do you?"

Taisie was called away, but as she went she looked back over her shoulder. "No," she said.

She mentioned her destination to her hostess before she set out the next morning.

"I wonder where Maurice is?" she said, with intent to deceive. "I'm sure Hetty would like to meet my husband."

"He went to the stables," Blair said and from the curt way he spoke Taisie knew that he resented this effort to cover their tracks.

"In that case there's no point in trying to drag him away," Taisie said. "Will you give me your escort, Blair?"

He nodded, his face grim. As soon as they were out of the house he burst out: "I hate it when you go in for that sort of play acting."

"I know, but it's necessary, for your sake if not for mine. Don't quarrel with me for being prudent. Tell me everything you've been doing since we last met."

"I seem to have spent most of my time thinking about you, missing you, wanting you day and night. You haven't changed your mind about leaving Maurice?"

Taisie shook her head, too close to tears to trust herself to speak.

"I'm a brute," Blair said remorsefully. "Forgive me, my darling. Frustrated love makes a man very short-tempered, I find. What have I been doing? Since the House resumed I've been very assiduous about attending. I've had a couple of interesting cases in the Old Bailey and got an acquittal in one of them against all the odds."

"I read about it in the newspapers," Taisie said. "I always look to see if you are mentioned."

333

"Do you? I don't know why I should find that so touching, but I do. All the same, don't you find it ludicrous, that we should be reduced to scanning the Society columns and the criminal news for a sight of one another's names?"

"There's nothing funny about it," Taisie said. "Let's talk about something else. I've been getting acquainted with your cousins. Augustus doesn't seem in good health."

"He's had some internal trouble and is coming up to London in a week or two to consult a specialist. They think it may be gall stones, apparently. Poor old Gus, he used to be such a robust fellow."

They walked on slowly, spinning out the time they were able to spend alone together, trying to keep off the painful subject of their feelings for one another. They were within sight of the row of cottages where Hetty lived when Blair said, with an abruptness that betrayed how much the subject had been weighing on his mind: "Does Maurice bother you much? I must know. It drives me nearly mad, thinking of you with him."

It was a question Taisie had long foreseen and she had her answer ready. "Hardly at all," she said steadily. "Put it out of your mind, my dear."

Blair turned her to face him. "I have a feeling you're lying, but I want to believe you too much to press you. How long are you going to be, visiting this friend of yours?"

"Only a few minutes, then we can take our time about walking back."

"I'll sit on this fallen tree trunk and wait for you."

Taisie moved towards him in mute invitation and he put his arms round her. They kissed for a long time under the cover of a group of elm trees and then Taisie drew away.

As Taisie had expected, Hetty already knew that she was staying in the "big house".

"Imagine!" she exclaimed. "Do you remember saying you wouldn't leave the stage unless you could have a house like that? We never thought it would come to pass, did we? Why didn't you bring your husband in to see me?"

"Maurice was visiting the stables when I left," Taisie said. "I knew it would take an age to get him away, so I came without him."

Hetty's face changed. "Who was that I saw you with in the park, then?" she demanded.

"That must have been Mr. Gregory, Maurice's cousin," Taisie said. She glanced quickly out of the small window of the cottage. Blair was completely hidden from sight.

"I was upstairs, standing on a chair to get some fresh linen out of the cupboard," Hetty said. "I saw the pair of you, kissing like you were demented. I thought it was a bit off, even then, when I took it for granted it was your husband. What are you up to, Taisie?"

"You . . . you must have been mistaken," Taisie said.

"Oh, no, I wasn't! Carrying on with another man already, are you? I might have known how it would be after the way you behaved with that Leonard, and you so young an' all. You should be ashamed of yourself."

"We love one another."

"Love! Is that any excuse? No, it isn't. You've got a decent, respectable husband.

336

Why can't you be content with that, the same as the rest of us? You're no better than you should be, Taisie Brown, and that's flat."

Taisie drew herself up proudly. "That's no way to talk to me," she said.

"Coming the fine lady now, are we? I was always one to speak my mind, as you very well know. I knew you when you were a nasty little guttersnipe the master brought in out of charity and don't you forget it. You've come a long way, my girl, but that's not to say you won't fall back again if you don't watch out."

Her voice changed and she put a hand on Taisie's arm, looking up anxiously into her face. "Give him up, girl. You know you're doing wrong. And he can't be much of a man, enticing you away from your proper husband."

"He's a wonderful person," Taisie said. "You don't understand, Hetty. If I've done wrong it's not in loving Blair, but in marrying Maurice."

She was shaken by Hetty's condemnation. Blair saw it as soon as she walked back to join him again.

"You've been quick," he commented.

"And something's happened to upset you. What is it, sweetheart?"

"Hetty saw us kissing one another."

"Will she talk about it?"

"She'll tell her husband. She won't be able to stop herself. But he's an outside servant. I don't think he'll say anything to anyone indoors. It was rather unpleasant. Hetty as good as called me a scarlet woman which, since it happens to be true, made me feel bad."

Blair put his arm round her, careless of who might see them. "All this could be avoided if you'd leave Maurice," he pointed out.

"When you've just been telling me how splendidly you've been doing in Parliament? No, my dear, I still say that's not the answer."

338

# 11

TAISIE and Maurice spent Christmas and the New Year at Starrid Hall, but this year Mrs. Gaymour did not join them and in spite of local festivities they were thrown very much into their own company.

It was a bleak winter. They were confined to the house by driving snow for weeks on end. The guests who were to have joined them found themselves unable to travel. Taisie, looking out at the swirling flakes and the black trees writhing in the wind, thought that the desolation outside was no worse than she carried in her own breast. Maurice was bored and restless and all too apt to turn to her for consolation.

"Ghastly weather," he complained. "Haven't had a decent day's shooting or hunting since I don't remember when. Nothing to do, no-one to see."

Taisie let him teach her to play billiards, which kept him amused for a time, but there were days when she found him as difficult as a fretful child.

The postal deliveries were uncertain because of the deep snow drifts. Maurice haunted the hall disconsolately, looking for letters and newspapers which did not get through. When their letters from London arrived they fell on them with the eagerness of exiles.

"The lawyers want to know what we intend doing about that Italian property of Desmond's," Maurice said. He glanced out of the window where the snow had given way to a steady downpour of rain and a sea of mud. "I must say the idea of a Sicilian villa is enticing at the moment, don't you agree?"

Taisie wrinkled her nose in the distaste she felt, but could not reveal, for anything that had belonged to Desmond Corley. "We've got enough houses already," she objected.

"Still, a pity to give it up without ever having seen the place. I remember Mother and Father visited it years ago when I was at school and Mother was in raptures about it."

Taisie did not reply and Maurice's mind

was instantly diverted by the news his next letter contained.

"I say, poor old Gus Akerne has snuffed it," he exclaimed. "Well, who would have thought it? Had an operation for what they thought was the stone and it turned out to be a malignant condition. Only lingered a week. It makes me feel quite queer. Poor old Gus. Not that we were ever very intimate, but it makes you think, doesn't it?"

"What a terrible thing!" Taisie exclaimed automatically, but her mind had turned immediately towards what this would mean for Blair.

"We don't have to go into mourning again, do we?" Maurice demanded. "No relation of ours, after all. We had an aunt in common, that's all."

"We might go into black gloves for a few weeks as a mark of respect," Taisie suggested. "Though buried here in the country it really can't matter."

"I tell you what, old girl, I wouldn't mind goin' up to London next week if the roads are clear. Brighten ourselves up a bit. What do you say?"

Taisie could only agree. It would be an opportunity to find out how Blair had been affected by this unexpected development in his life. To Taisie it seemed to put him further out of her reach than ever.

"It means Uncle Edgar will be the next Earl of Charlwood," Maurice said, pursuing his own train of thought. "Bit of a change from being a country parson, what?"

Taisie and Maurice travelled up to London the following week. It amused Taisie sometimes to look back to the days when she had been on tour with the Lamonts, shunting continuously from one town to the next on Sunday trains in third class compartments, with packets of dry sandwiches and bottles of tea passed round the company. Now she could always be sure of the seclusion of a first class compartment, a fur rug for her legs when it was chilly, a hamper full of delicacies if the journey lasted more than a short time. Someone else bought her ticket and saw to her luggage. She was always met on arrival. No more trailing round dreary streets in search of her digs. A warm house with all the lamps lit awaited her. She ought to be thankful, and yet she could not help feeling nostalgic for the companionship and the excitement of the days that were gone.

At Maurice's insistence Taisie sent a note round to Blair inviting him to dinner on the evening after their arrival. She was dismayed to hear in reply that his father was staying with him so there was only one thing she could do: invite them both.

"No other guests, just us," Maurice said when they arrived. "Taisie thought it would be best. Rotten news about Gus. We were very sorry."

"It's been a blow to all of us," Edgar Gregory said. "And not only because we were fond of Gus. It's meant an upheaval in my life, as you can understand. I am resigning my living. My father is very frail now and needs my support. As soon as it can be arranged my wife and I will go and live with him. He wants me to assume the courtesy title Gus held, but I'm in no hurry about that."

"What about you?" Taisie asked, looking up into Blair's face.

She thought he looked tired and sad, and preoccupied in a way that struck a chill to her heart, in case she had been right in thinking that this change would remove him even further away from her.

"For the time being I can carry on as before, but I shall always have it hanging over me that I'm the heir to an earldom—the last thing I ever expected or wanted."

"You'll have to get married," Maurice said with a joviality that grated on Taisie and Blair. "The family will be on to you to keep the line going, won't they, Uncle Edgar?"

"Blair knows my views on matrimony," Mr. Gregory replied. "It is not an estate to be entered into lightly."

There was a seriousness about his reply that silenced Maurice and which made Taisie suspect that he was thinking of the uneasy basis of her own marriage.

There was no opportunity for Taisie and Blair to be alone together. Only once did Blair take advantage of Maurice turning his back on them to seize Taisie's hand under the cover of her full skirt in a swift, painful grip. There was no need for her to look at him or speak. She knew that he sensed her concern for him and her continuing love.

Taisie was so sure that she and Blair had

not given themselves away that she was taken by surprise when Mr. Gregory called on her the next morning. She realized as soon as he spoke that he had deliberately chosen a time when he might expect to find her alone. Indeed, she had not long come downstairs when he was announced. She got up from her writing desk, leaving it scattered with the notes she was writing, and went towards him. He took her hand and looked searchingly into her face, but he did not say anything until they were both seated in front of the blazing coal fire.

His gravity alarmed Taisie. Without realizing what she was doing she put her hand up to her throat to touch the blue and gold pendant Blair had given her.

Edgar Gregory did not waste any time in polite preliminaries.

"My dear child, I must ask you what there is between you and my son," he said.

"Nothing," Taisie said, too quickly.

He continued to look at her in grave silence until she felt herself forced into speech again. "Why don't you ask Blair if you . . . if you suspect something?"

"Because I think that, for your sake, he

would lie to me. And that would be tragic."

With her quick understanding Taisie saw all too clearly that that would be true. For Blair to keep something concealed from his father was one thing, for him to be pushed into a deliberate lie would open up a gulf between them that might never be bridged.

"We love one another," she said.

"I feared it must be so. I knew there was something wrong with Blair, something more than the overwork he talks about so glibly. And then last night I saw a look on his face—only for a moment, you were both very guarded with one another—like a man dying of thirst who is shown a cup from which he may not drink."

He put up his hand to shield his eyes. "I grieve for both of you."

"Blair wants me to leave Maurice and live with him."

"That is something I could never condone, as you must very well realize."

"It would be more honest than the way we live now," Taisie said bitterly.

She struggled with herself for a moment

and then added reluctantly: "You needn't worry, I won't let him destroy his career like that."

"His career! Yes, I suppose that is important to him. My concern is for something deeper than worldly fame."

"Please don't preach at me," Taisie said. "I know you're a parson, but I don't see any reason for you to come religious over me when I'm already trying to be good."

"My religion is a part of me," Mr. Gregory said with a mildness that mollified Taisie. "I can't help looking at your predicament from the standpoint of the Church. I shall pray for you. However, it is for you to take the practical steps which will sever you and Blair. You must stop seeing one another."

"We can't. We're always meeting. If not here, then at other people's houses."

"It could be done if you were determined about it. It would need a separation of several months. It might be necessary for you to go abroad. And, of course, although I did not quite like it when Maurice spoke of it so lightly last night, he was right: Blair must marry."

"Turning himself into a breeding machine to keep a musty old title alive," Taisie said scornfully.

"It matters very little to me whether the title lives or dies. There is more to it than that. That is why I am giving up a life to which I dedicated myself in order to help my father. He is over eighty and the loss of two of his grandsons in the past year has bowed him to the ground. There is a large estate and many, many people dependent on it for their livelihood. If Blair dies without an heir it will be broken up. No matter what provision he tries to make the continuity will be gone."

"That's more important to you than it is to me. I don't think it matters all that much who's at the top. Some rich man will come along and buy up the old house and the people will go on working for him just like always."

"The prospect doesn't please me," Mr. Gregory admitted with a rueful smile at his own weakness. "I must have a more feudal turn of mind than I had realized. Very well, if that argument doesn't move you, what about Blair himself? Is he to be denied all domestic happiness?"

"If Blair marries some other woman while he still loves me no good will come of it. It'll be just as bad as me marrying Maurice."

"I think you are wrong in that," Mr. Gregory said slowly. "I believe Blair could marry out of duty and respect for the name he bears and find some measure of contentment in leading the life of a country gentleman, bringing up his children, taking a lead in the country, earning the respect of his tenants. He will have a seat in the House of Lords; with his abilities he could earn high office."

"You wouldn't talk about *contentment* if you'd ever loved anyone the way Blair loves me." Taisie dashed away angry tears. "And what about me, what about me? Who's going to stop me running on the rocks if I haven't got Blair to turn to?"

"Oh, my dear child!" Mr. Gregory was deeply moved by that despairing cry. "If you make up your mind to do what is right, you will be given strength. There is One above . . ."

"No, no, no!" Taisie said, covering her ears. "I won't have God dragged into this. He didn't help me when I was a little girl and I don't see any reason why He should start taking an interest in me now. The only reason I could cut myself off from Blair, the *only* reason, is if I was convinced it would be good for him."

"Can you doubt it?" Mr. Gregory asked gently. "Blair is burning himself up. To be free of any hope or fear of seeing you for a long period of time, to be told that you released him to marry if he sees fit, these are the only things that will give him peace."

Taisie got up and moved restlessly about the room, coming to a halt in front of the writing desk. With blind eyes she looked down at the mass of notes and invitations which had once held some importance for her. Without turning round she said: "You may be right. I will promise to think about it. Please go now."

She heard the door open and close and sank down on the chair by the desk. Hetty's condemnation of her conduct, Mr. Gregory's appeal to her for Blair's sake, both of these had had a profound effect on her. She told herself despairingly that they were both wrong, that the love between her and Blair was too strong to be denied or turned into any other channel, but in her heart she knew that there was some truth in what Mr. Gregory had said. If she were resolute in cutting the link between them then Blair would be capable of marrying someone else and finding some measure of fulfilment in the marriage. It would be a marriage of convenience, but that did not mean it would be totally unrewarding. He had been bred in the tradition of doing his duty by the family, the idea would not be so alien to him as it had seemed at first to her.

It took several small and apparently unconnected incidents to bring Taisie to a decision. The first was a renewed request from Maurice's solicitor for instructions about Desmond Corley's Sicilian villa, the second was a visit from her mother-in-law when Mrs. Gaymour spoke a little too pointedly about several friends who had become grandmothers, and the third was a querulous letter from, of all people, Laetitia Lawton. There had been a desultory correspondence between them ever since Mrs. Lawton had been the only non-theatrical guest on the bride's side of the church at Taisie's wedding. She had seen a notice of Mr. and Mrs. Gaymour's return to London reported in a daily paper and wrote in a reproachful way that Taisie was evidently too grand now to keep in touch with one who had befriended her in the past.

Taisie began by consulting a doctor about her childlessness. As she had expected, he was soothing and vague, but when, fixing earnest eyes on his face, she suggested that perhaps a change of air, a restful period in a warm climate might be the answer, he was quick to agree.

Taisie put it to Maurice in those terms and, although he was startled, he was also pleased by her desire to bear his child and the idea of visiting Desmond's villa appealed to him. With the promise that if they found the villa agreeable they would invite a party of friends out to join them he was very ready to journey to Italy.

Blair was not so easily handled. Taisie was anxious to get to him before Maurice blurted out the Italian plan. She contrived a meeting between them, knowing by his readiness to drop any other arrangement he might have had in order to spend half an hour with her that he was as near to breaking point as she was herself.

They kissed once with lingering slowness and then sat decorously side by side on the sofa, both conscious that they could not be quite sure they would not be interrupted by a soft-footed servant or even Maurice coming home unexpectedly.

"I've had a letter from Mrs. Lawton, who took me in when I was a child, and I mean to go and visit her before we leave London again," Taisie said. "She's in poor health—she always has been in poor health—but if I exaggerated it I could make it an excuse to stay overnight with her. To pretend to, that is. If I booked into a local hotel, would you come and join me?"

"Do you doubt it? It's like . . . like . . ."

"Being given a drink when you think you're going to be thirsty for the rest of your life," Taisie said, with her mind on her talk with his father.

"An oasis in the desert," Blair agreed. "My darling, I hunger and thirst after you, you know that, don't you?"

"I know," Taisie said.

The visit to Laetitia lasted no more than an hour. Taisie found her older and more faded than she had expected and for once she was inclined to credit Laetitia's complaint of being "so ill". She took her a bunch of hothouse grapes and a fine bouquet of flowers, which brought a flush of pleasure to Laetitia's cheeks. When Taisie got up to go she pressed her to stay and Taisie was conscious of an unpleasant feeling of guilt as she made her fluent excuses about her husband expecting her back for dinner that evening.

She walked to the station and took a cab out of the town. It was a relief to find Blair had not only arrived but was looking out for her and ready to pay off the cab.

"I'm not such a good plotter as I thought," she said as he took her up to their room. "Just as the cab stopped it occurred to me that I had no idea whether you had booked in your name or my name or in something quite different. I would have been in a terrible predicament if you hadn't already been here."

"I booked in my name," Blair said. "For this one night, my darling, you are Mrs. Gregory."

He took her in his arms, bruising her lips with the force of his kisses. When he took one arm away from her Taisie realized that he was feeling behind him for the door, to turn the key in the lock. With one accord they moved towards the bed, with hands pulling at buttons and fastenings, scarcely conscious of who was undressing the other. There was a tightness of unshed tears at the back of Taisie's throat but she put away from her the thought of what she meant to do and gave herself up to the delirium of love. Not yet, she thought, not yet; I'll tell him later.

When they had made love, in a confusion of half-shed clothing and Taisie's tumbled hair, Blair said lazily: "I suppose we must eat."

"I suppose so," Taisie agreed. "Are you hungry?"

"I was." Blair raised himself on his elbow and looked down at her, his dark face laughing. "And no doubt I shall get my appetite back again later."

"We must go down," Taisie said. "It will look so odd if we don't."

"Can you manage? Do you need any

355

help? I'm not sure what sort of lady's maid I'll make."

"Meaning you've never tried before? A likely tale! I know you for a bad lad."

"There were one or two girls before you," Blair admitted. He bent and kissed her shoulder. "No-one since," he said in a low voice.

Taisie put her arms round him and cradled his head against her breast. "You can't go on living like that," she said.

"What else am I to do?" he asked.

She did not answer him until much later that night, when the little inn was dark and still and they were in bed together. Then she told him what was in her mind.

"Marry someone else?" Blair said incredulously. "I can't do that. It would only double our difficulties."

"If I died you would marry one day," Taisie said. "From now on you must think of me as dead to you. This is the last time we will be together like this."

He argued with her in fierce undertones, refusing to accept what she said, pleading with her to say she did not mean it; he made love to her, his body tense with anger, and Taisie sensed that he was trying to bludgeon her into agreement with him. Against all expectation her resolve held firm.

"I am destroying you," she said. "We must part. I must go away for a long time and while I am gone you must find a good, sensible girl who will love you and give you children."

When Blair awoke from an uneasy sleep in the early hours of the chilly February morning he found Taisie in tears at his side.

"I wanted the last time you made love to me to be beautiful," she whispered brokenly. "Something I could hold on to and remember, to help me when it was difficult to stick to what I meant to do. But you were angry. You fought me as if you hated me. I spoilt it for both of us, what should have been our lovely memory."

"My heart, my treasure. Not your fault, mine. I'm not angry any more. Come, let me see if I can make it beautiful for you this time."

They were gentle with one another, tender in a way they had never been before, and if they did not quite reach the heights of ecstasy they had known when their hunger was unfed, at least the bitterness was assuaged.

When Blair separated from Taisie he kissed her softly on the forehead.

"I will try to do what you want," he said in a low voice.

# 12

THERE was more opposition to the plan of visiting the Villa Laurana than Taisie had anticipated. Having won Maurice over and torn herself away from Blair she had expected it to be plain sailing, but no-one else seemed to see it in the same light.

"You've been there yourself," she pointed out to her mother-in-law when she discovered that Mrs. Gaymour was horrified at the idea.

"We were cruising round the Mediterranean in a yacht and called in to see Desmond. We spent two nights with him and then went on. Entirely different from the journey you propose to undertake, and even that brief visit was enough to show that the island is shockingly primitive. Charming, of course. The villa is quite lovely and the scenery is beautiful and Taormina in its dilapidated way is a delightful town, but we were warned not to venture into the interior of Sicily

359

without an escort and even Desmond, who had lived there on and off for years, always carried a pistol."

Taisie was afraid that Maurice would be discouraged, but he decided to look upon the journey as an adventure and once he had made up his mind to go refused to be talked out of it.

All the same, there were times during their long journey when she suspected that he was sorry they had ever embarked on it. The March weather in which they started was unpromising. They ran into high winds and rough seas and until they entered Italy they saw more rain than sunshine. They had placed all their travel arrangements in the hands of Messrs Thomas Cook, who had been making such a name for themselves in arranging journeys across Europe, and in Naples they picked up a courier recommended by the company, who was to accompany them for the rest of the journey and remain with them in Sicily, since neither of them spoke a word of Italian and it was unlikely they would meet many people who could speak English.

The courier was a short, round man,

very quick in his movements, spinning round on his heels and gesticulating with his hands until he reminded Taisie of a child's top. He had thick black hair, arranged in careful waves, and a curving moustache which he fingered lovingly. He had introduced himself as "Cesare Capuana—entirely at your service, *signor*, *signora*. You have but to command me and it is done."

It might be theirs to command, but it seemed to Taisie that Signor Capuana intended to have things very much his own way.

"On arrival at Taormina we go to a hotel," he announced.

"But we've got the villa to go to," Taisie pointed out.

"Ah, but in what state? You have told me that the late Signor Corley—I have the name right?—was not resident all the time. You say he employed servants, sent money for the villa to be maintained, but who is to say whether his instructions have been carried out? They are not expecting you . . ."

"We wrote from London to warn them

we were coming. Had the letter translated into Italian an' all that," Maurice said.

"But have had no acknowledgement. Perhaps it has not arrived, perhaps the servant who received it cannot read."

He saw that they were looking unconvinced and went on, addressing himself mainly to Taisie, who seemed to him to have the quicker understanding of the two: "Imagine to yourself, *signora*, these servants left without supervision. They fall into careless ways, take liberties with their master's property, especially when they hear that he is dead. Suddenly the new master walks in. All their little badnesses are laid bare."

"They'd lose face," Taisie said.

"You have said it! And it is so important to them, the *bella figura*! These Sicilians, I know them; they are proud, so proud!"

"I don't see why we should concern ourselves about the feelings of a parcel of servants," Maurice grumbled, but Taisie over-ruled him.

"It'll be more comfortable all round if they've had time to make the place habitable for us," she said.

By the time they reached Taormina the

fierce southern spring had arrived, but the brazen heat of summer was still to come. The almond trees were in flower and there were new shoots on the vines. Taisie was enchanted by the view from the balcony of their hotel room high on the slopes of Monte Tauro, looking down over the rooftops and terraced gardens towards a sea which shaded from turquoise to violet.

"I didn't realize it would be so beautiful," she said. "Just think, Maurice, if we like the villa we can come here every year."

"Hold on," Maurice protested. "It's all very well for a novelty, but we're missing everything, coming away like this. We won't even be home in time for the Derby."

They went to see the Villa Laurana the next day, and even Maurice had to admit that it was as well they had not moved in straight away. As Signor Capuana had foreseen, their warning letter had arrived only just ahead of them and the servants were totally disconcerted by a development they seemed not to have anticipated.

"There are only three," Signor Capuana reported. "Caterina Buzzati, her niece

Maria, and her son, Giovanni, who works in the garden and is not, I think, very strong in the head. It is fortunate that you have with you your own maid, *signora*, and the *signor's* valet. At least your personal requirements will be attended to."

The house itself was beautiful. It lay on the slopes below the rocky ridge where the Greek theatre of Taormina stood in ruins. It had been built some thirty years before of marble removed from a tumbledown Renaissance *palazzo*, of a soft cream flushed with pink, like the inside of a sea shell. Because it was built on rising ground the principal rooms—drawing room, dining room and the master bedroom—were on a level with the rough track that led up to the front door, while there were additional rooms, used as bedrooms, at a lower level on the garden side. On both floors, facing the garden, there was a wide, roofed terrace supported on marble pillars. The three Sicilian servants were housed in a small cottage tucked in beside the iron gates which seemed to have been kept standing open ever since Desmond Corley had left for the last time.

"It seems that Signor Corley had the habit of bringing his own servants with him," Signor Capuana explained. "Caterina Buzzati is really no more than the caretaker, although she says that she can cook and is willing to do so."

"I think we should let her try. Don't you agree, Maurice?" Taisie said.

"Servants are your department," he said with a shrug. "It's quite a small place, isn't it?"

"Six bedrooms. I call that a manageable size," Taisie said.

It was certainly far smaller than any other house she had lived in since her marriage. To Taisie that made it all the more attractive. She had always wanted a house she could run herself. If only she could speak the language. More than ever before she regretted her scanty education. She had known that Siciliy was an island, she had known that it was Italian, though she had not appreciated that it had once been a separate kingdom; until she had got Maurice to point it out to her on a map she had no idea that it was so far south. The only other time she had been abroad was on her honeymoon and although

France had been a novelty it had not felt as completely foreign as this strange island, with its dark-skinned people and blazing sun. To look to the west and see the outline of Mount Etna and to know that it was an active volcano seemed so exotic to Taisie that she felt she could never grow accustomed to it. Every morning the first thing she did was to step outside and look towards the mountain to check that the strict cone was still as she remembered it, that—a troubling and thrilling thought—there was no smoke issuing from the crater.

Over and over again she turned to Maurice, her face sparkling with enthusiasm at the sight of a gaily-painted cart, a neat-footed donkey carrying an immense load, a woman in the striking local costume, only to be rebuffed by his indifference to everything that did not conform to what he saw as the established order. She was acutely disappointed by his inability to share in her pleasure, and all the more so because of the inner voice that whispered that Blair would have enjoyed the new experience as keenly as she did herself. There were times when she felt a physical ache for him so acute that she had to catch her breath and wait for it to subside before she could go on with her determined enjoyment of the passing minute.

They moved into the Villa Laurana with Signor Capuana still in attendance. He had been engaged to accompany them on the last stage of their journey and to remain until they were settled in the villa, but when he raised the question of departure Taisie begged him to stay on.

"Everything is so strange," she said. "I want to see how we go on with only Caterina and Maria to look after us. It may be necessary to engage extra servants and for that I shall certainly need your help."

Signor Capuana's round face was creased in a worried frown.

"As to that, there may be a little difficulty," he said. "I have tried to speak to your husband, *signora*, but it is difficult . . . a matter of some delicacy."

"It is to do with Mr. Corley?" Taisie asked.

"Ah, you already know something. It seems that the late Signor Corley was not popular."

"He molested a young girl and got half his ear shot away."

"I noticed that you do not say that he was accused of doing this thing, but that he did it," Signor Capuana said slowly. "I have every reason to believe that he was guilty."

"In Sicily this is very serious. All over Italy, too, but in Sicily it is a killing matter. He was lucky to escape with his life. There is more, which perhaps you have not heard before. Because Signor Corley was a foreigner, and because he denied that he had done the thing of which he was accused, the man who shot at him was sent to prison. This was not in accordance with the code of honour as the Sicilians understand it and it was very much resented. In their eyes Giuliano Arezzi had a right to revenge the wrong done to his daughter."

"I agree. I think it was a great pity he didn't kill Mr. Corley."

"You are very fierce, *signora*; it is not at all English. Now I must tell you the thing that troubles me very much indeed. Signor Corley continued to visit his villa while Arezzi was in prison, bringing with him his own servants. The last time he came Arezzi was free and once more he attempted to revenge himself. Again he was unsuccessful and this time Signor Corley seriously wounded him."

"I suppose it was self defence," Taisie said doubtfully.

"You may call it that, *signora*. But I must tell you this: if I had known this story I would never, never have allowed you and your husband to come to Sicily."

"You needn't be worried about us. We didn't like Mr. Corley. At least, I didn't, and neither would my husband if he knew as much about him as I do."

"You have not understood me, *signora*. Giuliano Arezzi may still want revenge."

"But Mr. Corley is dead, so nothing more can be done."

"I am not so sure."

Cesare Capuana felt the quandary he was in acutely. Signora Gaymour was a woman of sense; young, beautiful, and, unless he was much mistaken, of the people. If he explained to her his fears of a *vendetta* she would be quick to understand, but it was not a matter for a woman. Already he had said more than

369

was proper. It was to the *signor* that he should be addressing himself.

He tried, but as he had already discovered, Maurice was unresponsive to hints that his dead relative might have been a dishonourable man.

"Poor old Desmond. He may have made up to one of the maids, I don't say he didn't. Not quite the thing, of course, but we're only men and I dare say he had his little weakness like the rest of us. No excuse for shooting his ear away. Quite right to send the fellow to prison. As for trying it again when he got out, don't see what Desmond could do but defend himself."

"But you have not understood," Signor Capuana said in despair. "It is a stain on the honour of the family. The girl, Rosalia, she can never marry because she is not virgin."

"I say, that's a bit steep."

"It is so, I assure you. It may be that the family will feel that the insult has not yet been wiped out."

"They're out of luck with poor old Desmond dead, aren't they?"

"The *vendetta* can be transferred to

another member of the family, *signor*. Your own life may be in danger."

Maurice burst out laughing. "You Italian johnnies do exaggerate," he said. "Desmond was my second cousin. It's a bit far-fetched to think of killing me because he's no longer available, don't you think?"

"I have Sicilian blood in me," Signor Capuana said. "To me, it is not a laughing matter. Signor Gaymour, conclude your business in Sicily and go back to England with all the speed that is possible."

"Now I'm with you," Maurice said. "Very pretty place, an' all that, and I'm glad to have seen the property. My opinion is that we should get rid of it and go home, but my wife has taken a fancy to the villa. Wants to stay for the rest of the summer."

"Persuade her to change her mind, I implore you."

"Easier said than done. You don't know what Mrs. Gaymour's like when she's made up her mind to anything."

Because he treated it as a joke Taisie did not take Maurice seriously when he repeated the gist of this conversation to her. It sounded like the plot of an Italian opera, not something that happened in real life. She knew that Maurice was anxious to get back to England and suspected that he had exaggerated Signor Capuana's fears in order to persuade her to leave the villa. Taisie set her mouth obstinately and refused to be budged. It was too soon. If she went home now she would fly straight to Blair's arms and all the good she had meant to do him by going abroad would be wasted.

Besides, everything seemed to be going well. She had managed to achieve a form of communication with Caterina, a heavy woman in her fifties who wore perpetual black in memory of her late husband, but even if she had wished to do so, Caterina was incapable of conveying to Taisie how disconcerting it was to be saddled with a new master and mistress when she had thought herself safe from further upheavals. It was beyond Caterina to explain, or Taisie to understand, that Caterina had had to plead to be allowed to go on working at the Villa Laurana because she was a widow with a half-witted son and an orphaned niece to support and that she dreaded every day to hear that this dispensation had been withdrawn.

With the aid of a large dictionary, a few lessons from Signor Capuana and a word or two of English Caterina had acquired in the past, Taisie set out to run the first house she felt was truly her own since she had been married. The two English servants made difficulties and Taisie's maid spoke ominously of giving in her notice, but neither of them actually left because they were afraid of making the journey back to England alone.

Signor Capuana stayed on in the role of major-domo, half reassured because there had been no untoward incidents since they took up residence, and Taisie and Maurice began a life which would have seemed idyllic to Taisie if only she could have had a more congenial companion.

The day began early, when the milkman called, driving his cow before him to be milked on the doorstep of Caterina's cottage at the gate. It fascinated Taisie, who had never known anything but milk ladled out of a churn in the city streets or appearing on the table in a large country house without any reference to the animal which had produced it. He was followed by the vegetable and fruit sellers, the cheese and egg woman, the butcher. In her relief at seeing them still prepared to do business with the villa, Caterina entered into vigorous conversation with every one of them, whether she bought or not. It sounded like a running battle every morning, but since Caterina's plump face was wreathed in smiles as she shrieked after each disappearing back, Taisie judged that the noise was misleading.

Breakfast was brought to their room by Maria, fourteen years old and timid, who would smile shyly from behind a veil of black hair, put the tray down with a thump and run away without even replying to Taisie's newly-acquired "*Buon giorno*". Maurice would crawl out of bed, yawning and stretching, and come to join Taisie on the terrace, grumbling every morning because breakfast consisted of bowls of black coffee, a little jug of fresh milk, thick slices of the heavy, salty Sicilian bread and a saucerful of sticky jam, instead of the bacon and eggs he insisted he would have preferred, in spite of the heat.

374

Taisie had always had a hearty appetite, in spite of her slender figure, and she took to the peasant food Caterina produced.

"If you'd ever gone hungry you'd eat what was set in front of you," she informed Maurice when his finicky ways irritated her.

"I like to know what I'm eating," he said, poking at his plate. "What's this?"

"It's called *pasta colle sarde* and it's a sort of macaroni with chopped up sardines, pine nuts, raisins and fennel."

"*Pine nuts?*"

"That's what Signor Capuana said," Taisie said uncertainly. "I think it's ever so tasty."

"It's not bad," Maurice admitted. "But if we're going to stay much longer I think we ought to find a proper cook. Someone who can do a good roast instead of all these messed up dishes."

"You sound just like Jane," Taisie said. "She's always complaining about her stomach."

"Purvis looks down his nose all the time, too," Maurice said. "In fact, you're the only one who really likes the food."

"The vegetables are good and so is the fruit."

"But everything's cooked in olive oil. I can't get the taste out of my mouth."

It was only now, when they were thrown together all the time, that Taisie realized how much she had come to rely on Maurice's other interests to give her relief from his company. In the country he was out all day, shooting or hunting; in London he would spend part of each day at his Club, while she visited her dressmaker, interested herself in her charities, called on friends and planned entertainments. Often they spent a week or more apart visiting different houses and when they were reunited they had things to talk about and news to pass on to one another. They had separate bedrooms, too, and if Maurice came in late or Taisie was tired or menstruating he would sleep next door. Now they shared the same large bedroom on the first floor every night and it would have seemed unreasonable to suggest that Maurice should move downstairs for no other reason than that Taisie wanted to be alone.

He seemed to want to make love to her

more often and Taisie endured it with a stoicism which in the end even Maurice noticed.

"I don't know what's the matter with you," he complained. "When we were first married you were the one who was all over me."

"You didn't like it," Taisie pointed out.

"No, well, dash it all, not quite what one expects from one's wife. All the same, it's going a bit far in the other direction, being stiff as a log all the time. Not like you. You're feeling all right, aren't you?"

"Perfectly well, thank you."

He missed the tiny hesitation before she replied and went on: "Perhaps we should start thinking of getting some people to come and join us now that we've got settled in. I tell you who would like it and that's old Blair. He's keen on the Greeks and Romans and all that."

"He wouldn't come while Parliament's sitting," Taisie said stiffly. "I'll think about inviting one or two people and talk to Signor Capuana about a different cook."

She escaped, leaving Maurice to wander disconsolately into the garden and try to strike up a conversation with Caterina's son, who not only failed to understand but was frightened by this strange man who made noises at him. The little maid was more forthcoming. Maria was fascinated by these *inglesi* with their extravagant ways and drawling manner of speech. She would have been friendly with the two English servants, but they both stood on their dignity and treated her as someone who was far beneath their notice. The *signora* was more approachable than her own maid. She was beautiful and her clothes reduced Maria to breathless yearning. The *signor*, too, was always kind. He would stop and talk to her and his amiable attempts to speak a word or two of Italian flattered Maria, while his accent drew from her a spontaneous peal of laughter which covered her in embarrassment as soon as she realized that she was laughing at the master, and sent her scurrying away with a scarlet face and downcast head.

It was a relief when some of their wealthier neighbours called on them, but even that was only a partial success since so few of them spoke more than a smattering of English.

"We must take Italian lessons," Taisie said to Maurice.

"I didn't come here to go to school."

"It's only polite to speak a few words of the language. We're invited to dinner by the Contessa Petralassi tomorrow night. At least she speaks English."

"Old hag."

When Maurice was in that mood nothing pleased him. Like a spoilt child he demanded to be entertained and when the entertainment did not meet his expectations he sulked. Taisie began to consider abandoning the villa and moving on somewhere else, even though with Signor Capuana's assistance she had arranged to import a cook from the mainland and had drawn up a list of guests to be invited out from England.

"Why does the cook have to come from the mainland?" Maurice demanded.

"Because you don't like Sicilian cooking," Taisie said. "This man is French trained."

"That means he'll be expensive, I suppose?"

"Very. If you want the best, my dear, you have to pay for it. Do you want me to ask the Conways to come out next month?"

"They won't come at such short notice. You ought to have invited them before we left England."

"Not knowing what we were coming to? It wasn't practical."

"There's not room for much of a party anyhow. If I'd realized the villa was such a poky little place I'd have sold it without bothering to come and take a look at it."

Taisie put her list away without comment. All she said was: "The Contessa has arranged for us to have a trip round the coast to Syracuse. You'll enjoy that."

The yachting expedition was a success and only Taisie realized how much of a relief it would have been if she could have sent Maurice off for the day without her. His only complaint that day was that Taisie was exposing her face to the sun and getting a nasty brown colour.

Taisie looked at herself in the glass. It was true that her face was flushed with extra colour, but she did not think it unbecoming. Her hair seemed to have a lighter gleam to it, too, and her eyes looked large and green. As she gazed at herself she was seized by one of her helpless waves of desire for Blair. He would have liked her as she was now, he would have entered into her delight in feeling the warmth of the sun and the sting of the sea air on her skin. She leaned forward, her hands resting on the polished surface of her dressing table, her fists doubled up, waiting for the pain to go away.

"You've got a touch of the sun, if you ask me," Maurice said in a disapproving voice from behind her.

"Oh, do go away and leave me alone," Taisie snapped.

He went out, slamming the door behind him, and Taisie sat down, shaken by her reaction to his intrusion into her thoughts, Was she going to be able to go on with it, this separation from Blair? Never before had she realized how much she had depended on the possibility of seeing him from time to time. The stab of pleasure when she entered a room and saw that he, too, was invited to dinner that night; looking round a theatre in case he was in the audience; the dangerous thrill of knowing that they were sleeping under the same roof; even reading his name in the newspaper had been better than having no news of him at all. Was he feeling the same, or was he doing what she had asked and paying court to some other woman? The thought brought Taisie to her feet, frantic to know what was happening, and only the sound of Maurice's voice outside and the spontaneous peal of laughter he always seemed to be able to get from Maria brought her to her senses.

She and Maurice were alone that evening, Signor Capuana having been despatched by Maurice to make enquiries about hiring a boat of their own. Taisie seized on the idea eagerly, but when Signor Capuana returned he reported that he had had no success.

"It's difficult to believe," Maurice said, annoyed at being frustrated in something he had decided he wanted.

"I find it very worrying," Signor Capuana said. "I have told you before, Signor Gaymour, that you should consider your position here very carefully. I can only repeat the advice I gave you before: sell the villa and go back to England."

It was advice that Maurice would have been only too happy to accept, but Taisie, fighting her realization that separation from Blair had done nothing but make her love him more, pleaded for a further delay.

"At least you'll agree it's not a place we're likely to want to come back to every year?" Maurice demanded.

"I would willingly come back, but I can see it doesn't suit you. We'll sell, but do let me have a few more weeks first."

The days slid by. The heat grew more intense. They made one or two more expeditions and it seemed to Taisie that Maurice grew more resigned to the quiet life they were leading. Taisie pursued her Italian studies and began to find it easier to communicate with Caterina. It was unfortunate that just as she became more fluent Caterina retreated into a sullen withdrawal which Taisie attributed to the arrival of the new cook.

She thought that perhaps she had misjudged Caterina when the caretaker made her understand one day that she would like to be absent the whole of the following day, together with her son and Maria, to attend the funeral of a relative. Perhaps after all Caterina's strange mood had been due to anxiety and grief. Taisie

383

was quick to give her permission and she thought that the woman's expression softened momentarily as her dark eyes searched Taisie's face.

It was the day after the funeral that Taisie first saw a strange young man haunting the cottage by the gate. She might not have noticed him if he had not been unusually dressed, in a way Taisie associated with a city rather than a country district. His suit was of poor cloth, but very smartly cut, with wide shoulders and a pinched-in waist to the jacket. His tie, although it was black, like the rest of his clothes, was so wide and of such a lustrous satin that the effect was flamboyant. His hair was smoothed down with a pomade which Taisie could smell at a distance of several feet, and he wore his hat clinging to the side of his head. When he raised his hand to remove a cigar from his mouth she saw that his fingers were loaded with rings. He gave Taisie a considering look that lingered so long that she found it insolent, before he sauntered away. She asked Caterina who he was and had difficulty in understanding the caretaker's answer although she gathered that it concerned Maria in some way.

"What does 'zitamenta' mean?" she asked Signor Capuana.

"It is the Silician word for betrothal or engagement," he said.

"Oh, in that case I think Caterina was trying to tell me that the young man I saw was engaged to Maria. Is that possible? She's very young."

"Twelve is the marriageable age for girls in Italy."

"I didn't much like the look of him, but I suppose it's all right. Caterina said he was a man of honour."

She looked up just in time to see Signor Capuana crossing himself.

"*Signora*, are you sure that she said this?" he asked.

"Quite sure. I can understand her quite well now. It's words like '*zitamenta*' that catch me out."

"Describe this young man to me."

She did so, concluding: "And he wore the most atrocious shoes. I don't know how he could walk in them. Pointed toes and high heels."

"And they made a noise," Signor Capuana said.

"They squeaked as if they hadn't been paid for, as we say in England. How did you know that? Have you met him before?"

"I know his type. *Signora*, he was indeed a man of honour. Surely you have heard of the *Onorata Società*?"

Seeing that Taisie looked blank he added, almost under his breath: "The *Mafia*."

"Oh, yes, I've heard of the *Mafia*. It's a secret society, isn't it?"

"Not exactly. It is very strong in Sicily. Here, they look to the *Onorata Società* to redress their wrongs rather than to the government or the *carabinieri*. I do not at all like to hear that the little Maria is engaged to such a one."

Taisie told Maurice about it that evening. At least it gave them something to talk about and he had taken a liking to Maria.

"I hope they're not forcing her into it," he said. "She's a pretty little thing, but as shy as a deer. Turns red and runs away whenever I speak to her."

"She must be very poor and Signor Capuana says a dowry is still important on Sicily," Taisie said. "Perhaps we could do something for her before we leave, some sort of wedding present."

"If you're talking about leaving at last I'm certainly prepared to make a thank offering," Maurice retorted.

Taisie tackled Maria the next day, but she could get the girl to tell her very little about her young man.

"All I could get out of her was that the engagement was very new and that his name was Matteo Arezzi," she reported. "Apparently it was his father who died the other day."

"Arezzi? Wasn't that the name of the chappie who very nearly did for poor old Desmond?" Maurice asked.

"So it was! How clever of you to remember. Perhaps that's why Maria's boy looked at me so strangely. He can't have any reason to like Desmond's family. The girl who was involved must have been his sister."

It occurred to neither of them to discuss all this with Signor Capuana. To Maurice, the Italian was a servant with whom he would not dream of talking about family matters, while to Taisie Desmond Corley's life and death were still matters of horror and she avoided his name whenever possible. It had been a relief to find that the villa bore so little stamp of his occupation; if she had been reminded of him every time she looked round her Taisie could not have borne to stay there so long, however beautiful it might be.

The only incident that upset the quiet days was a sudden outburst from Caterina's son. Neither Taisie nor Maurice could understand what it was that had suddenly made him take exception to Maurice's friendly ways with his cousin, Maria. Maurice had been in the garden, idling away a few minutes before the light luncheon the new cook was preparing for them, when he had seen Maria and called to her. She came to him, with a degree of reluctance that reminded him more than ever of a shy animal who had to be coaxed to hand. There was a hibiscus bush near his elbow. Maurice broke off a blossom and handed it to Maria.

"*Bella*," he said, but whether he

referred to the flower or to the girl was clear to neither of them.

The boy Tomaso stopped working and leaned on his hoe to watch.

Maurice wanted to say something about Maria's engagement, but he did not know the right words. He took her hand in his, pointing in enquiry to her ringless finger, smiling in an effort to convey his good wishes. As always, he was fascinated by the bright colour that swept over Maria's face. She broke away from him, confused and ready for flight. There was a shout and Tomaso ran forward, brandishing his hoe, his thick speech incomprehensible, but obviously beside himself with rage.

"Fellow was like a madman," Maurice said afterwards. "If he carries on like that they'll have to put him away. I mean, it wasn't as if I'd done anything. Only meant to tell the girl I wished her well an' all that."

"You didn't kiss her?" Taisie asked, looking at him searchingly.

"Certainly not!" Maurice looked so offended that she was forced to believe him.

"I'll smooth it over with Caterina," she

said, but she found Caterina unresponsive to her halting explanation. Taisie felt dispirited when she left her. Until the new cook had arrived it had seemed as if Caterina was ready to be on friendly terms, but since then she had been silent and withdrawn. Or was it, as Taisie sometimes feared, that the death of Giuliano Arezzi had reminded her that Taisie and Maurice were related to the man who had wounded him and had him imprisoned?

Whatever the cause, this air of sullen resentment which now spoiled Taisie's visits to the little cottage had finally made up her mind that she and Maurice might just as well give up the villa and go home. By easy stages, if possible, and Taisie had the best of reasons for asking that their journey should not be strenuous.

She strolled with Maurice in the garden that night after dinner, enjoying the coolness of the air after the heat of the day. The moon had risen, an enormous silver disc casting a pathway of light on the sea far beneath them. There was enough light to see the white blossoms of the acacia tree and the jasmine which filled the garden with scent. When Maurice lighted a cigar Taisie regretted it, but she did not protest.

From the shadows behind the acacia there was a small sound, a squeak which, if she had noticed it at all, Taisie would have associated with one of the strange insects which haunted the garden. She slipped a hand through Maurice's arm as they halted by the wall at the edge of the terrace.

"I've got something to tell you," she said.

Behind them the man of honour moved again, giving his enemy warning that he was there. On his deathbed his father had made him swear to carry on the *vendetta* that had first sent him to prison and then left him with an arm that dangled uselessly by his side. As soon as the old man was dead his sister, Rosalia, thin and bitter, raging against the fate that had condemned her to remain unmarried since she had been despoiled by a stranger when she was little more than a child, had reminded him of his promise. And now the idiot Tomaso had seen the new *inglese* making advances to Maria. She had sworn that it had amounted to nothing, but she had not been able to deny that the man had touched her. Matteo had struck her, as a punishment for encouraging the foreigner, and had ordered her and Caterina and Tomaso to leave the cottage that night. Yet even now he was reluctant to act, while the man's wife held his arm.

"You may not like the place, but I think the Villa Laurana may have helped to give me something I've been wanting for a long time," Taisie was saying to Maurice. "I believe I'm expecting."

He always found it difficult to express his feelings in words, but she had not been prepared for his incoherent pleasure.

"I say! Well, by Jove! That's splendid. I mean, it's just splendid, isn't it? Imagine that. Me, a father."

Taisie laughed, touched by his delight. "It's much too soon to be certain," she warned him.

"You must be careful of yourself," he said. "I say, we ought to go home, didn't we? You'll want to see a doctor and I don't want any of these foreigners mucking you about."

"I don't need a doctor for a while yet, but I agree we should start for home. I'd like to travel slowly," Taisie said, making her point.

"Yes, rather. We'll take it as easily as you like. This heat can't be good for you. We ought to go north."

"I'd like to see Switzerland," Taisie suggested. "Can we manage that, do you think?"

"Of course we can. I'll put Capuana on to it in the morning. How soon can we leave?"

"By the end of the week, I think, don't you? I suggest you get Signor Capuana to go with you to see an Italian lawyer and put the sale of the villa in his hands."

She left him to finish his cigar, standing by the wall, looking out over the sea and savouring his excitement and pride. She felt suddenly peaceful, as if a great crisis in her life had been passed. Maurice would be a good father, she would find fulfilment in the child, she had done right in encouraging Blair to look elsewhere for a similar satisfaction.

Maurice heard the squeaking shoes and turned his head. He saw the moonlight glitter on the naked blade. He shouted and Taisie, just starting to mount the stairs to the terrace above, turned to see what he wanted. In the brilliant silver light she saw two dark figures by the wall. They seemed to blend into one and then they separated and she heard the sound of someone running away.

She started to run herself, towards her husband. Maurice staggered towards her, one slow, lurching step and then another. A terrible rasping noise was coming from his chest. As she reached him he collapsed on to his knees, his hands scrabbling helplessly in the dust, and she saw the hilt of the knife in his back.

# 13

BLAIR was in the middle of a particularly intricate case of fraud when he received Taisie's telegram. It was put into his hand by his clerk and he read it with half his attention still given to the examination of one of the witnesses. As the words in front of him sank into his mind the Court room seemed to fade away.

"Maurice seriously wounded. Little hope. Break news to mother. If you are free please come."

He was not free to leave immediately, but that was not what Taisie had meant and he knew it. He crumpled the telegram up in his fist with a harsh rustle of paper that drew a reproving glance from the Judge. Blair realized that he was being asked whether he had any further questions and, putting the telegram on one side, he glanced at his scribbled notes and got to his feet.

It was forty-eight hours before he could get away and that only after a prolonged and painful scene with Mrs. Gaymour, who wanted to accompany him. He succeeded at last in persuading her that he would travel faster alone and as he made his way across Europe he could only be thankful that he had left her behind. The journey seemed painfully slow, even though he travelled by both day and night whenever there was transport to take him towards his destination.

A small, plump Italian with a worried face was the only person Blair saw when he arrived at the Villa Laurana. There was what looked like a lodgekeeper's cottage at the gate, but it seemed to be unoccupied. The door of the villa stood open, perhaps to admit a breath of air. Blair, still wearing the clothes suitable for a cool English summer, felt his shirt sticking to his back. His throat was full of dust and he was stupefied from lack of sleep.

Signor Capuana led him straight out on to the terrace. Taisie was there, all alone, sitting in a light wicker chair, her hands resting idly on the arms, gazing out over the garden towards the sea and the horizon. She was dressed in black from head to foot.

She turned her head and Blair saw her white, still face and eyes which had lost all their green sparkle. As he went quickly towards her she got to her feet, looking at him uncertainly, almost as if she was not quite sure who he was. But when Blair put his hands on her shoulders she swayed towards him and, closing her eyes, laid her head against his shoulder.

He held her quietly for a few moments and then he said: "I'm too late?"

Taisie drew away from him. "Maurice died only a few hours after my telegram was sent."

"The funeral . . ."

Taisie shook her head. "Signor Capuana has been making arrangements for . . . for the coffin to go home by sea. I thought it was what his mother would want. Maurice, too. He was *so* English. He wouldn't have liked to be buried in foreign soil."

He made her sit down again and drew up a chair by her side.

"Tell me what happened."

She told him the story, as far as she had been able to understand it, but he sensed her disbelief that revenge could be carried to such extremes.

"It's so monstrously unfair," she concluded in a low voice. "Maurice, the one person who never did anyone any harm. Desmond was the one who did wrong. Maurice never even really understood how wicked he was. That was my fault. I ought to have told him. And I made him come here, made him stay when he wanted to go home. All because I'd fallen in love with you and been unfaithful to him."

"It was a valiant effort to make a fresh start," Blair reminded her.

"At Maurice's expense. Blair, it's been so dreadful. All the Sicilian servants ran away. My maid had hysterics, Maurice's man locked himself in his room and refused to come out because he thought we were all going to be massacred, Signor Capuana had to go to fetch a doctor. I was all alone with Maurice, bleeding to death, and I didn't know what to do. When he lived through that first night I thought we might save him, but he had lost too much blood, he was too weak. He just drifted away."

A change came over her face, the set composure wavered and she began to cry, in an uncertain, angry way, frowning as if she would still hold back the tears if she could. Blair knelt by her side with his arms around her, trying to still the paroxysms that shook her body.

He looked up and saw that Signor Capuana had come out on the terrace.

"It is good," the little man said. "Until now the *signora* has not wept, nor has she eaten. I came to say, Signor Gregory, that the *signora*'s maid has prepared a room for you and there will be food—not good, but such as I am able to provide—in an hour."

"Signor Capuana has been my lifeline," Taisie whispered. "I'll go and rest for an hour and then I'll join you again. And I will eat, Signor Capuana, I promise I will."

It was the evening, when the fearsome heat of the day had subsided, before Taisie and Blair spoke confidentially again.

"They wanted me to go to a hotel after Maurice died," Taisie said. "Perhaps it would have been sensible, but I was so afraid you would come and not be able to find me."

399

"I would have found you, no matter where you were."

"You understood what I meant when I asked you to come if you were free? Since you are here, does it mean that you haven't committed yourself to any other woman?"

He took so long to answer that she drew away from him, afraid of what his answer was going to be.

"I think I must give you the exact truth," Blair said at last. "I've been paying a lot of attention to Penelope Curtiss."

"That dull lump!"

It made him smile, to hear something of the old asperity in her voice.

"Have you proposed to her?" Taisie persisted.

"No, but I meant to and both Penelope and her mother must be expecting it."

"Do you want to go on with it?" Taisie asked in a low voice.

"You must know that I don't. All the same, I feel I've behaved badly. I've aroused expectations I now have no intention of fulfilling. The girl will be disappointed. But at least it's not as bad as if I'd cried off after an engagement had been announced."

"Would you have done that?"

"Yes, I would. I couldn't face a lifetime with Penelope once you became free."

Taisie did not respond as he had expected and Blair began to feel uneasy.

"It's too soon to speak to you about the future, I know," he said. "All I want to say is that after your period of mourning is over I hope that you will turn to me. I shall be waiting for you."

"There's a difficulty," Taisie said. "I believe I'm carrying Maurice's child."

It was something he had not foreseen and he had to pause to take it in. Taisie's body tensed as she waited for his reaction.

"I'm glad of it," Blair said at last. "Bear your child, my dear, and we'll marry as soon as we can afterwards. If we wait for a year we shall avoid giving offence to anyone. When he—or she—is born, Maurice's fortune can be put in trust and I can marry you and keep you as *my* wife. Did Maurice know?"

"I had just told him, only minutes before he was knifed. It made him so happy. I'm glad that he had that. Blair, I feel so guilty, so responsible for his death!"

"If you do, then you must be doubly glad that you are going to bring his child into the world," Blair said deliberately.

She thought that he had not fully understood the extent of her regret at having brought Maurice to this fatal place, and yet there was something in what he said.

"I suppose that's the thing I must concentrate on now. If it's survived what I've been through in the last few days it must be a tough little thing."

"Strong, like its mother."

"Am I strong? It seems to me I've been weak and foolish—and destructive. I've brought about the deaths of two men, Desmond and Maurice."

"Desmond richly deserved what came to him and I think we can lay Maurice's death at his door, too."

"I ought to have told Maurice the truth," Taisie said, speaking in a dull, obstinate way that alarmed Blair. "Perhaps then he wouldn't have married me and we would all have been spared a lot of unhappiness. I never told him anything. I even lied to you when I said I'd confessed to him about Leonard."

"If I'd known you better I would have

distrusted that innocent stare," Blair said, but even this slight attempt to lighten the atmosphere could not rouse her.

"Taisie, this is morbid. Maurice loved you and was proud of you. He never regretted his marriage, you know he didn't. Whatever I may have said against it in the past, I could never deny that it made Maurice happy. And your coming out here, breaking off with me, devoting yourself to him, that showed a strength of character that perhaps only I am capable of appreciating."

"When you talk like that, sounding so sure, I begin to believe that perhaps after all I wasn't solely to blame."

In the concealing darkness of the garden he ventured to put his arm round her. Taisie's head rested against his shoulder.

"This is the place where it happened," she said. "Strange, that I should be able to stand here and not feel any horror. Almost as if Maurice had forgiven me. I haven't been able to believe that before."

With a deep understanding of her need for that belief Blair went on holding her quietly until she said: "He will go on living in a way, won't he, because of the baby? Can you really love it, Blair, a child not your own?"

"A child of yours? Do you really doubt that it will be as precious to me as our own will be one day?"

He held his breath, afraid that his words might have jarred on her new mood of peace, but Taisie said: "Yes, one day" in a voice of calm acceptance that reassured him.

"It will be the new century before he is born," she said. "Nineteen hundred. How strange that sounds. A new century and a new life. Do you still believe that one day we can be happy together, Blair?"

"I'm sure of it. I'll be by your side all through the next year, helping you whenever I can. Everyone will see that it's the most natural thing in the world for us to decide to spend the rest of our lives together."

He sensed that at last she was smiling. "Even though it means I'll be a countess one day? Little Taisie Brown, the London sparrow?"

"Linnet," Blair said. "My lovely singing bird. You'll be the most beautiful countess in the entire British peerage, but much more than that, you'll be my wife, my love."

# THE END

# GUIDE
## TO THE COLOUR CODING
### OF
### ULVERSCROFT BOOKS

Many of our readers have written to us expressing their appreciation for the way in which our colour coding has assisted them in selecting the Ulverscroft books of their choice. To remind everyone of our colour coding— this is as follows:

## BLACK COVERS
### Mysteries

★

## BLUE COVERS
### Romances

★

## RED COVERS
### Adventure Suspense and General Fiction

★

## ORANGE COVERS
### Westerns

★

## GREEN COVERS
### Non-Fiction

# ROMANCE TITLES
## *in the*
## Ulverscroft Large Print Series

| | |
|---|---|
| The Smile of the Stranger | *Joan Aiken* |
| Busman's Holiday | *Lucilla Andrews* |
| Flowers From the Doctor | *Lucilla Andrews* |
| Nurse Errant | *Lucilla Andrews* |
| Silent Song | *Lucilla Andrews* |
| Merlin's Keep | *Madeleine Brent* |
| Tregaron's Daughter | *Madeleine Brent* |
| The Bend in the River | *Iris Bromige* |
| A Haunted Landscape | *Iris Bromige* |
| Laurian Vale | *Iris Bromige* |
| A Magic Place | *Iris Bromige* |
| The Quiet Hills | *Iris Bromige* |
| Rosevean | *Iris Bromige* |
| The Young Romantic | *Iris Bromige* |
| Lament for a Lost Lover | *Philippa Carr* |
| The Lion Triumphant | *Philippa Carr* |
| The Miracle at St. Bruno's | *Philippa Carr* |
| The Witch From the Sea | *Philippa Carr* |
| Isle of Pomegranates | *Iris Danbury* |
| For I Have Lived Today | *Alice Dwyer-Joyce* |
| The Gingerbread House | *Alice Dwyer-Joyce* |
| The Strolling Players | *Alice Dwyer-Joyce* |
| Afternoon for Lizards | *Dorothy Eden* |
| The Marriage Chest | *Dorothy Eden* |

| | |
|---|---|
| Samantha | *Dorothy Eden* |
| Waiting for Willa | *Dorothy Eden* |
| Winterwood | *Dorothy Eden* |
| Countess | *Josephine Edgar* |
| The Emerald Peacock | *Katharine Gordon* |
| Jane of Gowlands | *Anne Hepple* |
| Rebel Heiress | *Jane Aiken Hodge* |
| On The Night of the Seventh Moon | |
| | *Victoria Holt* |
| Wind on the Heath | *Naomi Jacob* |
| It Was The Lark | *Catherine MacArthur* |
| The Empty House | *Rosamunde Pilcher* |
| Sleeping Tiger | *Rosamunde Pilcher* |
| Under Gemini | *Rosamunde Pilcher* |
| Wychwood | *Nicole St. John* |
| The Reluctant Orphan | *Sara Seale* |
| To Catch a Unicorn | *Sara Seale* |
| The Truant Bride | *Sara Seale* |
| The Blue Sapphire | *D. E. Stevenson* |
| Five Windows | *D. E. Stevenson* |
| Kate Hardy | *D. E. Stevenson* |
| Sarah Morris Remembers | *D. E. Stevenson* |
| Sarah's Cottage | *D. E. Stevenson* |
| Summerhills | *D. E. Stevenson* |
| Adair of Starlight Peaks | *Essie Summers* |
| The Forbidden Valley | *Essie Summers* |
| Moon Over the Alps | *Essie Summers* |
| Not by Appointment | *Essie Summers* |

We hope this Large Print edition gives you the pleasure and enjoyment we ourselves experienced in its publication.

There are now more than 1,600 titles available in this ULVERSCROFT Large Print Series. Ask to see a Selection at your nearest library.

The Publisher will be delighted to send you, free of charge, upon request a complete and up-to-date list of all titles available.

Ulverscroft Large Print Books Ltd.
The Green, Bradgate Road
Anstey
Leicestershire
England